CHANGELING

When Hero Abrahams wakes up famous one morning, it is for the most unenviable reason: her husband, Tom, has been assassinated by a car bomb and she has become a macabre celebrity. Their marriage had confused everyone, not least themselves. Shy but determined Hero, recently released from college, made an unlikely partner for devastating, aristocratic Tom, with his mysterious job at the MoD. And it is only after his untimely death that Hero discovers just how little she knew about him . . .

CHANGELING

CATHARINE ARNOLD

This love will undo us all

A New Portway Large Print Book

CHIVERS PRESS
BATH

First published in Great Britain 1987
by
Hodder & Stoughton Limited
This Large Print edition published by
Chivers Press
by arrangement with
Hodder & Stoughton Limited
at the request of
The London & Home Counties Branch
of
The Library Association
1988

ISBN 0 7451 7142 7

British Library Cataloguing in Publication Data

Arnold, Catharine, *1959*–
 Changeling.
 I. Title
 823′.914[F]

 ISBN 0–7451–7142–7

For Liz Turpin
and Mark Ward

CHANGELING

PART ONE

CHAPTER ONE

Hero always remembered that day the news came. She woke to brilliant sunlight, leaves glittering in the prospect of heat and the telephone ringing downstairs. The caller didn't say much: he didn't need to. Hero knew the moment she picked up the receiver. Instead of the familiar pulse of the callbox came the measured tones of Gilby.

'Come here? Now?' she asked, already knowing why. He coughed at the other end. 'I'll be ready by the time you get here.' Hero realised battered old Gilby had been at a loss for words, afraid that in the circumstances she might embarrass him. As she replaced the handset, stillness flooded the room. Hero's feet were cold on stone flags, and the drawn curtains turned the low cottage into a shadowy labyrinth. Light was only visible in a thin pencil above the windowsill.

Hero had hurtled downstairs to the phone the way she always did, risking her neck on the narrow stairs. Now, it was a second or two before she recovered sufficiently to let habit take over. Like a sleepwalker she went through the motions of shower and change, pulling on old jeans and one of Tom's striped shirts, for comfort. She fastened his cufflinks with the deft ceremony of a soldier taking up arms. As she drew a jersey over her head, the implications of Gilby's call affected her: at once Hero knew, and did not know: realised, and refused to admit it.

The world was already confused. An incipient heatwave pressed against the windows, flooding the

3

Hampshire countryside with light, as though preparing for a high summer morning. But the March trees were bare, and condensation drops clung to the open lattice.

Hero combed fine red hair before the mirror, irritated as it spun with static. She rubbed foundation over her shiny nose, but avoided mascara. Cosmetics, like wearing Tom's shirt and links, gave her courage these days. Hero had the white skin, pointed cheekbones and fey expression which characterises certain redheads. However much she slept, persistent blue smudges underlined her eyes. Made self-conscious by her conspicuous colouring, at twenty-two Hero's gawky angularity and startled manner seemed almost adolescent, and she possessed a deceptively frail and otherworldly air.

Plucking stray hairs off the dark field of her jumper, Hero thought: *They've won. They've got him. They must have. I knew we couldn't last.* The old stoicism gripped again, as it had six years ago when the police arrived to announce her father's death. Then, as now, she had seemed astonishingly self-composed. It was useless to explain that any other actions would have been impossible for her. With the stoicism came a dogged determination. Although Hero possessed the redhead's requisite fiery temper, she seldom gave it an airing. The emotion that sustained her like a cold flame was a quiet stubbornness, which, unlike her looks, made her old beyond her years. It was a determination which would prevent her from breaking down in Gilby's presence, and in the past had overcome illnesses, won her a scholarship and several sporting distinctions against long odds. It was a

4

determination not to provide standard reactions, not to let *Them* know she cared, not to let *Them* hurt her any more.

She touched the cufflinks again, their rippled surface glinting like amulets in that sunlit room. She was armed against whatever news he brought. Tom would protect her.

Hero's courage almost failed at the last minute, seeing that bed, so broad and defenceless in uncanny March light. The knowledge that she had already spent so many nights alone there did not help. It was only sheer bloodymindedness which forced her downstairs again, to draw the curtains and let in morning, slam coffee on to brew, turn up Mozart on the stereo. It was only a desire to occupy herself with trivia that made Hero plump sofa cushions into submission, feed the cat and stack dishes, so that all other thoughts would stay banished from her mind.

★   ★   ★

Gilby arrived within minutes, parked, and approached the open kitchen door. Perhaps there was a little more tension in his face than usual, but Hero found it hard to tell. Lean and agile, with the yachtsman's weatherbeaten features, he could have been anything between forty and sixty. As far as Hero was concerned, he seemed sardonic, sometimes humorous, mostly stern: one of Tom's oldest friends, and the only one she halfway liked and trusted.

As Gilby walked towards her, Hero reeled inwardly with sudden vertigo. Panic made her brain pulsate. As her nerve plummeted down an imaginary liftshaft, she gripped the kitchen table for support. After a second the sensation passed, but Hero was wary: she didn't try speaking for a moment, knowing her voice would sound strange.

The way Gilby addressed her, as he stood in the doorway, summed it all up. She knew what he had to say before he said it because he called her 'Mrs Fitzgerald'. The title was an admission of seriousness.

'Yes?' Getting it out somehow, showing she remembered him in an official, not merely social capacity. 'Yes, Commander Gilby?'

'May I come in?'

She stood aside. Now she was Mrs Fitzgerald, identity concealed by rank. Mrs was never a prefix she'd adjusted to. Idly, she wondered if she'd continue to use it now. The exchange completed, she nodded him to a seat and put out cups and saucers.

The filter choked and spluttered to itself, lapsing into silence, just as the music died and the turntable clicked off. In the sudden stillness, Hero heard her heart beat loud as a drum.

Taking a seat opposite Gilby, she picked a sugar crystal and allowed it to dissolve on her tongue. Her hands were cold around the hot mug.

Finally, Hero resurrected enough courage to ask, despite that sensation of falling: 'What happened?'

'Mrs Fitzgerald—Hero—'

He paused and then continued. 'You know how—delicate—your husband's position was politically—'

Was? With that tense-shift, Hero was on what Tom called red alert. *Was?*

'For God's sake.' Real fear took over and

6

composure deserted her. 'For God's sake, just tell me what happened. *Please.*'

The sunlight outside, for all its unseasonal brilliance, no longer gave the illusion of warmth. It belonged to another world, screened by a wall of glass. She watched Gilby rallying all his sources of tact and diplomacy as he prepared to speak: and she no longer had any sympathy for him, after all.

He's waiting for me to work it out.

'Tom's car was mined last night in London. He was killed instantly.'

'Thank God.'

Gilby allowed himself to look shocked.

'Better than being maimed for life,' Hero replied, bitter at stating the obvious. Her voice was so cold that she sounded unconcerned, and the walls of glass were closing round her like the doors of a cage.

Once, climbing in the Lake District, Hero became so cold that all sensation left her. She observed her own body with detachment as it gradually froze, remaining aloof even when they came to take her to the hut and shroud her in blankets. This was how she felt now: overcome by spiritual hypothermia. With the remoteness of one whose heart had turned to ice (wasn't there some old story like that?) she said: 'Arrangements will need to be made. Do the Press know yet? Has the story broken?'

'It will. They've already got wind of the incident. Of course, we wanted you to be the first to know.'

'Good of you.'

Gilby ignored all this. Perhaps he had been surprised, Hero thought later, by her self-possession.

7

'No-one else was involved, fortunately, but there has been a great deal of structural damage. The parties responsible knew exactly what they were doing.'

'I expect they've had enough practice.'

Glancing at the clock, Hero couldn't believe that it was eight forty-five and her life had changed completely. She had woken on another morning, a different day: now she seemed trapped in one of those nightmares where you struggle to wake up but find you're still dreaming.

'Have they claimed responsibility yet?'

'We can't jump to conclusions.'

'It seems pretty obvious to me. Doesn't it? Tom is—was—in a very sensitive position.'

'Tom was involved in various activities, some of which you know nothing about. Some of which *I* know nothing about,' Gilby admitted. 'It's too soon to attribute the act to any one organisation. Added to which, any splinter group of extremists is likely to ring and claim they did it, in order to gain publicity.'

She could see sensation in his eyes now, carefully contained like a crowd of demonstrators, prevented from straying and disrupting his features into a display of emotion. Hero wondered why she wanted to hit this man for the news he brought, but comfort him because Tom had known him all his life, and he was vulnerable too. And equally skilled at concealing it.

A pins-and-needles tingle in her limbs threatened the return of normal response, and Hero knew she must get this man out of here before sensation engulfed her.

'So the Press will be told. Can you keep them off

my back? I don't particularly want to be bothered at a time like this.'

'Obviously, the Department will give you all the support you need. Details have been circulated. Tom's colleagues will be advised of the situation.'

Hero was to reflect on the mentality which led to her husband's assassination being described in the terms of a Civil Service memo.

'And what about his family? And all his relations in Waterford, and Langton Matravers?'

'Tom's people will be informed. Clearly, we had to to tell you first.'

'I appreciate that.'

Gilby finished his coffee, and his formal manner visibly returned. 'Of course, we won't be able to avoid publicity altogether, I'm afraid. You appreciate that once an incident like this occurs—'

'Yes. I suppose it's too much to expect for the Department to settle the whole affair quietly. I mean, when a young MoD employee gets blown up, it's bound to attract a bit of publicity, isn't it? We haven't *had* an outrage for a few months, and I guess it'll be a good excuse to whip up a bit of public hysteria about security and capital punishment. How could you pass up an opportunity like this?'

'Hero—' Even Gilby was astonished by her bitter command of language at a time when most women would be incoherent with grief. 'You're taking it very well,' was the best he could say. 'I'm impressed. I feel as if you're one of us. It really is like dealing with a professional. Your self-control is impressive.'

'I suppose that's a compliment, coming from someone like you.'

'I hope you'll be able to make the necessary public appearances. The Department will help you with any administrative problems, and there is a pension scheme.' These details seemed bizarrely inapposite. 'Exactly how long have you been married, Mrs Fitzgerald?'

You ought to know, you were there.

'Just under a year.'

'You're coping excellently.'

That's because it hasn't sunk in yet, and you're here, and I'm too proud to cry in front of anybody.

'I knew what I was letting myself in for.' Which wasn't strictly accurate, but sounded good.

'Perhaps you should go home for a while.'

'This is home.'

'To your mother's house. You might want to be—looked after.'

'You mean it would be easier to protect me in Oxford?'

Gilby looked restless. Hero had gradually adapted to the mysteries of his profession, and the full implications of what life as the wife of a 'Public Relations Officer' in an obscure branch of the Ministry of Defence actually involved.

Civil Service was a euphemism for the shadowy hinterland inhabited by Tom and his colleagues. Hero's research into the profession meant that, unlike other service wives, she was more conscious of the difficulties of her position. It was a world where suspicion and protection were taken for granted; where everybody thought twice, a world where 'security', which should guarantee liberty, made those administering it perpetually insecure.

'You're in a vulnerable position here. You must admit that.'

10

'I spent enough time on my own here before—before this happened.'

'I don't want to alarm you, Hero. I know you're not easily frightened, but—'

'Do you suppose they'll be looking for another martyr so soon?'

'Perhaps you could stay with Tom's family—'

'I'll think about it.' Cultivating an air of detachment, as though they were deciding how to spend the weekend.

'I've always considered this cottage to be rather isolated—'

'I *like* being isolated.' *Don't try and scare me. Mind you, I suppose it would make me more amenable if I was easily frightened. You'd be able to do what you liked then. You and the fucking Department. I couldn't give a damn if they shot me tomorrow. Whoever* They *are.*

Instead, Hero said: 'I'm going to find the public side of this difficult to take. Everyone will be so kind, and fascinated by it all—there'll be a ghoulish celebrity about me. God, it doesn't bear thinking about.'

'I'm confident that you will acquit yourself admirably.'

Hero wondered if he sat at home polishing up these headmasterly phrases for use on specific occasions. Perhaps he would have preferred a weeping female, primed with Scotch and Valium.

He was not the Gilby she had seen before: Hero preferred that wiry prototype of all ex-naval officers, the old family friend. As messenger of doom, she found him unappealing.

'What will happen about the funeral?'

'I expect we—I expect that the Fitzgeralds will

11

have the ceremony locally, and a Memorial Service in London.'

'But of course.' Hero did not comment on the opportunity for the expression of popular outrage which the Memorial Service provided: Tom, with his unorthodox PR career, would probably have been amused by the prospect. The Department, like the people who mined the car, always knew exactly what they were doing.

'The Department will take care of it.'

Suddenly, desperately, she needed to be alone. *Go away. Sod off. Get away from me. Now.*

But Gilby showed no signs of receiving this telepathic message.

'I'd better go and see if Black Bess is okay. She's been off her feed recently.' Taking refuge in rural practicalities, Hero walked out into that unfamiliar morning.

Black Bess, a phlegmatic dark brown cob who reminded Hero of an old-fashioned upright bicycle, cropped in her paddock, untouched by events. She condescended grudgingly to have her nose patted, as Hero wondered what the hell to do next. The cob, who had been Tom's for years, treated her with disdain, as a rival for his affections. Hero and Black Bess had a constrained relationship, reminiscent of that between Hero and her in-laws.

* * *

When she returned to the kitchen, Gilby was gone. She went to the front of the cottage and found him in his Range-Rover, preparing to leave. Slightly ashamed, as he must be suffering in his own way, she said: 'Thanks for coming. Don't worry about

12

me. I can look after myself.'

'You'll have protection. Someone will always be there, for as long as we feel is necessary. To prevent the Press from annoying you, if nothing else.'

'Is somebody here now?'

'He has instructions not to intrude on your privacy.'

'I'll ask him in for coffee if I get lonely.'

Gilby, amused in spite of himself, shook his head. 'I'll be in touch.'

He swung the car round and was gone, leaving silence to surge back like a tide.

For a second, Hero thought it had all been a dream.

As the telephone rang, she knew for certain it was another of the nightmares which tormented her recently. She knew Tom was on the other end, calling from God knew where—his movements were frequently unaccountable and she had learnt better than to ask. She knew it was Tom, tired and low and desperate to get home. Running to the phone, she lifted the receiver, anticipating the reassuring sound of his voice, faintly distorted by distance, his words, his presence.

'Hero?'

'Colonel Fitz—' She hadn't expected Tom's father.

'Thought I'd better give you a call. Gilby been round yet?'

'Gilby? Yes, he has.'

'Did he—put you in the picture?'

'Yes. Yes, it's true.' Forced to admit it. 'It'll be on the news this morning, and all round the world in no time. Tom won't be coming back. Not now. He's bought it. He's been killed.'

13

CHAPTER TWO

'I've got several sets of nine lives,' Tom used to say, with all that careless grace and schoolboy cricketer's grin. 'I'm on a winning streak.'

Soldiers never believe they'll die. Otherwise, why do it? Even the most cynical have a conviction of their own immortality. This assumption is applicable to the more arcane branches of the military world as well as the regular army. Stunning, anachronistic Tom, who resembled a pre-war fast-bowler from an old cigarette card, and acted like a character in Buchan, believed he'd always cheat death. The endless drills and training, designed to keep him alive, went disregarded. Deep cover, eavesdropping devices, checks and tactics, were a set of rules to be ignored. Tom was convinced defeat came from lack of confidence: 'You have to *know* you're better than the next man,' he said, in one rare serious moment. 'You must believe you're better, or the game's not worth the candle.'

The game, indeed. Tom treated his transfer—promotion was not the exact word—from a Guards regiment to the security services with supreme contempt. By the time Hero met him, Tom's concept of the activity had more in common with Kim and Hannay than the mundane preoccupations of electronic surveillance and interpretation of aerial reconnaissance photographs.

Hero had often speculated about her husband's persona, wondering if his gung-ho attitude was a carefully cultivated double-bluff, intended to give

14

anyone who guessed his occupation the impression that he was merely another cheerful moron who had strayed from Knightsbridge to Whitehall. She suspected a shrewder and altogether more calculating mind informed his actions, that he could on occasion be as devious and ruthless as anyone employed by the Department. Sometimes, watching him sanguine and blazing with malt whisky, she believed he was all that he seemed: that he was as upright, honest, and faintly naïve as he appeared to be.

'I've got several sets of nine lives.' Hero looked round the cottage, Tom's cottage. He would not be back now, yet she kept sensing his presence there, expected to turn and find him standing behind her, reading the overseas news or flicking through a magazine without seeing the pages, thinking of something else. 'You're in another world,' she used to say. And now of course he was.

After speaking to Tom's father, there had been a whole lot of nothing, a macabre state of oblivion, compounded of her reaction to the news and wretched sunlight pouring into the cottage with all the normal sounds of a country morning. The sensation reminded her of an occasion once when she got—accidentally—drunk one lunch-time, and attempted to manoeuvre her way through an ordinary day, each prosaic action becoming a bizarre and complex ritual, every object far out of reach, every step leading across a gaping abyss that threatened to swallow her. When Hero surfaced, she shook herself and made tea, in the time-honoured tradition. It was typical of her that she had not yet called her mother, or asked the local farmer's wife to come and keep her company. She

15

did consider offering a mug to the security man who must be posted outside, but with reversion to self-consciousness knew she looked too much of a wreck to show herself to anybody.

It had been wise to avoid mascara. Hero's pale northern skin did not recover well from crying, and her eyelids were swollen and puffy. With scientific detachment, she noticed how scoured her face had become. *It must be the salt in the tears*, she thought, as though they had been wept by somebody else.

Washing off death's contamination, she stood in the shower for over twenty minutes until her fingertips were ridged and bloated as her eyes, and her hair swung in drenched strings to her shoulders. Coruscated by water, she propitiated her stinging face with moisturiser, and found another of Tom's shirts to put on. It smelt faintly of his expensive sandalwood lotion, and was ridiculously large for her. But fresh jeans, and Tom's old combat jersey made her feel almost brave, almost capable.

Hero had not eaten since the previous day, but the congealed lamb and glassy vegetables in the fridge nauseated her. Unconsciously, she straightened the kitchen, stacking the books and bits of paper which seemed to multiply whenever her back was turned, and twice reminded herself that it would not be necessary to clear up before Tom came home.

Repressing emotion with manic activity, she cleared the fridge, rang the local farmer who kept an eye on Black Bess whenever she and Tom were away, and told him briefly that she would be absent for some time. She gave no indication of recent events. Drawing a breath, she pushed back

16

still-damp hair and knew she had little time before the Press arrived. There was no doubt that they would come. The story must break soon, and there could even be a special bulletin. Hero had seen enough footage of bereaved families to know that she would be a prime target, and planned not to be there when the cameras arrived.

She suddenly realised that she would have to drive herself to Oxford. Hero wanted no favours from the Department, and if her mother came to fetch her, she would never reach Hampshire before the Press did. Public transport was out of the question. The only solution was to bind her emotional wounds, as she had once strapped up her ankle in order to run a race, and get home somehow. Then she would let go. Then she would be nearly safe.

In the past, Hero had struggled against her body, forcing it to the limits of its endurance. Her almost belligerent determination had won sporting distinctions which seemed astonishing to those who were deceived by her frail appearance. Now, she battled to keep her mind. Distracted as she was, Hero knew she had to get away. If she put a foot wrong, it would not be to skim and glide through a trial into exhaustion and tranquillity: it would be to misjudge her distance, lose her balance, fall in the abyss that yawned out there, beyond the door.

It'll be an essay in surviving, the next few months. Two years, it usually takes. Or so they say. Perhaps longer for me. Perhaps never. It'll be like cross country. Imagine a race that lasts two years. Lumbering and stumbling on, long enough to qualify, long enough to get there. If something's at the end, so much the better. I mustn't let Them *think I can't do it. They* mustn't *think I'm giving up. It's just another obstacle. I've got to show* Them.

The ill-defined *Them*, whom Hero's entire life seemed dedicated to impressing, surfaced again. *They*, represented at various times by schoolmistresses, doctors, supervisors and Tom's family, were Hero's natural rivals, and infinitely variable. She was frequently in competition with the rest of the world. At present, *They* constituted not only Tom's assassins, but any group who expected Hero to collapse as a result of the event. Hero would show *Them* otherwise. She wouldn't allow anyone the satisfaction of thinking that she couldn't cope with whatever happened to her.

The feel of not to feel it. It was easy to shut down your emotions if you concentrated hard enough. She had done so when her father died. How easy to let the screens of glass slide close and wall you in. A little splinter of ice lodged in her heart.

Taking another look round, Hero checked the gun cupboard, which contained Tom's inherited Purdeys, her own 20a bore (for clay pigeons), and an automatic pistol. It was comparatively light, a .38 Beretta, and she had fired it previously at a range in London. Life with Tom meant weapons were no mystery to Hero: she had learnt to regard them as instruments, harmless in some hands, deadly in others, frequently lethal to those who did not know how to use them.

Without fully realising why, Hero wrapped the automatic, unloaded, in an aran sweater and put it in her holdall. She slipped nickel-tipped bullets into the clip, and stowed that away, too, with a spare supply of ammunition. *This is ludicrous. I don't need this where I'm going, and I'm not suicidal.* Yet,

18

feeling prudent and absurd, she packed the automatic about with jerseys, and locked up the cupboard.

Finally, Hero put the black cat—unimaginatively named Cat—into her basket, slung the holdall on one shoulder, and walked out into the bright cold morning. Light dazzled her swollen eyes. She allowed her guard to slip a little now, and a tear slid down her cheek as she unlocked the car and belted herself in. The Reactolites in their expensive frames were a gift from Tom. So was the little white Metro. She backed out of the drive apprehensively, as though expecting a posse of photographers to emerge from the shrubbery, and swung onto the narrow road. Concentrating on her driving, not allowing herself to think, she turned the radio up loud and headed home.

PART TWO

CHAPTER ONE

Love Affair With Life had been playing as Hero and Tom met, and it really was his signature tune. Hero's existence had been unremarkable before he came along, but she hadn't realised that. Within an instant of setting eyes on him, Hero knew something—or somebody—had taken control of her future, that suddenly, her life was out of her hands.

A few years later, after so much had changed—particularly Hero—it was impossible to explain the dimensions of her obsession. By then no-one visualised self-assured, composed Hero as the victim of hopeless infatuation. She found it difficult to believe, herself.

But it had happened, as it does to millions of lovers: the chance meeting, fascination, enthralment. They created their myth, their legend, with its feast days, rituals, periods of atonement. They had their sacred places: streets and pubs and reaches of the Embankment. Within a month of their meeting, Tom and Hero established an intimate mutual history, referring to *Remember that time . . . I'll never forget what . . . How about that night we . . .*

★　　★　　★

Happy ever after: that had been the assignment, reflected Hero bitterly, driving home. *Why didn't I remember that only fairy tales have fairy tale endings?*

★　　★　　★

23

Life before Tom had been humdrum, if not entirely conventional. Hero had grown up in shabby suburban academe, among broken-springed armchairs, yellowing journals and dusty bedrooms. Hero's mother, a successful sculptor in critical, if not financial, terms, taught art students at Oxford Poly; her father had been a philosophy lecturer and briefly, warden of his college, before an untimely death in a road accident when Hero was sixteen.

After Professor Abrahams died, and the family discovered how little money they possessed, Mrs Abrahams resorted to putting up students in the draughty, ramshackle house. But even among the adolescent tantrums, late-night Nescafé sessions and faint aroma of cannabis, and despite the distinction (at school) of being a bohemian orphan, Hero found life meandered tediously on, so that sometimes she longed to be overtaken by dramatic events.

There was little cause for rebellion in such a household, as her mother, who had run away from Ireland to St Martin's School of Art, had been a rebel herself. Maeve treated her children with liberality and was appalled not by their excesses (of which there were few) but their very conformity. Hero discovered early that passing exams and winning races made her safe: safe from what, she could not say. All she knew was that competing for the Girls' High School in regional heats, and gaining twelve O levels, insured her against the dangers of this world—and took her mind off her father's death. If she was ever lonely, or if she missed his fat, comforting presence, Hero was generally too tired to notice it. She was independent in her grief, as though asking for help admitted weakness.

Hero would have been happy to stay in Oxford, but her mother, believing the desire to stay at home to be aberrant behaviour, encouraged Hero to try for a history degree at Cambridge. The other university town was scarcely a dramatic change of scene, and so similar were her friends and activities at this new seat of learning that Hero wasn't homesick. Beth and Leah shared her preoccupations: they were all three reticent, isolated girls, with a melancholy streak of stoicism, and Hero spent her time in long discussions of potential research projects, and solitary runs across twilit commons with windows beckoning in the distance. Spindly Hero had an unexpected talent for athletics, despite annual battles with bronchitis.

At Cambridge she also developed an unexpected talent for sex. Hero had read enough psychology to know why she needed a man, but was surprised that she needed so many. Boyfriends, met in romantically unpromising locations such as the college laundry, and the University Library Tea Room, were inevitably reclusive young scientists, shy as herself. Other arts students, flamboyant and ambitious, frightened her, and Hero had an almost fetishistic penchant for thin, bespectacled young men with stars in their eyes and slide rules on their narrow hips.

There was comfort in their passionate intensity, their disregard for social activites (Hero, more slob than snob, possessed little smalltalk and less etiquette) and their wholehearted concentration on Hero during their trysts. They liked to believe they had sole access (even if Hero was seeing several boys simultaneously) and would turn silent and glaring if other friends of hers appeared in the pub. It never occurred to Hero that a party consisted of more than two.

Unable to hold her own in Hall among the socialites, who discussed skiing and ball-going and where to eat in Battersea, Hero was secure too in her capacity to understand SERC grants, quantum mechanics, and the latest advances in spectroscopy. She was secure too in the attentions of raven-haired Stephen Lewis, a twenty-three-old research astro-physicist who would appear, white-faced after twelve hours in the Cavendish, to descend on her room with Maltesers and Soave, and devote the same intense concentration to their love-making as he did to quarks and quasars.

When Stephen left for MIT, with much regret on both sides, there had been Colin, an aloof Scots chemist who specialised in crippling fell-walking expeditions and conducting their relations outdoors, even in the most unpromising weather conditions. And there had been their contemporaries and successors, David, Keith, Thomas, Michael, Peter, and what appeared to be the majority of the Pure Science Faculty.

This life continued for three-and-a-half years before Tom appeared. Hero was required to spend an extra year in Cambridge in order to take a degree in Art History, but she was content as she knew how, bedding her scientists, talking with Beth and Leah, running for the college and gaining a half-Blue. She became excusably selfish, as it is easy to do at university, allowing mealtimes, training, even sex, to revolve around work. She intended to do research, like all her friends, and had little

26

interest in party-going or cultivating an impressive CV. There was no active dislike between Hero and the college beauties, who fluttered to dances and drinks parties and charity balls. Hero's attitude was one of indifference, tempered by self-consciousness and fear of large gatherings. She was happiest being woken in the small hours by Stephen to go out and watch the stars; running alone along the towpath on a misty morning; disturbing the dust on forgotten books in remote libraries, and walking along the isolated country roads, formulating arguments for her dissertation on Russian iconographic art, Cyrillic lettering swimming in her brain.

If life after finals existed, it was only as a splash of sunlight beyond the mouth of the tunnel, a distant paradise where she would research, write learned articles and move in with one of her romantic scientists. When she went home for Christmas at the end of her last Michaelmas Term, it was with no more intention than to write up her dissertation and start revising before the festivities began.

For an agnostic household—Maeve was Lapsed, and Hero's father had been a non-practising Jew—they always put a lot of effort into Christmas. Relatives of all types and conditions descended on the house once the students left, and there were always lively cultural exchanges between Maeve's family from Donegal and the Abrahams contingent from Manchester.

But when Hero first returned, the house was quiet. Her brother and sister were not yet back from London, and her mother was preoccupied with a new spot-welding technique developed at Cowley. She had turned one of the garages into a studio, and spent most of her conscious time there when work was going well.

Hero settled to comfortable isolation in her attic room, savouring the silence after the uncarpeted clangour of college life. The ramshackle Victorian mansion in North Oxford had wind-tunnel corridors and no central heating, but Hero had a fondness for its decayed grandeur and vast, high-ceilinged rooms and had almost developed an immunity to the Thames Valley damp. Unless her mother re-married—which with her taste for poverty-stricken young men from the Polytechnic and her headstrong independence seemed unlikely—the house would always be like this. Hero found it reassuring, though she sometimes envied the richer lives glimpsed at Cambridge.

From her chilly eyrie, she looked down at the snowy suburb, where other dilapidated houses bore the scars of academic occupation and one or two had been restored to japanned elegance. Women plodded past, assignable at a glance to the species of Town or Gown. Dishevelled dons' wives led their loaded bicycles like mules along the slippery pavements, as smart provincials, whose husbands did not rely on the University (or the Poly) for a livelihood, defied ice in high heels and frost in flimsy jackets. The house on the corner—the most beautiful and expensive in the street—glittered with light, like the set for a seasonal commercial. It was actually called 'The Residency' as if, Hero's mother commented, its occupants felt obliged to maintain order among an anarchic subject race. The title was derived from its original, ex-colonial inhabitant, but The Residency still possessed an establishment air absent from its neighbours. As Hero watched, an

28

expeditionary force clad in Puffas and Huskies left The Residency, laughter echoing in the frosted air.

This could only mean one thing. Stretching, getting up, and leaning through the window, Hero realised Flora was back. Hero hadn't seen Flora since the summer. Once close friends, they had not quarrelled, but had little in common now. On leaving school, Flora had opted for London, and acquired a daunting metropolitan glamour, working up her regular features to conventional beauty and capitalising on her natural vivacity so that she was always good company. Flora had an instinct for pleasing men, a batlike radar system which sensed and tracked a likely admirer, and a gift for manipulation which both frightened and impressed Hero.

She kept these criticisms to herself, since it was evident that she and Flora were destined to lead different lives. But she was fascinated by the other girl, and enjoyed her company. Flora knew the fashionable brands, the right labels, the names on the swing-tags, the price of everything. She had no time for the romantic bespectacled Stephen Lewises of this world.

Flora had arrived home from LSE earlier that year, accompanied by a group of staid young men in shooting jackets and shoes with snaffles. Hero nearly cycled into them on her way from the Bodleian, as they sauntered past in a laughing crowd, and had been seized with a rare but acute fit of self-pity.

Now, she watched a similar party make a *sortie* down the road, talking, shouting, throwing snowballs. The amount of noise such groups generated always surprised her.

29

Ten minutes later, the telephone rang, with Flora at the other end.

'Hero—we saw you at the window. When did you get back?'

'Oh—about three days ago I think. Yes.'

'Well, listen. I'm having a party. New Year's Eve. You absolutely must come.'

'I'm—I don't know what I'm doing that night.'

'Studying, probably. Give the books a rest for once and come over.'

'Well—maybe—'

'Is your friend Colin coming up? Would you like to bring him?'

'Colin's at UMIST now. I'm seeing him later—'

'*Where?*'

'University of Manchester Institute of Tech—'

'Manchester! God, how awful! Then you *must* come!'

'I've got nothing to wear—'

'Oh, you must have. Do come.'

'I'll see what I'm doing.'

'You know you never go anywhere.'

This was an incontrovertible truth.

'Come and have a drink with us on New Year's Eve. And meet some *real* men.'

★   ★   ★

Hero's mother eventually persuaded her to go. New Year's Eve arrived on a night of freezing fog, when even walking down the road was an uninviting prospect. Uncomfortable in skirts, she put on a black velvet dress provided by her mother two years earlier 'for an emergency', which made her look slim but not bony. Nothing could alter her pallid

30

freckled arms, and the pale lipstick (Flora's) made her a wraith. But the black and white provided a foil for Hero's vivid hair, though she was not the vivacious redhead of popular fiction. Instead, with her unfamiliar clothes and apprehensive air, she seemed like an extra-terrestrial uncomfortably trying to pass for an earthling. And she knew she would feel like something from outer space all through the party. She always did.

'You look like Mary Queen of Scots,' pronounced Maeve, when Hero finally came downstairs. 'Try to smile a bit. Why, when I was your age—'

'You were living in Chelsea on a houseboat and dating Keith Richards. I know.'

'At least I *enjoyed* myself,' replied her mother. 'Really, you do look *most* extraordinary.' Maeve Abrahams had not retained her brogue, but she still had a distinctively Irish syntax, speaking English with the formal eccentricity of an immigrant.

'So you go to the party.'

'I will not. I'm expecting people here myself.'

'*You're* having a party? Here? Why didn't you tell me?'

'We'd not be able to enjoy ourselves under the scrutiny of the young. An exemplary daughter such as yourself would inhibit the whole undertaking.'

'Yeah, I don't give you much cause for concern, do I?'

'None of you do. I could say I'm disappointed.'

The children resembled their father. Diligent, academic, scholarly, and worst of all, quiet. Cassandra, Hero's younger sister, had announced her intention of becoming a doctor at the age of ten, and was now at Guy's. Philip was at the Royal School of Music, having decided in a similarly

31

uncompromising fashion to make his living as a violinist. It had never occurred to him to consider any other occupation.

'It's genetics, no doubt.' Hero's mother spoke with mock-gloom, a favoured mode of expression. 'Here was I, expecting some black sheep, and I end up with some nice middle-class professionals. Where did I go wrong?'

Hero laughed, patting her mother's head, and the greying red curls which always reminded her of a red setter's coat.

'All right, I'll *go* to the party. Perhaps I'll meet someone suitably depraved and run off to a life of sex and drugs and rock and roll.'

'I think you're more likely to marry a nice Jewish boy.'

'Don't be too sure.'

A little self-conscious for the addition of cardigan, wellingtons and sheepskin jacket, Hero set out, seldom-worn high heels in her pocket.

The reason that she looked most extraordinary was her sense of discomfort in female clothes. It was almost like being in drag. Flora had made an attempt to persuade Hero into changing her image, but somehow she drifted back every time to jeans, trainers and shirts inherited from her father.

Snow was falling as she stepped into the street, hardened ridges of ice buckling the soles of her boots. Crystals drifted aimlessly and settled on her mittens, sprinkling the bottle of wine she carried with glitter. The stars shone against the blackness, and Hero tried, whilst moving warily along the pavement, to pick out the constellations, chart the planets and trace the famous figures in the sky. The heavens were like one of those children's puzzles

32

where you joined the dots.

For the first time in a long while, she missed Stephen Lewis, and wondered what he was doing now. She had resolved not to regret anybody for long, but Stephen had been the first, and they had been happy. Letters were exchanged, and an agreement made that they had no claims on each other, now. There were tentative plans to meet the following year, when he came back from Massachusetts, but no threats or promises.

Hero thought of the dreamy eyes behind misted glasses, the childlike absorption in the mysteries of the universe, the spiky hair which never lay flat, and she missed him. She did not miss his parents, who, gradually reconciled to the fact that Hero was only half Jewish, and on her father's side at that, so it scarcely counted, had been suggesting to both that it was time they settled down.

Get married, indeed, she thought, skidding along the pavement in the dark. *I've got no plans for that, either to a nice Jewish boy or anyone else.* Which made it all the more ironic that six months later Hero found herself married.

CHAPTER TWO

The Residency blazed with light, an advent calendar with all the doors wide open. Hero geared herself for the assault made on her senses by the gamut of people, the noise, the steady thump of music as she was ushered to the drawing room. Flora, fashionable and intimidating in scarlet and black, greeted Hero as though she had just returned

33

from a solo expedition to the Amazonian rain forest and introduced her to a group of men in pinstripes. After a brief exchange, Hero headed for the drinks tables.

She found this the most successful way of withstanding such events, and drank two glasses of wine very quickly. Flora's parents were in abeyance, and the house had been given over to revelry. Hero looked about for a quiet niche where she could settle until the worst was over, as a fell-walker will take refuge from a rainstorm, and headed for a bookcase. There were yards of unread classics in beautiful bindings, but Hero chose the *Ordnance Survey Road Atlas Of Great Britain* and concentrated on the best way to get to Manchester. One day Hero hoped she would be too old to have to bother with parties.

Drinking her wine, which was excellent (one of Flora's beaux was a shipper) she glanced occasionally at the milling guests, the deafening talk almost drowning the stereo. Hero now knew why these occasions were known as a *stand up and shout*.

She was on the outskirts of Salford and speculating about a T-junction when she sensed someone standing over her. At that moment a lull in the conversation allowed her to hear the lyrics of *Love Affair With Life* and she looked up into a face which seemed familiar.

But it couldn't be: or Hero would never have forgotten how they met before.

'I'm sorry—what did you say?'

Because she hadn't been able to take all this in, and listen too.

'I said, I don't think we've been introduced,' he said, settling beside her on the floor, with his back to the bookshelf. For an instant, Hero's undoubted attraction to him was overlaid by her automatic dislike of the English upper-class male, a prejudice based more on theory than fact. Yet he had such a strong aura of charm, of reassurance, that she was prepared to overcome her reservations. Tall and lean, with good looks of a quintessentially English variety—blue eyes and ash-brown hair—he was the type of man whom Hero usually ignored. This was because she believed (erroneously) that her own looks were deficient and that she never stood a chance with conventionally handsome men. Hero had resolved to avoid any opportunity of rejection.

He must think I'm somebody else. That's what. In a minute he'll realise he's got the wrong girl, and go away.

Intrigued nevertheless, she tried to concentrate on the atlas. Hero was completely unconscious that her apparent indifference constituted a challenge to the stranger. When she looked up again, to the accompaniment of *Where do I stand now? In the rain* . . . he was still there.

'How about another drink?' he asked, hair flopping over one eye.

This came at a lull, when it was possible to hear oneself talk and think. Hero was about to reply, when the loud volley of an in-joke was succeeded by a rattle of baying laughter. He asked her something else, but Hero could hear nothing. Finally, he scribbled on a receipt produced from his pocket, handed her the message, got up and walked away.

Meet me in the kitchen? she read.

Mesmerised, and vague with drink, Hero put away the atlas and raked back her hair before setting off through the house, which was as

35

labyrinthine as her mother's.

Whoever this was, he certainly seemed worth having a drink with. The fact that he was interested in someone like her was pretty bizarre, of course, but it could be an opportunity. It might even fall into her mother's category of an emergency. How right she had been to make Hero come to the party: and in the black dress. Hero wouldn't have been able to face the stranger in her lived-in Levi's.

But halfway to the kitchen, the other Hero had already destroyed her own excitement and analysed it half out of existence. *He was probably just another upper-class twit*, the small voice whispered, *patronising and chauvinist and out for a quick screw. Why automatically follow him anyway? Who did he think he was, leaving messages like that? He was just another of* Them.

Hero was never entirely certain about the origins of Other Hero, and the carping little voice with which she destroyed her confidence. She suspected that she had conjured up this inner critic some years ago to guarantee her against undue optimism, an internal defence system. The voice's principal function seemed to be to remind Hero that life was a contest: Hero *v* The Rest Of The World.

In a curious state of ambivalence and excitement, Hero walked into the kitchen to find the man sitting on the table, relaxed and in control and looking as if he was about to address a press conference. He stood up as she came in.

'Don't tell me you wanted help with the washing up,' she said, looking at the usual party chaos.

'Absolutely deafening in there. I couldn't think straight. I'm getting too old for this sort of thing.'

'Me too,' said Hero, with complete seriousness,

36

although his remark—he must have been about thirty-five—would have been the cue for polite astonishment in more formal circles.

'I hate parties,' she added. 'I always say I'll never do it again—and then I go to another one.'

'You must be a friend of Flora's.' The bright kitchen lighting revealed a weather-beaten, open face, putting Hero in mind of Test cricketers and actors who specialised in adventure films and costume dramas. There was something faintly old-fashioned and reassuring about him.

Hero shrugged, watching him open a bottle of champagne with the negligent expertise she had thought restricted to barmen. Other Hero tried to chip in with a few comments about heavy drinkers, but Hero managed to stifle her critic by watching the way the man's hair fell into his eyes, and approving the lean athletic body emphasised by a guernsey sweater and corduroy jeans. She was always impressed by someone else who hated dressing up.

'We—we're neighbours,' she got out at last after a gulp of Moët. 'We've known each other years. But we don't have that much in common, now.'

'I really don't know Flo very well at all. We met at a party just before Christmas. I came over really because—well, I haven't got anything better to do.'

Hero found that hard to believe.

'It happens sometimes. It doesn't seem right, being on your own for New Year's Eve, so I drove up here.'

Hero realised, with mingled disappointment and relief, that this must be Flora's new boyfriend, or a prospective candidate for the post. She didn't want to be undiplomatic, and show the knowledge might

37

be disheartening (*told you so*, said the inner voice) and loyally if naïvely agreed:

'Flora's very attractive, isn't she? She's always good company and she's got so many friends.'

He looked at her curiously.

'Well, she seems popular, I'll give you that.' He refilled her glass. 'But not exactly the polished hostess yet, I fear.'

'But there's lot of food and wine, and everything.'

'And bottles of champagne lying around. Yes, all well and good. But she hasn't introduced *us*. That's a major oversight. Especially as I begged her to. Twice.'

Steady on, went the inner voice. *Don't get carried away*.

'We'll have to be very informal and do it ourselves.' He stuck out his hand, so that Hero had to come closer. 'I'm Tom Fitzgerald. And I think it's time for the mystery guest to reveal herself.'

'H—Hero. Hero Abrahams.' Offering stiff fingers (tight with fright) in return. 'And I've heard all the jokes before.' *You tell him*, agreed her inner critc. Honestly, it was as good as taking your best friend on a date with you.

'That's a lovely name, but bad news for anyone you meet called Leander. I suppose at least people can spell it.'

Perhaps it was the champagne, perhaps it was the surprise of finding someone who wanted to talk to her, but Hero relaxed, and became good company herself.

'Where are you at school?' asked Tom, at one point.

Hero was used to this, being one of those people

who look preternaturally young.

'I'm in my fourth year at college, actually.'
Ektually. She would sound like Flora at this rate.

'A levels?'

'Er—well actually—' *There we go again*, said
Other Hero. *Trying to make yourself sound like one of
Them*. And Hero could already predict the outcome
of this conversation. Men—apart from the ones who
were already there—were invariably put off by the
fact she was at Cambridge. And once she mentioned
her intention of doing research, discussion had
usually been terminated. Hero explained what she
was studying and where, and was impressed when
Tom did not back out of the room as though
retreating from a ghoul.

'I was there myself for a while. A few years ago,
now. I got chucked out of Magdalene.'

'Whatever you did must have been pretty bad for
them to complain.'

'I just didn't work, that's all. Just wanted to have
a good time and get pissed. Christ, you're only
young once.'

'So what did you do—when you got sent down?'

'Went into the army. My father's regiment.
We're rather a traditional family.'

So he's not only a berk, he's a killer psycho, said
Other Hero at her most maniacally unreasonable.
Hero shook involuntarily, as though trying to brush
her other self away.

But he's a nice bloke, she thought. *He's kind and
friendly and he likes me, which is something. Doesn't
meant he's a monster just because he was in the army.
Stephen Lewis's cousin is in the Israeli army. He's
okay. That's different*, retorted Other Hero.

'Are you cold? Goose walked over your grave?'

Tom asked with concern, seeing Hero shudder.

'It's nothing. I've just got something on my mind.' *Or I'm going out of it.*

'Do you actually want to stay at this party?'

Hero looked round the kitchen. 'Well we're not exactly participating at present, are we?'

'I mean, did you come with anybody?'

'Oh—another guy, you mean?'

'Yes, or your sister—or whoever.'

'No, no I'm not with anybody.'

'Do you fancy going for a drink?'

'There's enough here.' She hadn't intended to sound pert.

'What I *really* would like to do,' declared Tom, with the conviction of someone making an electoral address, 'is go out to a pub in the country somewhere, and have a drink there. And perhaps something to eat. Best way to celebrate the New Year.'

'That appeals to me,' admitted Hero. 'And it's so loud here—'

Flora came in at that moment, visibly bewildered by the spectacle of her shyest friend monopolising the star guest in the kitchen. Tom and Hero were sitting side by side on the table by now, a second bottle of Moët between them.

'There you are, Hero!' Flora's tone was more accusatorial than she intended. 'I thought perhaps—Tom, I'd like you to come and meet—'

'Actually, Flora, I'm going to be very rude and make my apologies now.'

'What do you mean?'

'Hero and I are going out for a bite to eat.'

Hero was totally unequipped to deal with such a social dilemma. She had never been accused of

40

stealing anybody's man before, and felt uncomfortable in the role of siren. Though it might be worth getting used to, she admitted to herself, smoothing the black velvet down over her knee.

'That's settled then.' Tom kissed astonished Flora and thanked her for a wonderful party. Hero, expecting one of Flora's outbursts—or at least one of her Looks—was equally surprised by the sudden change of mood this kiss induced in their hostess. Flora smiled, charmed, and concentrated on getting more bottles out of the fridge, while Hero went upstairs for her coat.

I suppose that's what they call masterful, she thought. *But why not? Even with Stephen, I had to ask him for a date. It could be fun and here's someone who really knows his way around. Be daft not to go, really.*

Pleased with herself, because everyone likes to make a conquest, Hero patted the velvet dress and brushed her hair in Flora's mirror. The wine had given her face a febrile intensity, and it shone with a festive glow. So did her nose. Covering it with some of Flora's foundation, she snatched up her sheepskin and rushed out. Catching sight of herself in a glass on the landing, Hero thought: I look pretty good. And Other Hero was quiescent.

Walking downstairs, where the partygoers thrashed around like organisms seen through a microscope, Hero noticed Tom waiting by the door. He really did look attractive, but she began to doubt his interest in her again. *Perhaps he's just being kind.* But Hero walked downstairs with an air of confidence which transmitted itself with subliminal magic, so that people glanced up who had not bothered previously. The reassurance of

41

having someone interested gave Hero presence, and she practically swept past Flora, feeling chic and suave despite the sheepskin mittens. Thanking her hostess politely, she walked out into the fog with Tom.

★   ★   ★

Mist swirled and billowed around the street, obscuring mundane details of bus stops and fences, so that only shadowy outlines of gables and branches remained. The iced road glittered as they got to Tom's car, and the night had a hushed, enchanted quality which made Hero feel she'd strayed into the wrong context. These things didn't happen in real life. Or not to her.

'It's very foggy,' she said. 'Are you sure we—'

'I'm a good driver, and we'll drive *slowly*.'

She got into the passenger seat and arranged her skirt, nervous and apprehensive away from the fuzzy warmth of Flora's house. Tom's face looked older in the muted undersea light, worn and determined as he concentrated on driving. They went deeper into the countryside, wraiths of mist springing at them from deserted roadsides, an occasional gleam of yellow eyes as some animal vanished into the shadows.

'I'm grateful to you for getting me away from that party, Hero. Much more of Flora's friends and I'd have got out the *Standard* crossword. Terrible, this obligation to mix.'

'I would have thought you were a great mixer.'

'I suppose I'm friendly enough until I meet someone I like. And then I want them all to myself. For a while, at least.' He turned and smiled, but

42

Hero wasn't entirely reassured. There was danger in the air, a hint of menace. For the first time she appreciated that she was sitting in the car of a complete stranger, driving God knows where after a couple of hours' acquaintance. With the mist outside, and the faintly spooky atmosphere of New Year's Eve, she could almost visualise herself as a trusting, red-haired riding hood, smooth-talked by a well-spoken wolf.

But it's an adventure, she told herself, as they moved into the night, through the shimmering fog. *It's an adventure.*

CHAPTER THREE

And so I was swept off my feet, to spend New Year's Eve in the arms of a perfect stranger. Too romantic by half. Completely impossible. Things like that just don't happen. But it was different. After Stephen and Colin and all the other nervous academics, perhaps I needed someone like that to come along, rescue me, take control. It can be attractive to be looked after—if you allow it. And how flattering it was, to be taken up like this, made much of, complimented and praised. And how addictive.

How could anybody have resisted all that? All that charm, all that glamour, all that fun. And the sensation of power—seeing him genuinely bewitched and besotted, singling me out for his sole attention. They talk about whirlwind courtships—but it was more like being in the rays of a great benevolent planet. One of the Plantagenets was referred to as The Sun In Splendour. He must have been very like Tom.

43

*   *   *

And of course it had all been too perfect. Unlike most relationships, where both parties generally start by having commitments elsewhere, demanding jobs, travel difficulties or constant misunderstandings to complicate their involvements, and it may take a couple of weeks or months to develop an attachment. Hero and Tom fell in love practically overnight. At first, there appeared to be so few obstacles: Tom seemed (mysteriously) unattached; Hero still mourning Colin's defection to Manchester; and being a student allowed her plenty of time to visit Tom in London and Hampshire, and sit around thinking about him, a necessary activity for those with romantic interests, and a novelty to Hero.

*   *   *

Their journey on New Year's Eve had ended at a country pub, with logs flickering in the grate and a mixed clientele of rustics and advertising men. Tom demonstrated his ability to establish an effortless rapport with total strangers, who made room for him at the bar, bought them a round, and jostled and winked as the couple sat huddled by the fire like eloping lovers.

Hero ate crisps, and steak sandwiches, and drank too much whisky, and basked in the glow of Tom's fascination with her. Their conversation was still reticent, as though they sensed that more personal details could be discussed later. Instead, they chatted about books and films, the difference

44

between pubs in Oxford and Cambridge, and very briefly, Tom's job. He described himself as a civil servant, and glossed the activity over so that it sounded as boring an occupation as Hero had always suspected.

She noticed him staring at her hair—people always did—and that his eyes kept wandering back to it so that he seemed to lose track of the conversation. But it was not until midnight when behind bolted doors the remaining drinkers linked arms and sang *Auld Lang Syne*, that he actually kissed her, chastely, as though embarrassed by the reckless embracing that went on around them.

'I've been wanting to do that all evening.'

'I won't try and stop you.' But Tom shook his head slightly, restricted himself to touching her hair, and said it was time they got back to Oxford.

'Where are you staying tonight?' she asked, when they drew up outside her house. It had crossed her mind that he might stay at Flora's.

'Oh, I'll get back to London.'

'But it's so late now—and you've had a lot to drink—'

'I need to pop into work tomorrow morning. But listen, are you busy tomorrow—I mean tonight?' looking at his watch.

'I don't think so. I usually work during the day and then watch TV.'

'Good. We can have dinner. Properly, this time. I'll pick you up at eight.'

'Well—I don't know if—'

Fancies himself, doesn't he? commented Other Hero. *Just automatically assumes you're available. Well, I am*, Hero pointed out.

She watched him drive off, taking a little of

45

herself with him, and swayed unsteadily indoors, hoping for a quiet bed and a cool pillow. But celebrations were still in progress at the Abrahams'. *They observed every festival of the year, Christian, Jewish and Pagan*, she reflected bitterly—and Hero was prevailed upon to sit up and drink more Jameson's until four a.m. before staggering upstairs.

★   ★   ★

The prospect of dinner with Tom did not appeal to Hero when she woke on New Year's Day with an aching head and clouded eyes. In fact, it appalled her. After the success of the previous night, she could not see how it could fail to be a disaster. She forced herself to run five miles until the alcoholic cobwebs had blown away, and spent the day agonising over what to wear. Eventually she settled for an Indian muslin dress, busy with paisley, which Stephen had brought from Cambridge market. With its high waist, handkerchief hems and billowing sleeves, the dress seemed uncomfortably arty, but it was all she could find. The indigos and cobalts showed off her hair, but beneath the sheepskin jacket she felt dowdy and crushed, a faded flower child.

'I wasn't sure you'd come,' she said as she stepped into his car, and immediately regretted the remark.

'I don't believe *you've* ever been stood up.'

'It could happen.' Other Hero reminded her of that all the time.

'You're extraordinarily insecure, Hero.'

'Just realistic.'

46

*   *   *

Dinner with Tom was not like trips to the vegetarian diner with Stephen Lewis. Coats were whisked away, wine lists produced, and an attentive buzz surrounded them the moment they stepped through the door. Hero's previous experience of the restaurant had been restricted to staring with disbelief at the prices displayed outside.

Seated opposite Tom, Hero flicked back her hair with a gesture of Flora's and was convinced that the entire room must be able to hear her heart pound with anxiety.

'How was your day?'

It was one of Tom's characteristics to speak in clichés as in phrases new-minted, but at that time Hero found the habit endearing.

'Oh—well—I wrote up a bit of my dissertation, did some revision, went out for a run. That sort of thing.'

'The running sounds intrepid.'

'It's the best cure for a hangover.'

'Not that you get many.'

'You'd be surprised.'

'Have you spoken to Flora today, Hero?'

'Er—no. No, I meant to ring her—sort of apologise for going off last night.'

'I gave her a call.'

Hero was momentarily consumed with jealousy and apprehension.

'To say thank you,' Tom continued. 'That's all. And to wish her Happy New Year. I didn't mention—us.'

'*Is* there an us?'

'I hope there can be.'

Glancing up to see if their food had arrived (she wasn't used to dining out and couldn't feign Flora's sophisticated indifference), Hero noticed other people watching them, as though at a play. She realised that being in Tom's company involved high public exposure: he radiated warmth and fascination.

And there was an element of performance, too. She knew intuitively that fantasy, some element of pretence, governed his behaviour. Did he lean forward to stroke her cheek like that because he really wanted to, or because the other diners, glancing frequently, expected it? Were the gestures, comments, jokes, asides designed for Hero alone—or intended to amuse everybody present?

After another Campari Hero didn't care. She had entered the game herself, held in romantic thrall. They could be in love, they could be pretending to be in love—or a little of both.

Over dinner, Tom told Hero about his Cambridge days. These were so different from her own that they could have been at university on different planets. He mentioned the antics of his dining club, the girl who pushed him out of a punt, the grapefruit juice and vodka drinking contest. It was a Cambridge which Hero knew dimly, a parallel universe which never overlapped with her own. Throwing people in rivers, letting off fire extinguishers and dropping statues in lakes seemed pretty inane to Hero's friends: but perhaps her friends were stuffy, lacking in youthful exuberance.

'You've never done anything like that?'

'It didn't occur to me.'

'I suppose girls are different.'

48

'Yeah. We're not so immature.'

'What a serious girl you are, Hero.'

'It's a serious world.' These were Other Hero's words. Quickly, she tried to change the mood. 'I like this place. It's very glamorous, though.'

'You fit the surroundings.'

'Hardly.'

'Look in the mirror if you don't believe me.'

Hero generally looked in mirrors to see what was wrong. But this was evidently an enchanted glass: in the tinted reflection on the other side of the room, she and Tom appeared as a golden couple.

'I don't ever go to places like this.'

'We'll change that.'

'I mean, Flora sometimes wants to—you know, with a whole group of people—I don't really get on well with them. I don't like what they represent.'

'Including me?' Tom sounded jovial, but his slightly hooded eyes had a way of becoming threatening.

'No—no, of course not. I just meant—all those silly Hoorays and Henriettas—'

'I haven't much time for them either, come to that. But you *are* different, there's no question about it. Something sets you apart.'

'Probably my background. Half Jewish, half Irish. I get the worst of both worlds.'

'Or perhaps it's your sense of humour. And you're very attractive. You must have so many boyfriends. I was surprised to hear you were going to stay in.'

Hero shrugged. She might be in love, but she was also, suddenly, very hungry, and wanted to concentrate on her prawns.

'Isn't there somebody at the moment?'

'No—not really. He's gone to Manchester.'

'Hence the road map.'

'Oh, you noticed that? Yes, I might go and see him later in the vacation.' *But I probably won't.*

'I hope you'll be able to come up to London before term starts. I'd like to show you round—show you off, I should say. And I get so bored during the week.'

'I'm no good at meeting people, Tom, and I hate parties. You ought to know that much by now.'

'This would be different.'

'You're such a change from the girls I usually meet,' Tom commented, later in the the evening. Hero had slid into a relaxed mood, Other Hero in abeyance, and she was starting to enjoy herself. But at this comment, her normal preoccupations returned.

'What sort of *girls* do you meet?' she asked, annoyed both by his casual reference to women and the prospect that he probably had many admirers.

'Oh, you know. London girls. Sort of grown-up versions of the ones who went to the secretarial college in Cambridge.'

'Dumb, you mean.'

Hero sounded arrogant and she knew it.

'They're insipid, quite honestly. But they generally have a good sense of fun.'

'All jolly hockeysticks and ra-ra-ra.'

'You could say that. They can be tedious after a while.'

'They probably get bored with you too.'

Hero had intended to stay polite that evening: to be Good Company, have a Sense Of Humour (something conventional men claimed to be absent from anyone halfway feminist), even to try and

50

entertain Tom as he entertained her. She had resolved to be Flora for the night: to compromise. (Or be a *hypocrite*, as Other Hero remarked.)

'So why aren't you here with one of your secretaries now?' she went on, as Tom did not respond to her earlier comment.

'Because you're more interesting. Most of the girls—women—' with a nod '—who I see are all alike. They're so dull. They want to get married and—' He shrugged dismissively.

Hero was torn between contempt for Tom's attitudes and sexual fascination. Her temper won.

'The other women are only like that because men like you made them that way.'

'That's a point,' Tom conceded, conscious perhaps that he might lose ground with Hero if he pursued the argument. 'You may yet change my attitude.'

'I doubt it. Everything's too convenient for people like you as it is.'

'I'm really fascinated by the way you fluctuate between shyness and aggression. Honestly, Hero, I'm getting confused. One minute I think we're getting on like a house on fire, the next I expect you to hit me. I can't make you out at all.'

Hero was astonished by this speech, but had enough presence of mind not to answer. She allowed him to place his large hand over her own.

'I don't think you're really very impressed with me, are you?' Tom said.

'I've certainly never met anyone like you before,' she replied, with truth.

* * *

51

The evening had been concluded in a certain mutual fascination and irritation. Hero realised she could get away with a lot, and that he found their verbal skirmishes exciting. There was a style, a quality of glamour about their banter which had been absent from the good-natured companionship of previous lovers. She and Stephen had dined out with the compatibility of an old married couple. Tonight Hero had wondered if they would actually get through the meal without one or the other walking out.

'Will you come down to Hampshire this weekend?'

Tom was attractive in the darkness of his car, and she enjoyed the sensuous scratch of his overcoat against her arms.

'Yes. Yes, I'll come.' Away from the restaurant, and with the reassuring sound of her mother hammering away in the garage/studio, Hero had become more tolerant.

'I can show you the countryside. You don't know that area well, do you? And perhaps there'll be snow. Do you ride?'

'Ride what?'

'Didn't you learn, as a little girl?'

'Of course not. Sorry, that was rude. No, I've never been on a horse in my life.'

'Then you can learn. I think you'll take to it easily. You're fit, and you're very light. We've got a super pub in the village, and—well, I'd just enjoy your company. It gets a bit lonely down there. I go most weekends, but I don't always take somebody. It doesn't mean—anything you don't want it to mean.'

How innocent it all sounded, especially his efforts

to put Hero at her ease concerning sleeping arrangements. It made a change for anyone to assume that she would *not* automatically sleep with them.

'How do I get there?'

'I'll collect you. I have to be in London for the rest of this week, but I'll call for you around seven on Friday, and we'll drive down together. Will that be all right?'

'That's lovely. I'll look forward to it.'

And Hero meant what she said. In spite of herself.

*   *   *

Tom's cottage was surrounded by snow on Hero's first visit, but warm with central heating as they went inside. It seemed like the home of a much older person, with its Stafford dogs, faded bindings and worn Persian rugs. There were low beams on which even Hero—five foot four—bumped her head, and a faint smell of lavender. She was amused and slightly touched by the domestic clutter, with back numbers of the *Field*, and Benares brassware which invoked the shade of a long-gone Anglo-Indian colonel.

'I'd expected something more—cool,' she explained. 'Dimmer switches, low sofas, tapes of mood music that come on when you open the door.'

'Not quite my scene, I'm afraid. The cottage belonged to my aunt, that's why there's still all this stuff lying around. I like it, to be honest. There's a little garden at the back, and a paddock.'

Tom dragged a hairy sweater over his head, having discarded the London jacket and tie almost the moment they walked through the door. The wool crackled with electricity, and, hair rumpled, eyes a little red, Tom was more human and approachable. Hero told him so.

'Ah well. Perhaps I'll win you over, after all,' he said, sinking back into the sofa with a sigh.

'You have a chance,' she agreed, settling beside him.

★   ★   ★

Broad daylight streamed through the lattice window of Tom's bedroom, and Hero could see the distant outlines of snow-laden branches against an oyster-grey sky. Lying still, so she would not wake him and have to talk, Hero gazed at the morning. Tom stirred, and she held her breath, unwilling to be drawn into speech or any other activity. But his gesture was merely to wrap an arm around her, securing her to his body like a load, before slipping back again into the journey of sleep. Hero lay close, trying to get used to a different shape folding itself into hers. Tom's was the sort of body Flora admired, the sort most women and some men photographed and adored. For some reason, although she liked its owner well enough, it didn't really appeal to Hero.

★   ★   ★

It was as though people's appearances represented the reverse of their sexual behaviour. Pale, nervous Stephen Lewis, who looked thin and languid, had been a passionate and sensual lover. Although his study of the subject had been chiefly theoretical

54

until meeting Hero, he had caressed and fondled, shivered exquisitely like a cat and buried his face in her golden triangle. Stephen haunted the lingerie department of Marks & Spencer's, spending his grant on stockings and garter-briefs which he dressed Hero in for the pleasure of taking them off again. And he was comically priapic. Hero, as he was her first lover, assumed most men behaved in the same way. She had derived secret satisfaction that on seeing him flit about the darkened streets like the Scholar Gypsy, it was impossible to guess their activities. Her sensational underwear remained hidden under layers of sensible jerseys.

Colin too had found relief from the pressures of biochemistry in frantic coupling, and had greeted Hero's sexiest underwear with excited incredulity. With characteristic diligence, they pored over manuals together, and expended energy on their erotic accomplishments much as another couple might practise duets.

Hero's more casual lovers had also been enthusiastic, eager to please, and shown an appropriate academic willingness to explore the topic. She had often slept with men because she was generous, she enjoyed it, and she hated turning them down. It was only later that she realised how fortunate she'd been, and how many bored, frustrated people there really were.

*   *   *

So when Tom embraced her vinously after dinner, slipping a hand inside her striped shirt and cupping her breast, Hero did nothing to stop him. And he

55

had been attractive, the ash-brown hair unkempt, the warmth of his body against hers. But she had been surprised by his inhibition, the lights switched off, the clothes removed before getting into bed, the tentativeness. Hero knew the first time with somebody different—or somebody special—can be traumatic, so she expected little. A long week, a long drive, too much wine, take their toll of most men, and she knew that the very fact that he was so attracted to her made Tom nervous.

Tom in bed was a more anxious, conventional and hesitant man than Tom fully clothed and holding forth in a drawing room. She thought wistfully about Stephen Lewis long after Tom had fallen asleep.

*   *   *

But it had been remarkable, and touching, to hear the things he said on waking, the expressions of tenderness, the intense gratitude with which he stroked her hair and kissed her. Hero realised that she had power over this grown man, and that was a reward in itself.

Tom had remained inhibited, slightly self-conscious, to the end of his days. He had been ill at ease with public displays of emotion, curtailing any serious discussion with a joke so that he would not be betrayed into revealing himself. It was only with Hero that he occasionally clung in desperation, holding her as though on the verge of tears, and showing such anxiety and defencelessness that she often wondered which of them was stronger. His vulnerability, the sudden irritational panics that she had assumed to be a legacy of his military career, moved her, though he would never tell Hero the cause.

CHAPTER FOUR

'I don't believe it!' Flora was bright and intimidating, flushed face vying with her viridian dress, highlighted hair falling across one cheek. 'You might have told me before!'

'I was afraid to.'

They were sitting in Flora's kitchen, sharing a bottle of wine on their last night before returning to their respective colleges. The house already reminded Hero of her conquest and at her insistence *Love Affair With Life* played in the background.

'But it's wonderful! I mean, I do rather fancy him myself, everybody does. Though he's a bit old.'

'Only thirty-one.'

'And such a change from your usual type.'

'Bit different, yes. But he makes you feel special. As if you're doing him a favour just being there. And he's so attentive. Notices what you wear, and things like that.'

'But you've never bothered about clothes, Hero. Why would anyone want to notice what you wear?'

'Tom does.'

'It'll be nice for you to have a proper boyfriend. I mean someone to take care of you, who you can have a good time with. Who's got a car.'

'Colin used to take me out in the van.'

'To Tarkovski double-features at the Arts, and protest meetings.'

'It was interesting enough.'

'But I bet Tom's more fun.'

The concept of someone being fun was new to Hero.

'So what happens next? When are you seeing him?'

'This weekend. I'm supposed to go and stay in London. He's got a flat in Hans Place.'

'And what about poor Colin?'

'I've written to poor Colin. I just said I was too busy to see him. Which is true, in a way.'

'And what about last weekend? How did that go?'

'Well—it was *different*. And I'm not telling you everything.'

'Don't Tom's parents live in Hampshire?'

'Yeah, but I haven't met them yet. I hope I don't have to. I imagine they're really snobbish and county.'

'But they're very well connected, Hero. Tom's maternal grandfather was a peer.'

'Brighton or Southend?'

'Hero, sometimes I think you fell in with a really chippy crowd at Cambridge. I hope Tom straightens you out a bit.'

'So what, so they're well connected. I bet they're as thick as paint.'

'And you're intellectually arrogant.'

'Anything else? You've already criticised my clothes.'

'Okay. But—you know what I mean. There's money in that family, Hero.'

'I realise. I think he must have some sort of private income. I shouldn't think civil servants get much, and he's so generous—did you ever have dinner with him?'

'Me? No, I wish I had. I'd have grabbed him at the first opportunity. All that happened was we met at a drinks party in London, and, since I fancied him, I asked him to come over on New Year's Eve if he was free.'

'But you had Rufus coming—or was it Adrian? I can never remember all your boyfriends.'

'Anthony, actually. Yes but that doesn't stop me inviting him. The rule is, that if I invite him, he'll invite me to the next one he gives—or out for lunch or something.'

'Is that so?'

'Hero, you're really naïve, sometimes. Don't you know anything about organising your social life?'

'Not really, no.'

'Tom isn't a moment too soon. You'd probably have gone off to live in a feminist collective or something, if he hadn't arrived.'

'What's wrong with that? And anyway, you're such a gold-digger, Flora.'

'I need to be. I'm not going off to do research, like you. Though I must say, there were some gorgeous young men in that merchant bank I'm joining. When they showed me round I thought I'd died and gone to heaven.'

'I can imagine.'

'Well, I think it's absolutely super that you two have got together. I mean, I suppose before long you'll be back to grey scientists, and all those thin boys who know everything about alpha decay but can't get good service in a restaurant—'

'Oh, piss off, Flora!'

'I think it'll be rather fun. Tom and Hero. Hero Fitzgerald. Imagine that. Have another glass of wine.'

Hero accepted, thinking about Flora's rather antiquated views of correct female behaviour. The chastening thing was that all her manoeuvres seemed to be successful. Flora always had an adoring retinue of men, willing to lunch, dine, and if required, marry her, whom she treated with condescension and scorn, knowing that if one defected, others would soon take his place. Flora was so confident, so pleased with herself, so delighted to be Flora, that admirers were attracted helplessly to her, as though by some law of physics. She did not regret the loss of Tom, knowing he would soon be replaced by another eligible, well-bred bachelor.

'Anyway, you're no different,' Flora commented, turning over the cassette. It was as though she knew what Hero had been thinking. 'You dropped Colin pretty sharpish.'

'But—Colin's so far away, and—'

'You were never really serious about him, were you? I mean, not *really, really*?'

'Well, it was the usual thing. He wanted me to settle with him, maybe get married, and I just didn't fancy the idea.'

'You'd rather have been a mistress.'

It was another of Flora's dated words. Hero was sure no-one had mistresses any more, or if they did, they were referred to as girlfriends. A mistress was a fictional creation from Flora's paperback-ridden youth, all jewels and camiknickers and illicit assignations. Hero found it difficult to imagine herself 'kept' in the hot-house of a flat like a rare orchid, occasionally visited by a Tom dripping diamonds and champagne.

'No, I just want to get on with my research.'

But the faded books began to lose their old appeal; Hero struggled to retain her interest, and half-heartedly completed the application forms for research that spring, as it became increasingly difficult to think about anything but Tom. Hero knew she loved him because, although he could be irritating, she missed him desperately when he wasn't there. She had forgotten how quietly enjoyable Life Before Tom had seemed. All that mattered now was his passion and protection, warm arms around her, the constant brilliant sequence of events in which she took a role. How could she possibly refuse to visit him when he rang, how could she work when she could be with him, how could she lose that mainline of love, cut off the supply which fed her addiction?

She had forgotten her aloof independence before Tom ruled her life, the cosy isolation of college rooms, and libraries on windy nights. She had forgotten the ambitions once entertained, to see her name in learned journals, or be on the platform lecturing, not sitting in the hall taking notes. She had forgotten the camaraderie of evenings with Leah and Beth, or nights with Stephen. Now, somehow, she was desperate to please, desperate for approval, desperate for his attention when he wasn't there.

And Tom frequently wasn't there, and wasn't anywhere she could find him. His lapses and absences, failures to telephone and one broken date, went unexplained. These disappearances were sporadic and irregular, inspiring a precariousness and anxiety in Hero, so that her relief on hearing from him again convinced her that she loved him. It was as though they were governed by some malignant force, which strove to drive them apart, and this element of mystery fascinated Hero.

*   *   *

It was only after he proposed to her that Hero learnt of her future husband's real occupation, and the reason for his curious disappearances. When they first met, Tom had described himself as a civil servant. Pushed, he added that his job was in public relations, which Hero assumed was something to do with organising press conferences and holding receptions. But she was accustomed to talking with her men about their work, listening to complex accounts of laboratory procedure and rival theories. Tom's refusal to discuss his activities perplexed Hero, and she kept asking why the telephonists sounded wary and evasive when she rang him at work. Tom eventually admitted that he worked for the Ministry of Defence, but this scarcely seemed unusual for a former major. Hero had to be satisfied with this information, but there were still unexplained absences, evenings when nobody knew where he was, when those friends whom Hero dared telephone replied that they hadn't seen him in a week. There were weekends when, having promised to telephone and perhaps visit, he did neither, and the staircase callbox remained silent as Hero paced her room like a tiger in a cage.

Irritation, anger, finally anxiety would seize her, driving her out onto the streets of Cambridge in search of sights and activities which would distract her. Leaving copious messages with friends, and lists of instructions taped to the telephone, Hero would cycle off into the fens, or walk restlessly around the town, trying to wear away her frustration and fear.

*   *   *

The days of Tom's absence had been clear blue spring days, bright and cold, with vapour trails etched across the high East Anglian skies. She had squelched through water meadows in the chilly breeze from the river, or ridden along narrow fenland roads, spending hours in cold isolation which should have been spent at her desk.

She had ranged through Cambridge, when the town was prosaic and going about its business with no knowledge of her pain. Market stalls glistened with fruit, students turned over second-hand books and moons of cheese shone on marble counters. Tourists sidled through Hero's college, unconscious of the events occurring behind its walls. Photographers, oblivious of her suffering, and that of many others snapped the red creepers of St John's and the windy courts of Trinity.

Remembering those anxious days, Hero realised later that they had been good preparation for bereavement.

*   *   *

Tom always did ring. Late on Sunday evenings, or perhaps one lunch-time, the message would come, a quick apology, no explanation, and a firm date to meet again as soon as possible. When he suggested

63

they marry, Hero saw some means of ending this cycle. Perhaps if he really did commit himself, these absences would stop, he would be reliable and constant and give her that blazing adoration to which she had become addicted.

Tom had proposed marriage after reappearing from a particularly long excursion into the unknown, which had lasted five days, and Hero had accepted immediately, out of relief. If this was what she had to do to keep him, well: she would suspend her judgement, ignore her principles, dismiss her doubts, and marry the man.

*   *   *

One afternoon some days later, as they sat in Hero's room after lunch, Tom said: 'I've got something to tell you.'

You've changed your mind, suggested Other Hero. Her bitter inner critic had not received the news of the impending wedding with equilibrium, but then kept her mouth shut.

Both leant on their elbows, hands propping their chins, staring at each other across wine glasses which shimmered with condensation. Silver beads of moisture vapour trickled down the stems, and late afternoon sunlight poured through the casement, bouncing off a tarnished silver trophy. Hero listened to the strains of Jean Michel Jarre drifting through the quad.

'Hero, I haven't been quite fair with you.'

'No, but it doesn't matter.' She was charitable to Tom where she would have been barbed and abrupt with Stephen Lewis. Losing Tom seemed so likely, whereas Stephen had always adored her.

64

'Well, it does. I think I should put you in the picture.'

'You don't have to talk about it. I don't really want to know.'

'That's not true. You're a very inquisitive person.'

'Yes—'

Hero couldn't tell him how much the disappearances affected her. There were no means available to convey her sensation of loss when he failed to ring, the stricken quality with which she greeted empty days. There was some cliché about dying a thousand deaths every time this happened, and it described Hero's feelings perfectly.

'I'm going to give you some indication of what I do, but not much. I shan't tell you a lot, or anything which could be dangerous for you to know. Do you understand?'

'I think so.'

'I never really left the army. I work for the MoD now—'

'You mean Intelligence—'

'Don't jump to conclusions.'

Tom was more serious than Hero had ever seen him before; older, too. The carefree, brazen quality had disappeared, and been replaced by someone altogether more unguessable. It was as though another face looked out at her after a carnival mask had been removed. The Department, he explained, dealt with a variety of security matters, internal and overseas. It had links with other major organisations, but its operatives were considered a race apart. 'A bunch of mavericks,' Tom said. 'Officially, we don't exist. You perhaps know that there's a great deal of rivalry between the different

65

branches of Security. The established services look at us askance. But they still use us.'

'That's fascinating, Tom. I bet it's exciting, isn't it?'

'Humdrum, most of the time. A lot of it is just meeting and greeting, making sure things run smoothly, getting people what they want. It *is* like public relations really—or private relations. But it means I work peculiar hours, and sometimes I can't contact you, and—that's why, well, in the past—'

'Is there a lot of travelling?'

'Sometimes.'

'So that's why you've been—'

'I can't say much about it, of course.'

'And is it dangerous?'

'Prosaic, most of the time. You're taking this very well, Hero.' As he touched her hand, to the haunting strains of electronic music and the echo of laughter from the quad, Hero felt as if they were doomed lovers in a spy film.

'I don't scare easy,' she replied, playing her part.

Tom relaxed, smiling for the first time, and visibly becoming *Tom* again, lines and folds settling into a different pattern on his face.

'Some of the wives go on a sort of—course, when people in my line of work marry. Just to teach you how to look after yourself. But I don't think that's necessary. You may want to ask me a few things, and I'll tell you what I can, but there will be times when—times I can't talk about.'

'That's okay.'

And Hero wasn't frightened, either. Fear didn't seem an appropriate response. Most people travelled, these days. Most ambitious people worked long hours. Why should intelligence work

66

be any more disturbing than Flora's brother, jetsetting for BP, or Hero's cousins, who virtually lived at the advertising agency they worked for in London?

'It means we won't see too much of each other and get bored,' she said.

'You've got the right sort of character, which is important. You're a bit bolshy, of course, but you don't panic, and you're resilient.'

'Wait a minute, are you marrying me or recruiting me?'

'Perhaps a bit of both. I must warn you, Hero. Once you've joined the family, life is never quite the same again.'

'Things have never been the same since I met you.'

★　　　★　　　★

'Don't ever mention this in conversation will you?' Tom said later, as they lay on her narrow bed watching the sky change colour.

'Of course not. Never volunteer information, right?'

'Right. But there is one person—don't say *anything* unless he mentions it first, and even then, be careful. It's Alex Gilby, who lives near us in the country. You met him at that drinks party a few weeks ago.'

'But he was *nice*.'

'We're not all monsters, you know.'

'I'm sorry, I didn't mean it that way.'

'You can trust him, Hero. If anything does—go wrong, he's the one to turn to. He'll see you're looked after.'

'But nothing will go wrong. You said yourself. It's a tame world, these days.'

'Accidents can happen. Even in the best regulated families.'

★   ★   ★

Hero had not been entirely surprised by Tom's occupation. It explained his frequent absences, the defensive receptionist, the peculiar working hours and his not inconsiderable talents as an actor. But, being a scholar, Hero devoted her spare time to reading Professor Hinsley and Christopher Andrew on the history of the British Intelligence Service—none of which mentioned the Department—and supplemented these books with Deighton and le Carré. Tom assured her the real thing was far more prosaic.

★   ★   ★

If the secret life with Tom held no fears for Hero the public life certainly did. Hero had always hated parties, and had only attended them with the greatest reluctance. However often Tom reminded Hero that one party had brought them together, she could not overcome feelings ranging from anxiety to cosmic dread at the prospect of a room full of people. Hero couldn't convince Tom of the terror which overcame her as she walked through the door, the suppressed panic, sweating palms, the urge to turn and flee. No doubt a psychologist would have something to say about her choice of running as a sport.

She couldn't explain either the crippling

68

consequence of these occasional but virulent bouts of shyness to someone as bold and extrovert as Tom.

Part of the fear was that London parties were full of adept and polished London women. Hero knew she was in competition with them, and wondered how long she could continue to amuse and distract Tom, before the novelty faded, and someone else became the object of his attention; someone with glistening lips, polished nails, and who wore the right sort of shoes and brushed her hair without being reminded.

'But you're *you*,' he had said, one night at the cottage when Hero voiced these anxieties. 'You're special. I don't care what you look like.'

'Well, thanks a lot.'

'What I mean is that you're more important to me because of who you are, not because of any superficial attractions. And some of those women you're so jealous of are no spring chickens,' he added. 'You're much younger and prettier.'

'But people like Carina Villiers—I mean, she's very *elegant*.'

'Yes. Carina's elegant, all right.'

Carina Villiers, tall and slender, would have been beautiful if she were not quite so cadaverous, battered by the sun like an expensive piece of luggage. Her hair was blonde and fine as a child's, contrasting strangely with the black in which she habitually dressed. Carina was present at many of the parties they attended, and her warmth towards Tom, and coolness towards Hero, irritated Hero profoundly.

'Carina can be a bit funny sometimes,' Tom said. 'It's just her way. I'm sure she likes you really.'

'I always get the feeling she's a bit—off—about my name.'

'I think you're over-sensitive, Hero. Carina was brought up in Capetown—'

'So she *is* a fascist, after all.'

'What I was going to say was, Carina knows many Jewish people. I hardly think she was being prejudiced. Besides, you've got to avoid these snap political judgements of yours, Hero. The fact that she was born there doesn't mean that—'

'Okay, okay.'

Hero was conscious that Tom liked Carina, had perhaps more than liked Carina in the past, that Carina didn't like her, and that nobody could do anything about it. So Hero kept her thoughts to herself, remembering Carina's artificial laugh, strong teeth and large blue eyes. Carina had not taken to her. Tom was secretive about his past life, and scarcely ever mentioned former girlfriends, unless it was to account for some object in the cottage, or an inscription in an old book.

'This isn't *Rebecca*, you know,' he said once, when Hero asked about the provenance of a lavishly-illustrated coffee-table volume signed *All my love, Nerissa*.

'I'm just curious.'

'Remember what that did to the cat.'

Hero was silenced.

★　　★　　★

'There's an independent streak I like about you,' Tom said that night in the cottage, once they had disposed of the subject of Carina Villiers. 'Sometimes I'm even frightened of you!'

70

'You like that?'

'I'm honoured you put up with me, to be honest.'

Hero hit him with a cushion.

'See what I mean? You can take care of yourself.'

'Except at parties.'

'Yes. Yes, I do wish you enjoyed them more. But it's important, for my job. And I've known some of these people for years.'

'I can't understand why I have to go, as well. I mean, you never talk to me.'

'But Hero, I can always talk to you. You know I'd *die* for you. But one has to circulate.'

'I *hate* circulating. I can't carry on conversations about skiing or who I met at Hurlingham. I just don't fit in.'

'You can learn to ski, next winter. You took to riding as if you were born to it, and you know you enjoyed that point-to-point I took you to.'

'That was different. There was something to look at, something going on. It's all this standing round nattering which I can't get used to.'

'There speaks my little bluestocking.'

Hero hit him again with the cushion.

'You *are* refreshing,' he replied, picking off feathers. 'And everyone says what a nice quiet girl you are, too.'

'I'm not quiet. I just can't be bothered to talk to them.'

It had occurred to Hero at this point that Tom must consider her something of an exception. Most of the girls she had met—and some of the men—had been won over instantly by his charm. It must have been unusual to find someone like Hero, who fought back, and occasionally fought dirty.

'Anyway, you said *you* didn't like parties, when

71

we first met.'

'I don't, darling. I mean, we only go to three dinners and about one drinks party a week. I wouldn't call that excessive. Believe me, I'd rather be here with you, but we can't always do what we want. Can we?'

'Why not? Though I quite enjoyed that reception we went to. At the embassy.'

'You mean the one where you spent the evening chatting up the cultural attaché.'

'It's not often I get the chance to practise my Russian. I've done so little studying recently.'

'Our friend was most impressed. We'll have you defecting next.'

'Yeah, well. As long as they don't force me to go parties in Moscow.'

'You'll grow out of your nerves, Hero. You'll see. It's simply that you didn't have much practice at socialising when you were younger. It'll come, in time.'

But it never did come. Hero knew that her refusal to make the effort (as Tom called it) and stand in a circle patting back and forth the conversational ball, was pure arrogance. But she couldn't bring herself to believe that the discussions of holidays, personalities and restaurants contributed anything useful, and was amazed that other guests derived such satisfaction from reinforcing one another's prejudices. Other people realised this and left Hero alone.

As their life together developed, Hero advanced to the stage of finding one other person in the room and spending most of the evening in his or her company. They were often the isolated guests, the ugly girls nobody spoke to or the ones considered

72

dull but asked to make up numbers. Hero's singling out of the socially inept earned her an erroneous reputation for charity, so that she was considered a Social social worker.

But how often at those parties she had drifted off into her own world, gazing at a flower arrangement or at the evening sunlight golden over a garden square. She had longed to be outside, anywhere with Tom but without his retinue. She would watch him from a distance, still entranced and hypnotised by his features, still astonished that he had chosen her, and touched by the knowledge of his secret dependence, as though she were an illicit drug.

It had never been like this with Stephen Lewis, who though attractive, had never trapped her by her own responses. Hero didn't feel sure enough of Tom's continuing love to risk incurring his displeasure and slip away, walk out into that golden garden square, or leave early and go home to television and a dish of scrambled eggs.

CHAPTER FIVE

Tom and Hero were married at midsummer. Events unrolled with a narrative fluency that left Hero almost frightened, as though life shouldn't be this simple, as though at any moment her transformation to an easier, more privileged existence would be denied. She lay in bed at night, sometimes alone, sometimes beside Tom, waiting for him to wake and announce he'd changed his mind, waiting for the return of some old girlfriend (the shadowy Nerissa or the aggressive Carina), waiting for the telephone to ring with some dreadful message when he wasn't there.

It was on these nights that Hero was haunted by a different Tom. A figure, conjured out of shadows, this other Tom appeared in her dreams, often dressed in combat clothes (she had never seen him in military kit) hard-faced, narrow-lipped, cold and cruel. He inhabited some dark arena of swirling mists and damp forests, and, without being physically violent, rejected her in some way or another. Often he would appear with a crêpe-clad Carina Villiers; at other times he would shout something she couldn't understand, and walk away, vanishing into the darkness. And Hero would wake beside him—the real Tom—sweating and confused and unable to decide which was which. She never told anyone about these dreams.

And none of Hero's forebodings were vindicated. Admittedly, Maeve Abrahams was a little surprised by the rapidity of Hero's path to the altar, and asked why Hero felt an anachronism such as marriage to be necessary; and Hero's Cambridge girlfriends were surprised to find a former cynic transformed to a romantic, going for fittings at Belleville Sassoon and flashing an emerald ring. But no bad fairy actually appeared to deny the union, and it seemed unlikely that a mad wife, trailing attic cobwebs, would appear at the little Hampshire church to forbid the banns.

*   *   *

Occasionally, Hero admitted to herself that self-interest played as much a part as did her love for Tom. Research jobs are hard to find these days,

74

and Hero knew her chance of any sort of university teaching post would be slim, even if she were admitted for a PhD at Cambridge. The prospect of a house, a loving partner with an excellent income, and the chance to do what she liked were as good a reason as any for the match.

'I think you're very clever, Hero. And very lucky. No girl in her right mind would turn down Tom Fitzgerald.' Flora, perceptive beneath her voluble exterior, did not criticise Hero's decision. 'Besides, you'll be able to live at home, do some research into your Russian icons or whatever, without having to go to work like the rest of us.'

And there was another reason, which even Hero could not yet acknowledge. In her relationship with Tom, tough, warmhearted, rich, she was proving to them that she was as capable as the Floras of this world of landing a man. It was some months before Hero recognised this reversion to base competitive female behaviour, and by that time it was too late.

Hero's only moment of doubt, apart from the nightmares which she tried to ignore, came at Henley Regatta. Through an alcoholic haze, stunned by sunlight and the sea of blue and white in the Enclosure, Hero found herself thinking: *How did I get here? Last year I wouldn't have been found dead at an occasion like this, now I'm here with the best of Them.* It was like accounts of amnesia, where victims regained their memories in alien surroundings, and wondered how they got there.

I told you so, murmured Other Hero, whose dissenting voice had been absent recently. Hero had almost missed her.

'I am doing the right thing, aren't I?' she said aloud.

'Everything okay, darling?' Tom walked over, not hearing what she said for the burst of cheering which went up suddenly.

'Yes—yes, of course.'

'You seem rather sad and wan. Or have you just had too much to drink?'

'This stuff's lethal, isn't it? And it looks so innocent.' Hero finished her fifth Pimm's.

'Just like you.'

'Thanks a lot.' She felt giddy: the brilliant colours and green landscape had merged like an Impressionist painting, with the occasional bold stripe of an awning standing out against pale canvas. Someone lost a helium balloon, and it fled upwards, a vanishing globe of red, buoyed by thermals into the stratosphere. Seeing it disappear into the blue, Hero was moved by a sudden grief, and tears sprang to her eyes as it sailed out of sight.

'Hero? What is it? Too much sun?'

'No—' She brushed wet eyelashes with her hand. 'It was nothing. Nothing at all.'

'Nerves,' said Tom. 'It's only natural.'

Was it perfectly natural, Hero wondered, to wish that she could have fled like that, buoyed on currents, far away above the earth, free as air? And was it nerves which suddenly made her see Tom, in profile with his lips stretched tight, turning away from her, as a someone she didn't know? Was it nerves which made her feel as though she were in the presence of a complete stranger?

*　　　*　　　*

On the night before the wedding, Hero surprised herself and her sister Cassandra—an extremely reluctant bridesmaid—by bursting into tears.

'I suppose you've come to your senses and want to call the whole thing off,' said Cassandra, administering gin. She often sounded exactly like Other Hero.

'It isn't that at all,' Hero sniffed, scrubbing her face with a tissue in the unfamiliar spendours of Mrs Fitzgerald's guest room.

'You must stop crying. You can't go on tomorrow looking like that.'

'Cassandra, it isn't amateur dramatics. Tomorrow's for real.'

'All the more reason you've got to give a good performance.' Cassandra, outspoken and slightly humourless, was a taller, thinner version of Hero, but without the otherworldly quality. Hero's alien charm had been replaced by a ruthless and practical attitude which boded well for Cassandra's future medical career. 'Come on, you've got this far. You might as well go through with it.'

'Oh, it isn't that. It's nothing to do with Tom at all, in fact. Actually, I'm really upset about not hearing from Stephen Lewis.'

'Imagine getting upset about that!'

Hero had written to Stephen soon after getting engaged, inviting him to the wedding if he was in Britain at the time, and hoping they would keep in touch. She knew that he was due to visit his family in Beckenham during the summer. Stephen never replied.

'He might be on a course, somewhere,' Cassie pointed out. 'Perhaps he's at some isolated research station in New Mexico. And anyway, you haven't seen each other for about eighteen months.'

'I know. I just miss him, occasionally. The idea
77

of him. His company.'

'Well, you could have married Stephen instead, you know.'

'That was different. I'm doing this because it's the only way I can keep Tom. With Stephen, getting married seemed totally irrelevant.'

'You're just being self-indulgent. You're transferring your anxiety about tomorrow onto something else, namely Stephen. And what about Colin? You didn't even mention him.'

'Colin was very upset about it. He wrote me a long letter and said he couldn't bear to come tomorrow.'

'Well, you have enough admirers, I'll give you that.'

Cassie, too busy for a boyfriend and contemptuous of men—she was surrounded by them all day at Guy's—was nevertheless impressed by the Fitzgeralds' house, a large Georgian cube, and Hero's wedding dress, the cost of which, as she said, would have kept a family for months.

'Borrow it,' Hero said. 'Have it. God knows what I'm supposed to do with it afterwards.' She pulled herself up on the bed and poured another drink, fishing ice from the chilled tub with tongs. Such refinements would have been unbelievable at home, where the Jamesons bottle lived on the same shelf as the toolbox and the disinfectant.

'I think you're a bit frightened of the ceremony, that's all. Remember how you hated school speechdays, even when you were getting the prizes.'

'That's me all over. I'm afraid someone will turn up at the last minute and say: There's been a mistake. I won. Hero came second.'

She wandered over to the window, looking out at

the deep blue midsummer evening which would never get completely dark. She could hear the clap of woodpigeons' wings as they roosted for the night in the great chestnut trees beyond the lawn. Tom was playing an old recording of Vaughan Williams' *The Lark Ascending*, and the notes drifted out into the darkness across the ghostly white marquee.

'They're paying for everything, you know,' she told Cassie. 'The wedding, my dress, your dress. Everything.'

'Just as well, after that estimate Mum got for the roof. I can't approve of all this, but it must be nice not to have to worry about money any more.'

Hero nodded, catching sight of herself in the mirror. Until now, she had felt like the soft-featured heroine of an old movie, Grace Kelly perhaps, or Joan Fontaine. The female counterpart of the men Tom reminded her of, in all those faded black-and-whites, watched on wasted Saturday afternoons. But her reflection was pointed and eerie as ever, her hair blazed unnaturally red, and tears and alcohol, which normally blunt the face, had further refined her ethereal quality.

'I look a vampire, Cassie. Tomorrow will be awful.'

'No you don't. It's just your surroundings. Ireland is full of people who look like us. So's Jerusalem. It's only here you seem out of place. Your face doesn't fit. You're a changeling.'

'I certainly don't feel like the future Mrs Fitzgerald.'

*   *   *

For someone who hated parties and was mortified

79

by public attention, Hero's starring role at her wedding was a triumph. She had several glasses of champagne before leaving for the village church, and carried off the occasion with a certain startled charm. Tigerlilies had been twisted into her hair, and the cream-coloured silk scratched and rustled, but she stood, in the woodpigeon-haunted stillness, spoke the words they had rehearsed, and hoped the rest of the congregation could not hear her panicked heart beating.

Behind Hero the guests—she almost thought of them as the audience—were vivid in morning suits and hot pastels. The scarlet tunics of Tom's old regiment added a theatrical brilliance to the occasion, and the air was heavy with scent. The sun beat down outside, and Hero pictured waiting footmen, arms folded and off-duty, until the signal to begin had been given. Even Carina Villiers, in navy with white polka dots, stood silent, gloved hands folded and face perfect beneath a dark straw hat. Hero stole a quick sideways glance at Tom, who looked unusually serious, and wished he had looked back at her.

The hands of the clock reached two fifteen, and Hero Abrahams became Hero Fitzgerald.

PART THREE

CHAPTER ONE

'The twisted wreck of Thomas Fitzgerald's new BMW was all that remained after the blast ripped through his car in the early hours of this morning,' droned the reporter, as Hero watched the coverage of the event on television later that day. The whey-faced commentator spoke to camera, his voice in deliberately impersonal tones, with an acceptable undercurrent of outrage. Beside him a desultory group of anti-terrorist squad men turned their faces away, as though embarrassed.

The car was a tortuous modern sculpture, a Moore fallen warrior struck by lightning: impossible to believe that it had ever been a vehicle, that she had driven it to Winchester yesterday morning, that it had served such mundane purposes as taking her to Sainsbury's. It had become the stuff of nightmares.

So had Ovington Square. The area looked familiar on screen, larger and seedier than Hero remembered, transformed from the prosaic to the dramatic, from ordinary Ovington Square where Carina Villiers gave her protracted dinner parties to a place of conflict and murder. The adjacent houses were blackened by smoke, and windows had been blown out. A familiar street had entered the realms of a television thriller.

The vans were there, men in uniform (police and military) fluttering fluorescent cordons, the inevitable ghoulish spectators. Above the metal carcass, frayed remnants of Carina Villiers' drawing-room curtains fluttered in the breeze.

'Those in the vicinity were unhurt, and damage to property was minimal—'

Hero's mother stood up to switch off the set, but Hero restrained her. She watched as a shaken Carina, dressed in advantageous black, condemned the outrage. Next, a government spokesman deplored political violence, a senior police officer pointed out that nobody is one hundred per cent proof against bombing, and a journalist who had been at a rival dinner party across the Square gave his account. Hero found it ironic that Tom, whose profession had been shrouded in secrecy, should die in such a spectacular fashion. No death can be more public than assassination.

★   ★   ★

Hero accepted a third cup of coffee and sat, speechless, in the room overlooking the garden, half-conscious of the noise emanating from the street outside. The Press arrived soon after she did, but their presence seemed to have nothing to do with her. Oxford is frequently invaded by camera teams, and the tumult and shouting meant no more to Hero than if they had been shooting a commercial down the road.

'Hero, you will *have* to go out soon. Just to give them something. Just to keep them happy.' Maeve possessed an understanding of press psychology. 'Say something. Then they'll be away, phoning it in or whatever it is they do.'

Hero didn't reply.

'It's tough on the rest of us. The students cannot get in and out the house.'

Hero tasted the coffee. Every substance repelled

her, and she let the cup cool alongside the others. She had no memory of the journey home apart from a fierce concentration on road signs and traffic lights. If she had arrived safely it was not through any conscious attempt to stay alive.

★   ★   ★

The world outside was a cold, dead place, and the spring burgeoning beyond the garden windows bright and sterile as paper flowers. Hero hated her life because Tom was no longer in it, Tom whose existence had become a justification for everything she did. For Tom, meals were planned, excuses formulated, books neglected, evenings prepared. For Tom, make-up must be worn, hair washed, shoes repaired and special food ordered from the local shop.

Now, sitting alone in Oxford, it seemed as if time had come round in a loop, that she was seeing the second showing of the film at the place where she came in. At any moment, Flora would ring and invite her over; or Tom would call, enquire after her mother, wonder if she was home for long or simply collecting books. And then he would suggest she take the fast train and meet him at the flat in Hans Place.

The year's events reeled past, bright images standing out like clips from a main feature. There were stills everywhere she looked. And where Tom had been, a glowing planet with his own moons, occupying a significant place in the solar system, there was now a black hole, emotional anti-matter which she orbited, a lonely satellite.

CHAPTER TWO

I miss
I miss
I miss you

cried the voice on the stereo, softer now, almost tender after the harsher emotional excesses of the preceding lyrics.

All day through
No-one else will do
I miss
I miss you

Extraordinary how a rock song could catch up and pierce the heart, Hero reflected as she dressed for the funeral. How the cracked intonations seemed to reveal exclusive knowledge of her own grief, as if extending a secret message. Extraordinary that she had listened quite dispassionately to a symphony concert on the radio last night, and now felt moisture brimming on her lids. They had danced to this song, or rather pushed each other languidly about the floors of nightclubs, on hot summer nights last year.

I miss you

Hero heard Maeve scolding the unfortunate student who had put the record on, and shrugged. She hoped somebody played music she liked before *her* funeral. The gesture didn't seem disrespectful, indeed the mournful track seemed quite appropriate to the day's events.

I must be going mad. Whoever wrote that has no idea who I am, and what I'm going through. Just a good commercial song, that's all. But somehow it gets to me. I must ask if I can hear the album.

It was the first positive thought Hero had had for days.

The black hat crouched like a crow on the bed. Conscious that she was about to perform in a public spectacle, Hero fastened her black skirt, tied the stock of her black blouse, pulled on uncomfortable high-heeled shoes. The emerald engagement ring, always cumbersome, seemed too loose for her thin finger, but she couldn't bring herself to remove it. Many times, when it interfered with her left-handed writing, or became caught in Black Bess's reins, she had slipped it into her pocket. But Hero wouldn't take it off now.

Christ I look awful.

Hero had lost weight—*how*, when she was already so thin?—and her face was taut and strained. She applied make-up, but still looked unearthly, her pallor accentuated by the black hat which she pulled down over her eyes. The trilby style complemented her black suit, cut on Forties lines, which Maeve had bought yesterday. Going into shops and trying on clothes was beyond Hero.

The reflection of her thin, dark-clad figure, the pale face beneath the halo of a black hat, reminded Hero of some rock icon, glimpsed on posters and other people's bedroom walls. She couldn't put a name or gender to the figure, but the stylised portrait was echoed in the glass. *Now everyone can be an icon*, she realised, recalling her own black-and-white features on the cover of the *Sunday Times*.

Fame at last.

*   *   *

'Hero! Are you ready or what?'

Maeve's voice, issuing upstairs as she tapped across the hall in black stilettoes. Hero imagined her mother attempting to fix her disorderly hair, brushing stray red threads from her shoulder, tightening a belt above flat hips.

'I'm coming down now.' Tonelessly, as though nothing mattered much any more. Which it didn't. Well, did it? What was so dreadful about being late for a funeral? Tom wouldn't care.

Hero went into the kitchen, where three of the students, anxious and at a loss, competed with one another to fetch her coffee that she wouldn't drink. Outside, spring sunlight poured breathlessly onto the green grass, warming the belly of Cat, who rolled unregenerately on the dusty path, oblivious to the atmosphere of mourning. She was Hero's cat, hot and happy, and she loved Hero, and did not deplore the death of Tom.

But many people did, people from whom Hero had not heard in months or years. She had attained a melancholy distinction and was ironically amused by the number of friends from school and Cambridge who found it necessary to write after long silence, expressing their sadness and concern. Hero had become that anachronistic and somewhat embarrassing phenomenon—a widow.

*   *   *

88

It was five days after Tom's assassination, and Hero had given three interviews, permitted the cameras into her mother's sitting room, accepted numerous telephone calls, and read through a sack of mail. Maeve Abrahams, work suspended, demonstrated a hitherto unexpected capacity for dealing with ordeal by media. She fielded freelances and repelled photographers with élan, while Hero felt as though the house was under siege.

Hero had not intended to speak to anybody, but on the evening following Tom's death Gilby had arrived in Oxford and persuaded Hero to talk. He spoke of her role in representing Tom, of the need to let the public see that she was not afraid. He spoke of her duty to show Tom's assassins the grief and devastation they had caused, and that their action would not go unpunished.

Whilst Hero doubted that nationwide publicity would deter terrorists in the least (surely they rejoiced in it?) agreeing with Gilby seemed preferable to arguing with him. And Hero discovered a macabre, unprecedented talent for performing before microphone and camera. Journalists, accustomed to the devastated ravings of political widows, were disconcerted by her deadpan, articulate composure and the unhesitating, relentless tones in which she described her reaction to the news of Tom's death. 'She's like someone from an early Warhol movie,' said the man from the *Guardian*. 'I can't believe she's for real.'

Hero didn't feel for real. Although her languid demeanour resembled a drugged trance, she refused to take any sedatives apart from the occasional whisky. Even this was in moderation, as too much on an empty stomach made her sick. After her arrival home, Hero had sunk into a tearless gloom, a bereaved sulk from which she surfaced to speak to ITN, the BBC, and the local stations.

*   *   *

One of the students offered Hero a biscuit, and she nibbled round the edges of one fragment, breaking the rest to sawdust. The prospect of any proper food, particularly meat, filled Hero with horror. Diced chunks of flesh, laden with sauce, were reminiscent of human remains, swept into a bodybag, recovered from pavements with a broom. An oozing steak, traces of blood on a trout's gills, induced nausea. Hero was becoming an involuntary vegetarian.

Hero often felt sick these days, and several times after Tom's death had to rush away and vomit. She was not pregnant, as the familiar drag of cramps in her lower back testified. Nausea was simply a response to Tom's grisly death, and the sordid accounts of bombings remembered from newspapers.

'You should let it all out,' her mother said. 'Much healthier for you.'

'There's nothing *to* let out,' replied Hero, getting up from an untouched plate of lettuce, or a book at which she had stared without turning the pages. 'Nothing at all.' And she would look for another part of the house, where no-one could reproach her for a lack of conventional response.

Time had passed strangely, grief providing a new concept of relativity, in which hours flashed by in

90

seconds, or minutes dragged in tortuous intervals. Sometimes Hero was astonished by the speed at which a day shot by. Sometimes a morning lasted months. All the normal methods of measuring time were gone. It was impossible to concentrate on the Novgorod School, or the Iconoclastic Controversy, and her notes lay in the cottage now, gathering dust. A paper held Hero's attention for no longer than five minutes. Television palled, and she had no memory for the plots of novels. Conversation lagged, as even Hero's articulate household had no arsenal of words and phrases with which to combat the horrific nature of the event. Trapped in her aloof despair, incapable of pushing back the invisible walls of glass, she allowed the splinter of ice to freeze ever colder in her heart.

*   *   *

Inappropriate sun dazzled windscreens, and, as guests stepped out of cars clutching hats against a playful breeze, the setting seemed fitter for a wedding than an interment. As at the previous ceremony, Hero felt as though she had walked onto a film set. Cameras were grouped in the churchyard, and fat cables slithered through grass between headstones. Sunlight gleamed lichen and moss with a supernatural glow, and the Hampshire trees carried a stippled weight of almost unleaving buds. The funeral, rich, slick and well organised, was a superb exercise in public relations, the black limousines gleaming as though they had just driven from a display window in Berkeley Square.

Measuring her steps Hero walked up the crunching gravel and past a gamut of Nikons,

Canons and Olympuses. In the front pew, reserved for members of their families, she discovered Carina Villiers, resplendent in black Italian leather.

Standing up had suddenly become difficult, and Hero leant on Maeve's arm for support. Carina caught Hero by her free arm and fixed her with one glittering eye.

'Of course you don't object to my being here,' Carina stated. 'Tom and I were so close. Almost members of the same family, you might say.'

'Is that so?' Hero was too weightless and vacant to argue. At any moment she might float away, like the helium-filled balloon at Henley.

At that moment, other members of the Abrahams family arrived as reinforcements, grouping powerfully around Hero and shooting uncomplimentary looks at Carina Villiers. Hero's brother Philip looked grave and sacerdotal in the few black garments he had been able to piece together. Cassandra, hair scraped back, was fierce and angry, the personification of outrage.

The Fitzgeralds maintained a sad hauteur, and only Colonel Fitz, stooped and ghostly, seemed to register the appropriate weariness and bereavement which Hero felt. How strange that when people were stricken, they behaved like bad actors in a soap opera. How little originality there was in real life: Carina Villiers, long-nailed and steely, like a mistress from one of Flora's paperbacks; Flora weeping openly and charitably, mascara smudged and disregarded, nose red. And several shadowy men in dark suits, characterless and etiolated beside the members of Tom's old regiment who attended in full uniform—just as at their wedding—and bore his coffin up.

Services and ceremonies, performances and
rituals—how Tom had enjoyed them. Hero tried to
concentrate on the soaring seventeenth-century
prose of the Psalms, the bluff, gruff address given
by Tom's old commanding officer, the extract from
The Lark Ascending.

But Hero was unable to keep her mind from
running on more macabre details, the charred
remains and fleshy embers which had somehow
been gathered together, and lay now in that coffin.
Impossible to imagine his ash-brown hair,
weather-beaten face, powerful body mangled and
destroyed—yet her brain continued to conjure
repellent images.

Hero was relieved to see Tom buried at last, the
box lowered into the gaping earth, handful of soil
drumming down on the coffin lid. She was
reassured by the thought of that scar being refilled
soon, the clogged edges soothed, flowers growing
over the grave. At least they could do no more to
him now, and what remained of Tom would be
absorbed into the Hampshire earth, nitrates and
trace elements mingling with roots and worms, as
the grass waved above him.

After tentative comments, and restorative gulps of
alcohol, the reception at the Fitzgeralds' house
became loudly convivial. *Tom would have enjoyed
this too*, she realised, watching the mourners, their
outrage and grief forgotten as they bumped into old

93

friends, caught up on gossip, exchanged lunch invitations and business cards. One of Tom's nephews was even chatting up Cassandra. The bizarre nature of the occasion almost brought tears to her eyes.

Flora, make-up restored but eyes still puffy, came and drew Hero to one side, her third glass of wine flushing her cheeks with warmth.

'It's so awful. I don't know what to say, Hero.'

'Nothing. Don't talk about it.'

'When I saw the news I just couldn't believe it. I was coming back from lunch and saw the *Standard* headlines. It was a nightmare.'

'Except I'm never going to wake up.'

'You're so calm about it. If that happened to me—I don't know what I'd do.'

'Let's talk about something else. How are you getting on in London?'

'Oh, brilliantly. Seems ages since I came round to dinner with you and Tom at the flat—sorry—anyway, you know I started with the bank after finals, they're training me and I'm doing really well. And there are the most *gorgeous* young men in merchant banking, Hero. You should go in for it.'

'They wouldn't have me. I don't add up.'

'How are things in that direction? I mean—'

'You mean money? Well, I have to see the family solicitors on Monday. I've signed on in Oxford.'

'Signed on! Really, Hero!'

'I've no idea what the arrangements are. He might have left it all to the family.'

'Tom won't—Tom wouldn't have left you high and dry.'

'I might have to find a job.'

'You'll be all right, I know you will. I say, Carina

94

Villiers is a bitch, isn't she? Fancy coming and sitting with the family like that.'

'I know. Well, the Fitzgeralds can't stand her either, so she perched on the end of our pew, eventually. I do resent the way she always implies that there was something between her and Tom.'

'Perhaps there was, before you came along.'

The reception—wake would have been a better description—buzzed around them, with the familiar baying cries and jungle shrieks. The event was indistinguishable—with the exception of sombre clothes—from any other drinks party.

Tom's nephew, Douglas, pink-faced and loose-lipped, came over to them, ears still ringing from a clash with the caustic Cassandra. Hero had only met him once before, at the wedding.

'Hero, this is appalling. I can't say how sorry—I won't try. I hope they hang the bastards.'

Hero nodded, too exhausted for talk of revenge, and introduced Flora, his real object of interest. They shook hands, mutually captivated, and Hero left them to a discussion of Douglas's arduous military career at Sandhurst. She was wandering away, hoping to find a quiet room, when someone tall stole up beside her, pressed a glass of hock into her hand.

'Can I talk to you for a moment?'

'What for?'

'I'm an—an old colleague of Tom's.'

'I don't want to know.'

'No—you—you mis-s-understand.'

'I don't want anything to do with your lot.'

'I don't work for them any longer.'

'Is that a promise?'

'It's nothing official.'

'Everything to do with the Department's official.'

'I—s-simply want to speak to you.'

This conversation had passed without Hero looking directly at her interlocuter, though she took the glass of wine. The hock had the chilled, thin quality of the sunlight outside, that shone without warmth. Beyond well-stocked tables, damask stained with red, french windows revealed brilliance bouncing off the lake and the dark shapes of two young mourners treading gingerly across the lawn. Hero recognised Douglas and Flora, relieved and smoking, shaking off the constraints of grief as though stepping away from a dance floor.

'W-well?' the voice asked, and Hero turned to look at him. To look up at him, in fact. He was taller than Tom had been, six four perhaps, height accentuated by gangling angularity. Dark and beaky, and funereal in his black suit. Hero wondered momentarily if he was an undertaker, or a lawyer.

'Who are you? What do you want?'

Despite intensive training by Tom, Hero's manners were still shaky. Graciousness frequently deserted her on testing occasions, to be replaced by the old cold insolence.

'Alistair Urquhart,' extending a bony hand. 'I can't tell you how s-sorry I am about all this.'

'We all are.'

'I'd like to s-speak to you. Just an informal discussion.'

'Does it have to be now?'

'It s-seems as good a time as any. May I get you another drink?'

'If you want.' She watched him disappear through the noisy crowd, moving in a way which

96

indicated a tangential relationship with the material world, as though his body had been entrusted to the direction of remote control while his mind concentrated on the real work. As he knocked a tray from a waiter's hands, Hero wondered how such a character could have been Tom's colleague.

'S-sorry about that,' looking warily over his shoulder. 'Had a bit of an accident.'

'Don't worry. This can't wait till Monday, can it? I'll be up in London then.'

'I would prefer—just for a moment—'

Hero sighed. He was a nervous man, about the same age Tom had been, but with tracks of anxiety driven into an aquiline face. Perhaps Gilby had instructed this poor creature to talk to her. He induced pity in Hero, and she was unwilling to hurt his all-too-evident sensibilities.

'All right. Come into the library.'

*   *   *

The library, a chaotic room contrasting strongly with the ruthlessly well-ordered interiors of the remainder of the house (Mrs Fitzgerald dabbled in interior design) seemed to soothe Alistair. He leant his head against the buttoned back of a leather armchair, nursed his wineglass, and stared at the pale, sunlight-bleached fire in the grate.

'Tom was a wonderful man, Mrs Fitzgerald. One of the b-best.'

Hero waited, wondering what would come next, if anything. Did he, as others had, want to deliver himself personally of his feelings, confide them to her, as though his grief were particularly harsh? She drank more wine, losing all feeling until she was

97

scarcely there at all, body barely held down by gravity, a balloon straining at its moorings. Alistair remained silent, and with a sensation of *déjà vu* Hero remembered being taken out of another party, led aside, spoken to and cajoled by articulate Tom. It all seemed so long ago now.

'One of the best,' repeated Alistair at last. 'I'd—I'd like to be able to help you, Mrs Fitzgerald. What can I do?'

'I don't know. I hadn't really thought about it.'

'We—I—I wondered where you're planning to live. Do you have anything s-special in mind?'

'I've no plans.'

'Will you stay in Hampshire? Or move to London?'

'I've no idea. It depends on Tom's family.'

'I don't work for the Department any more, Mrs Fitzgerald. I really have nothing to do with them. I used to s-see Tom because we were old friends.'

'So why are you so keen to help?'

'I only met Tom on two occasions after he—after he met you, but I've heard all about you, Mrs Fitzgerald. All about you, and I'd—I'd like to help you, if there's anything—if there's anything—'

'What do you do now?'

'I—er—I'm a sort of academic. I do a little research—that s-sort of thing.'

Hero couldn't believe Alistair Urquhart did much at all. His old, discreetly expensive clothes and beautifully polished shoes indicated another of those private incomes which so many of Tom's friends still possessed.

'You've left the Department. I don't suppose you know if they're any nearer finding who did it, yet?'

'I'm not much wiser than you, I'm afraid. I

s-suppose you've s-seen the papers?'

'Yes, but who believes what they read in the papers?'

'Mrs Fitzgerald—'

'It'll all be forgotten in a month or two. Until it happens again. And about five different groups have claimed responsibility. I think it'll be like the line in *Casablanca*: "*Round up the usual suspects*".'

'You s-seem unduly cynical, Mrs Fitzgerald.'

'I got to know the Department pretty well, while I was married to Tom.'

She looked at Alistair Urquhart, who had hooked his feet up on the fender and was studiously toasting the soles of his shoes. He had one of those long, Scots faces, and unexpectedly warm eyes the same colour as his hornrims. Even now, relaxed in front of the library fire, he had an air of tension and constant wariness, as though anticipating attack. Hero noticed that he had selected the chair in the corner, commanding a good view of the door and french windows, so nothing could surprise him as he sat.

'Would you be able to help me find out who did it?'

'The authorities are doing everything in their power—'

'I s-suppose you're right.' Regretting the words almost as soon as speaking them, Hero slumped down. Growing warmer, she reached up and removed her hat. Until that moment, she had not even taken off her dark glasses, and now the freed hair dropped limply to her shoulders, floating and making her sneeze, the way it always did. 'I suppose they'll eventually catch up with whoever did it. I'm past caring.'

99

'You're very brave.'

'Brave? What does brave mean? I haven't been difficult and made a scene in front of everybody. I couldn't be bothered.'

'Will you meet me in London?'

'What for?'

Alistair looked hurt.

'I mean, why?' Hero amended.

'Perhaps we—we could have lunch, s-some time.'

Hero was filled with remorse. Poor Alistair. It must be so terrible just being Alistair Urquhart, without people like Hero sounding surprised whenever he invited them to lunch.

Alistair had got to his feet, and fished out a card by this time, but they spent a further ten minutes trying to decide where to meet.

Really, this is awful. He's got such an infectious s-stammer and he just can't make up his mind. Lunch was so simple with Tom. See you there. One o'clock, Thursday. But Tom was a pretty simple person.

'Perhaps you might like to come to my flat, and we could decide where to go then? It really depends on what you feel like, and how hungry you are, and—'

And whatever else you have in mind, put in Other Hero. Her reappearance was reassuring.

'I have to see the solicitors on Monday. I'll come round after that.'

Alistair looked concerned.

'I'm s-sure there'll be no problems with money. The Department will—'

'I don't want any of the Department's lousy money.' Though Hero knew that she might be in no position to refuse it.

'I do s-so want to help you,' Alistair said

100

confidingly, when the plans for their meeting had at last been finalised. 'I want to be your friend.' He shook her formally by the hand before leaving the library. Exiting, he caught one foot in a Persian rug and almost tripped, before edging out with an anxious nod.

Hero Abrahams. Hero Fitzgerald. Hero Abrahams-Fitzgerald. Really, I can't go through life called that. Chilled wine soaked into her system, and she floated languidly in the chair, lethargic and light-headed. *So what's it to be? Miss Abrahams? Mrs Fitzgerald? Ms Abrahams-Fitzgerald? The Widow Fitzgerald? Having two names can be useful. A double barrel has snob value. Gets you a seat in a restaurant, though I wouldn't have bothered about that once. Perhaps I could just be known by one name, like celebrities. Colette. Bardot. Hero.*

*   *   *

Dozing, Hero was eventually retrieved from the library by her mother. Hero replaced the hat and glasses, and took her leave of the mourners, remaining unmoved by black garments and anxious faces, the powdery female kisses and stalwart masculine pats which assaulted her on the way to the car. Turning slowly, she gazed back at them all through the glass. Flora's face appeared, near then far, and she was swallowed up into the crowd again. Cameras flashed, and a few drops of rainwater spilt, as though on cue, from an overhanging branch, spattering silver on the windscreen.

Hero's eyes remained dry behind dark lenses, though her mind swarmed with images. She was conscious only of a huge commotion, a bustle

101

reminiscent of a hunt meet, as the car drove away leaving mourners and photographers baying in its wake.

CHAPTER THREE

The sad eyes of a madonna gazed at Hero, filled with sorrow and pity; stylised, slightly Asiatic features reminded Hero of the Venetian women seen on her honeymoon. The gold leaf, the manner in which the colours had faded, the inscription—everything indicated that the icon was a fifteenth-century original.

'I had no idea—' she began. 'I've seen nothing like it outside the Fitzwilliam.'

'I'm—I'm glad you like it,' said Alistair Urquhart, handing her a sticky sherry glass. 'Tom told me that—that you were—s-something of an expert.'

'Not an expert, by any means. But where did you get it?'

'I inherited it. My grandfather brought it over before 1917—he was with the British Consulate in Moscow. One of the reasons I sort of—wanted you to come here today was s-so that you could look at it.'

Entranced by the icon, Hero only gradually began to take in the rest of the room. Dust motes floated in the sunlight, above layers of books and papers. Crammed shelves held hardbacks, many with Cyrillic lettering on their spines.

'I'm—I'm s-something of a Slavophile,' Alistair confessed, clearing a chair for her and then sitting down himself. It was a complicated operation, and he settled carefully, like a cat. 'Most of my time with the Dip was spent in the s-satellite states.'

How unfair, with that s-stammer, commented Other Hero.

'Then you were in the Diplomatic, like your grandfather?'

'And my father. It's—traditional in our family.'

★   ★   ★

Alistair Urquhart seemed to have grown since Hero last saw him, or perhaps he had simply shrunk to more manageable proportions in her imagination. He wore an old navy sweater with fluff adhering to it, and grey flannel trousers which did nothing to disguise the thinness of his legs. Hero suddenly realised why she found him reassuring: Alistair was what all those spindly young men from Cambridge would look like when they grew up.

'I'm s-so glad you could make it today, Hero. I didn't think you'd come.'

That really inspires confidence, thought Hero. There was an awkwardness and hesitation between them: both knew they were there for reasons other than discussing iconographic art and Alistair's career, but both were tentative about admitting it.

'So you're an academic now?'

'I went back to Oxford for my doctorate—St Anthony's—but I don't do s-so much now. I decided to concentrate on the odd article, a little editorial work, reviews—you know the s-sort of thing. Perhaps the sort of thing you p-plan to do. I'm writing a Georgian grammar at present.'

Hero understood. But Slavonic studies could only

provide a modest income. Alistair Urquhart must survive—as she would now—on someone else's money.

Sunlight illuminated more clearly the thin lines on Alistair's face, and the lean bones, softened slightly now by a smile. His dark hair and heavy eyebrows were Gaelic and imposing, contrasting strangely with the anxious, learned air.

He does have a certain ravaged charm. If you like that sort of thing, added Other Hero. Hero did.

'I thought we'd—go to a place round the corner from here, if that's all right. Do you like s-sea food?'

'God, no!' with involuntary horror. 'I mean, I'm sorry, it's just that I know the place you mean, near Draycott Avenue, and I can't bear it. Tom used to have to drag me past. It's where all the lobsters and things live in a tank by the window, waving their whiskers and trying to escape. I couldn't take it.'

Taken aback by Hero's sudden outburst on behalf of crustacean rights, Alistair nodded sympathetically, as though familiar with the strong aversions and anxieties of people in Hero's position.

'I can understand that,' picking up the telephone. 'I'll cancel the table. What about the Bombay Brasserie?'

'That'd be wonderful.'

'Used to go there w-with Tom?' Alistair's eyes could be disconcertingly penetrating.

'No. That's why.'

★   ★   ★

The lunch was a success, though Hero had eaten little, picking through mounds of rice and relish,

104

toying with the shards of a poppadum. She watched, trying not to show surprise, as Alistair put away two double gin and tonics, the majority of their two bottles of wine, and a couple of generous cognacs, without being noticeably the worse for it. Hero, who seemed to have lost her resistance to alcohol, stuck to Perrier after one glass of wine but still felt giddy.

After halting pleasantries, Hero told Alistair of her morning with Tom's solicitors. It had been a less traumatic event than she feared. The old Hero Abrahams, to whom her grant cheques had seemed dauntingly large sums, would have dreaded such an occasion. Hero Abrahams would have hoped for a small annuity, some of the silver, and provision for Black Bess. Mrs Hero Fitzgerald, after only a year's acquaintance with the landed gentry, had asked composed questions about inheritance tax, death duties, and property which disconcerted the sympathetic young partner assigned to deal with her case. He had praised her courage, shaken her thin hand with his burly rugby-player's grasp and invited her to lunch next time she was up in London.

'S-so you'll be all right, as far as money is concerned?'

'Well, it's funny,' tracing patterns on the tabletop, and disconcerted by Alistair's hot eyes on her. 'I mean, there's more than enough for me. Enough so as I don't need to worry about work, as long as I'm careful. And I get the Hans Place flat, *and* the cottage. It's an amazingly generous will, when you think of what some widows go through. But I thought Tom had much more money, somehow. I mean we had an incredible standard of living. Compared with what I'm used to.'

'P-perhaps he fiddled his expenses,' suggested Alistair lamely.

'Oh come on. There's a limit to how much of that even Tom could do.'

'The Department's very flexible about s-such things. In Tom's—profession, extraordinary expenses do crop up—regularly. A new car, a sudden trip to Hong Kong, other less conventional requirements—'

'So that's what taxpayers' money goes on.'

'What do you think you'll do now, Hero? will you go on with your s-studies?'

'I really don't know. I can't seem to summon up much enthusiasm for anything. But it was nice of you to ask me up to see your icon!'

Alistair had an engaging laugh, unexpectedly loud. Warmed by cumin and cardamoms, and channelled towards his pet topic, he seemed to come alive, and they had the vivid, noisy and enthralling discussion which only near strangers can enjoy, absorbed by mutual enthusiasm.

'Let me lend you some books,' he concluded, stammer diminished by relaxation and alcohol. 'When will you be in London next?'

'I'm going to stay at the flat for a while. Oxford's driving me crazy, all Mum's students are getting ready for exams, the whole town is like a hot-house. It's too late to register for a doctorate this year, so I'd have to wait until next September.'

'That's a pity. But you could do a lot of reading for it. And travel. You're in the ideal position. And you got your 2.1. There shouldn't be any difficulty if you're p-prepared to finance yourself.'

'I know. But I can't seem to take advantage of it.'

'I hope we can meet—next time you come up.'

'I'd like that.' Her head swam. Hero felt vague and listless, floating off to another world again. She had a vivid image of Alistair stretching out, as though with a boathook, to catch her as she drifted from her moorings.

'I say, are you all right?'

'Fine. Perhaps I drank too much.'

'But you've only had one glass of wine. And sherry at my place. Have you taken some tranquillisers? They d-don't always mix—'

'I haven't taken anything. I don't like—taking things, except maybe antibiotics. As for anything else—I tried smoking dope once, but it just gave me an almighty headache.'

'Would you like to come back and lie down? Christ, that s-sounds ghastly, I didn't mean—'

Hero found herself laughing for the first time since Tom's death. And it didn't seem sacrilegious. Tom would have enjoyed the Freudian slip.

*　　　*　　　*

They stumbled out into afternoon sunlight, blinking a little as though emerging from a cave.

'What time is it? I have to get the train.'

'Four fifteen.' Alistair looked down with concern, eyes hot behind the hornrims.

'I've *got* to get back. My mother'll be worried, and—'

'Relax, Hero. You can ring your mother, and you know that—'

'I know I'm being shadowed,' she agreed. It was something Hero had got used to, very quickly. A man from the Department followed her everywhere, keeping a discreet distance. She had watched him spinning out his meal at a table in the corner of the restaurant, and knew he was watching her inconspicuously now, pretending to gaze into the window of an antique shop. Although the man was there for her own protection, Hero felt ambivalent about his presence.

'Perhaps some coffee—' Alistair began.

'We've had coffee.'

'I know. I thought perhaps—a little cognac.'

'I have to get to Paddington—'

'Are you sure it wouldn't be better to come round to the flat? Until you feel a bit s-steadier on your feet?'

'I'm all right. Really.' She caught his passionate glances, wondering whether to attribute the intense glow to cognac, vindaloo, or her presence.

'Hero—I did s-so enjoy today.'

'So did I,' she said, trying not to sound too surprised. 'Can you see a cab?'

'Will you ring me when you're back in London?'

'Yes,' she conceded, as the taxi sidled up and she sank into hot upholstery. 'Yes, I'll ring you.'

He leant towards her, and Hero half-anticipated, half-dreaded a smouldering kiss. But he was only closing the door, and gazing earnestly through the glass.

*　　　*　　　*

Hero arrived at Hans Place the following Monday, and propped Alistair's card on the mantelshelf, where Tom's dusty invitations still stood, summoning him to functions he would never attend.

She was drawn to Alistair, the juxtaposed burning eyes and library hornrims, and the thought of being entwined by those long, lean limbs was both comforting and attractive. But Hero wanted nothing to do with the Department, or anyone involved with it, past, present, or future. In fact, she did not really want to have anything to do with anyone, not for a long time.

★   ★   ★

Yes, she would call Alistair. But only when she felt ready.

CHAPTER FOUR

I miss
I miss
I miss you.

That song again, coming like a secret message to her over the airwaves. She only switched on the radio with a listless flick and there it was. *I miss you.* She waited patiently, anxious to find who sang it, who wrote it, where she could buy it, but the track was immediately followed by another, from a different artist, then the headlines, and she switched off in frustration.

Hero stood alone in the gloomy splendours of the Hans Place flat, gazing out at dim April skies where heavy-bellied clouds romped, leaden Olympians, across the west London skyline.

I miss you. Oh, the potency of cheap music. How

right Coward had been. The song haunted her, calling to her unexpectedly as she passed a pub or sat in a minicab, as though some mysterious ally were sending her coded reassurance. *I miss you.*

And of course she did. More than she had ever expected, when she considered how their last weeks together had been spent. Impossible to say how much, and she could not begin to put it into words, as that songwriter had done.

Fetching another cup of overpowering coffee from the *cafetière* in the kitchen, she sifted through *The Times*, still delivered every morning.

Hero had been living in Hans Place for a fortnight now, despite opposition from both families, who were concerned for her mental stability. Eventually, ignoring their advice, she had packed a few bags and driven to this fortress of isolation, with nobody for company but the cat.

Setting down her bags she had breathed in the dusty atmosphere like an alpine breeze, and fallen into a chair with relief. Alone at last. Great slaking draughts of solitude, no-one to talk to, no-one to bother with, except of course Cat, and she was a tolerant companion.

But it would not be accurate to depict Hero as entirely alone in her luxurious eyrie. Flora rang from time to time, as did Maeve, and Colonel Fitz, who, far from being a gruff ex-officer, was a gentle and melancholy man possessed of almost clerical gravity. Hero shopped for groceries, and discovered even Knightsbridge, shoppers off the scene, could be a village. The same people bumped into on the stairs, familiar faces at the delicatessen, the honest-to-God golden-hearted call girl who lived across the landing and always had a kind word for her when they met. People knew who she was now, and though nobody bothered her in the street (the security men took care of that) local traders treated her with sympathy and regard, old ladies nodded sorrowfuly to her at the Oratory.

Hero didn't know why she had taken to going there, but it offered solace, and reminded her of infrequent visits to Mass with her mother during childhood. Hero was astonished by how much of the service she actually remembered, and it gave her comfort to add another candle to the ranks of lights flickering in the scented darkness.

Superficially, Hero recovered in her splendid isolation, and soon evolved a daily routine of running in Hyde Park, reading or listening to music during the morning, running again at night before a hot bath and early bed. She was amused by the fact that her running caused headaches for Security, who had to find someone capable of keeping up with her gruelling sessions.

She seemed to require an enormous amount of sleep, as though recovering from an operation, and, having exhausted her body with exercise and living on inoffensive little meals of salads and cereal, she grew ever thinner. She found it impossible to sleep without holding something in her arms, and, if her cat was not curled up beside her, would cling to a pillow.

The flat in Hans Place was thick-walled and silent, and she seldom heard anything except the crash of the liftgates. At night she bolted the door carefully, the locks a tribute to Tom's security-conscious mentality—and sometimes she would sink, helplessly, into the depths.

Nobody told me there'd be days like this: strange days indeed. Lines from a posthumous John Lennon song, released during Hero's time in London. She often muttered them aloud, relishing their appropriateness.

For they were strange days, and strange nights too. Nobody told her about the fear, the panic attacks when she took a bus alone, or stepped into the Hades of the Underground, to travel the Piccadilly line which shot through London like a bloated vein, when footsteps echoed behind her in Brompton Road, or someone joined her in the lift. She experienced that irrational (or rational?) stomach-gripping, blood-pounding, absolute terror, which made her fingers tremble and her hands quiver, her voice shaky and her movements sporadic.

Am I paranoid, she used to wonder, *or do I have good reason to be afraid? Is the Department watching me, or someone else? Are they trying to protect me—or what?*

Hero became suspicious, defensive, unwilling to enter into conversation. What a relief it was to be inside the flat, with the door fastened and the windows bolted. She trembled when the telephone rang, nerved herself to answer, having learnt from Tom, or seeming to remember she had learnt from Tom, of remote control devices detonated by someone lifting a receiver. When fear shook her, like physical cold, and she lay in bed trembling with a chill no hot-water-bottle could overcome: when she objectively, with scientific detachment, found herself debating the relative merits of suicide techniques; then Hero knew she had stepped out of her normal life, out of the wonderful predictability of Cambridge and the suburbs of content, into a terrifying new world. Stammering, anxious, frightened, with a nervous headache thudding and fingers clumsy, she sat it out, for hours at a time, waiting for the fit to leave her.

*   *   *

Alcohol was a poor friend, and one she learnt to avoid: it could trigger an attack or strengthen an incipient one. Hero learnt the delights of Ovaltine, experimented with herbal teas, read soothing old favourites—when she could concentrate—such as *I Capture The Castle* and *The Wind In The Willows*.

Occasionally Hero let go, stretched out flat on the floor, arms spread in abandon like a small child, sobbing desperately, whether for Tom or herself it was hard to know. Emerging from the sessions she would be embarrassed but revived, muscles flooding with relief, as they did after the buzzing short-circuit of a nightmare, when she woke crackling with psychic electricity.

*   *   *

Nobody told me. Why didn't someone warn me, give me some indication? she cried, though there was no-one there to hear. *Why didn't you tell me about this desolation welling up inside like a smothered cry, this teasing out of the senses, tantalised tears brimming on the threshold of the lid? Why didn't you tell me about the sorrow when beauty strikes, a drop falls from a leaf after a storm or the last note of the violin dies*

113

away? Why didn't you tell me what it was to stand by a window in the rain with tears silent down my face? Why didn't you tell me the memory of pleasure would bring pain, random associations would fracture the present like shreds of nightmare fading at the break of day? Why didn't anyone mention that remembered trivial details acquire enormous significance, every discarded day a lost empire? Simple reminders of a visit to the sea, windsurfers flying like butterflies, fragile and ludicrous, challenging the elements. Why didn't you tell me that epitomised you, Tom, rising and ducking the almighty breaker, dancing along the wave's back in the wind, until one moment you appeared once more and then were gone? Why didn't you tell me how precious those days were when they happened, not afterwards? Then I wouldn't have agonised over pebbles in my shoes, or been intimidated by your friends.

Why didn't you tell me of those lunatic impulses to open the car door in the slipstream, turn the wheel into oncoming traffic, convinced I saw you stand before me in the middle of the fast lane? Most of all, why didn't you tell me I'd lose my reason, my powers of distinction, become a weeping, cringing, mindless emotional mess, moved to tears by a vapour trail scrawled like an autograph across the sky? Why didn't you tell me about this sense of complete loss and isolation, so remote and so alone? No more joking, no more puns, no more jollying me out of it; no more waiting at the flat for you to come home; no more watching the shadows lengthen across Brompton Road before you returned noisy, bouncing, funny and too good to be true.

★   ★   ★

But they hadn't told her either about the relief once

such crises passed. The sigh, brisk rubbing down of the face, post-exertion chill: just like a race. They couldn't have conveyed the physical sensation of catharsis, the pleasure of a shower and hot tea, having just run home through her own personal thunderstorm.

*　　　*　　　*

Hero's ambivalent feelings towards Tom in his lifetime did not make her grief any easier: she had not realised that it was possible to be so devastated by death. But her sullen anger rallied her, and she determined, with a trick of the old rage, that she would survive. That would show *Them*.

*　　　*　　　*

One Saturday afternoon, after a particularly devasting attack, huddled in her bathrobe and drinking a restorative mug of Earl Grey, Hero rang Alistair Urquhart and invited him over for a drink.
　　Within ten minutes of her call, Alistair's voice was at the entry phone, and Hero stood composed and polished, pressing the buzzer to let him in. She did not appear panic-stricken or tearful. As soon as Alistair agreed—enthusiastically—to come round, she had rushed to the bedroom to change and make up. For some reason it was necessary to face him looking poised, as though, in Tom's phrase, she had 'made a bit of an effort'. Life with Tom made Hero conscious of her appearance. She checked ritualistically now, as if a stray hair or dangling thread could provoke misfortune. Yet she could never get it right: Hero lacked that rich gloss

115

associated with Tom's friends. Something always came untucked, she forgot to brush her hair or wore the wrong shoes. Even the black woollen sweater dress had little white feathers stuck to it now (where she had attempted to plump the cushions) and her pumps needed a polish. Anxiously she rubbed her toecaps against the back of her calves, to remove a layer of dust.

'Hero! I c-came as soon as I could. What's the matter?'

'Nothing's wrong. I just wanted a bit of company, that's all.'

I'm not telling you I was strung out on that hearthrug an hour ago, weeping hysterically. I don't suppose I'll tell anybody.

'I've been waiting to hear from you. I've been s-so worried.'

'I'm still here.' She led him into the drawing room. 'I suppose you've visited the flat before?'

'S-some time ago. Ages ago.'

'It's a bit of a mess, I'm afraid.'

Alistair seemed reassured by the mild disorder, as if it provided a background for his own dishevelled appearance. His casual old clothes were sadly lacking, and he wore a shabby overcoat he could have spent the night in. 'I came right away,' he said in mitigation, as Hero stared. 'I didn't think you'd—'

'Oh, never mind. Would you like a drink?'

'Actually, I brought this. I thought—'

'Glenlivet. How kind.' Taking his coat and fetching glasses, Hero wondered suddenly what she was going to do with Alistair now that she'd got him here.

After a year of marriage, she had lost her touch

with other men. Yes, she *fancied* Alistair—that useful term which covered a multitude of sins from mild attraction to passionate romantic love—but she still didn't need involvement. It was just that Hero wanted—a bit of company.

'You've been spending too much time alone.' Alistair's opening comment was uncharacteristically direct.

'What do you mean?'

'I don't think it's s-such a good thing, staying alone like this.'

'But I like—'

'Don't you ever get out at all?'

Hero took an emboldening swig of whisky, sat back in her chair, facing Alistair who had spread himself over the sofa.

'I enjoy spending time on my own.'

'But you get very—very frightened sometimes, don't you?'

'What do you mean?' Curious how she often got lost for words in her conversations with men. They made her defensive, reserved and sullen, always probing, always knowing what was best, always offering the wrong advice.

'Aren't you getting a little exhausted by it all? The s-security people outside, the Press, that feeling that s-someone's watching you?'

'I don't understand how you know—what that's like.'

'I worked with Tom. And I recognise the symptoms.'

'What symptoms?' For God's sake, she had invited Alistair here to make her feel good about herself, and now he sat watching Hero intensely, his gaze occasionally dropping to her

117

black-stockinged knees and making her uncomfortable.

'When people spend too much time alone—s-say because of something they're doing for the Department—they get rather—their reactions—'

'You mean they become paranoid?'

'A similar type of anxiety.'

'Well, thanks a lot, Alistair. I thought you were supposed to cheer me up.'

'But Hero, I am. It's s-simply that I feel you must occupy yourself in some way—find something to do. Even a job in a s-shop would be better than this perpetual isolation. It's not good to be a recluse.'

'How do you know what's good for me?'

'I can only s-suggest my own experience as an example.'

'So what's so special about you?' Hero was insolent now, annoyed by his refusal to offer her that passionate admiration which he had shown previously. Though there was still a glow behind the glasses, according strangely with his foreboding words.

'I left the Department—and consquently the Foreign Service—on medical grounds.'

'Too much of the hard stuff?' Hero raised her glass, noticing Alistair had downed and refilled his with despatch.

'No—although I did drink heavily. I was involved in—well, I won't go into that. I resigned from the Department after having a nervous breakdown.'

'I see. I'm sorry, Alistair. I didn't mean to be so flippant.'

'It doesn't matter. But I can tell you that I

118

recognise all the signs. Everything gets so—out of proportion in our world. Especially after what you've been through.'

'I know you're right. It's just—I can't bear to have people fussing round me, ringing up to see if I'm all right. As though they're saying *What, you're still alive*! As though they think I'm harmless because I don't run around like a chicken with its head cut off.'

'You're too proud.'

'Too stubborn, more like. I hate exposing my weaknesses. Can I have some more Scotch?'

He stooped over her glass and a current of electricity leapt across the space between them. You got used to sex—even indifferent sex—and Alistair's proximity reminded Hero that it was weeks since she'd made love.

'S-so—what do you suggest?' *Damn, I'm catching that stammer again.*

'You must get out and about, s-see people. Do more. Running in the park isn't enough.'

'How do you know about that?'

'I've s-seen you a couple of times. In fact, more than a couple of times.'

'Why didn't you say hello?'

'I didn't want to intrude—until you were ready to s-see me.'

I should have sat on the sofa, she realised. It was difficult for a shy man to make a pass at anyone encased in an armchair. Though he was not so very shy. Hero had come across these superficially nervous, essentially sensual men before. *Remember Stephen Lewis.*

'Sometimes I feel so lonely,' Hero confessed, leaning forward, red hair tumbling over her white

119

hands, fingers across her eyes. 'So isolated.' Making it easy for him, there, he would take her in his strong thin arms and comfort her, venture through the walls of glass bringing rescue. Hero knew her fine stockings enhanced her slender legs, that the brilliant strands against her pale neck and black dress made an irresistible composition. And she realised she had become skilfully manipulative during the last year, adept at putting on a show.

'Hero—' Alistair crouched beside the armchair as though on starting blocks, looking up into what he could see of her face behind the hair. Hero peered out from under her fingertips. 'Please—don't be s-sad—'

'Not sad. Just wish people would leave me alone.'

'You don't want *me* to leave you alone, do you?'

'I'll make an exception.'

Moved by Hero's semi-artificial vulnerability, Alistair took her hand in his, stroked her soft, angora-covered shoulder. After weeks of feeling sad and mad and lonely, she derived unexpected atavistic comfort from a man's touch, something she had not anticipated.

'Come and s-sit here,' he suggested, drawing her up and moving to the sofa. 'It's more s-sociable.'

It was also more intimate. But there was no immediate rush, no fumbling urgency as with Tom. Hero shored up against his fluff-ridden sweater, as though they were a long-acquainted couple settled for a night of television.

'Tell me what happened,' she said, lethargic and languid with whisky.

'I'd rather not. It was—s-something that went wrong. Someone turned up where they s-shouldn't—'

120

'And got killed?'

'We don't use that word.'

'How tactless of me. Eliminated, wasted, terminated with extreme prejudice—'

'That s-sort of thing. The details aren't important. It happens more frequently than people realise. I just couldn't c-cope—that's all.'

'I don't see why anyone but a psychopath should be expected to cope. The things the Department does are completely unjustifiable.'

'This is no time for a discussion of ethics.'

'You're right there.'

*   *   *

Alistair did turn out to be passionate. Removing his glasses, Hero took off a mask, and discovered somebody different underneath. He was powerful, strung tight with sexual tension—as she was, allowing sinuous fingers to delve between her thighs and stocking-tops, his weight unexpectedly heavy above her on the sofa.

'Come next door,' she invited, having tidied the room in advance and turned up the radiators. Hero stage-managed everything these days.

'Hero—perhaps we're rushing things—if you'd rather not—'

She smiled at his token reservations, as he pulled her dress off over her head, and they subsided onto the duvet. Lying back, Alistair suddenly exclaimed and sprang to his feet, producing a .38 automatic from beneath the covers.

'Christ Almighty! Hero!'

'Careful. It's loaded.'

'Is this in c-case you go off me?'

121

'Put it in the bedside drawer.'

'Do you always sleep with a gun under your pillow?'

'It's something I took to recently. It makes me feel a little more secure.'

'I thought I'd s-seen it all.' He unloaded the clip, put the gun gingerly away, and washed traces of oil fastidiously from his hands.

'Where did you find it?' he asked, professional courtesy getting the better of him as he curled round Hero.

'It's Tom's, of course.'

'How strange.'

'What's strange? Why?'

'I wonder what he was doing with a Beretta, that's all.'

'Is that important?'

'Not at this very moment.'

★   ★   ★

'How do you feel?' he asked anxiously, lying beside Hero, nursing her with one hand, a glass with the other. It was astonishing he managed to do anything at all with that liquid intake, but he was a sensitive and more considerate man than Tom had been. She had watched his shoulder muscles knit and bulk in the light of the bedside lamp, and observed that he made love like a drowning man. *Or fucked for dear life*, as Other Hero commented, crudely.

'I feel sleepy,' Hero replied, 'very sleepy, very relaxed.'

'I haven't—it's been a long time since—'

'Don't worry.' Oh, if he would only stop talking.

Hero wanted to sleep and sleep and sleep. She was not a gifted post-coital conversationalist, and possessed the philistine, generally masculine attribute of rolling over and dropping off the moment the activity was concluded.

'Do you want me to s-stay? I could spend the night here.'

'No—please don't.' That sounded harsh. 'I mean—'

'When can I see you again?' Peeling away from Hero, dressing haphazardly, never shifting his eyes from her huddled form.

'Ohhhh, soon. Ring me tomorrow.' She spoke into her pillow, wrapping her arms round it, as though clinging to a raft which would bear her away on a tide of sleep.

She was conscious of him kissing her again, desperate goodbyes, and heard Alistair let himself out. She realised the door would not be double-locked, and that she hadn't bolted the french windows onto the balcony, but she didn't care. Full of sex and whisky she let sleep take her down, down, down, into warm darkness, and the best night's rest she had known for months.

*   *   *

And if only that was it, Hero reflected, lying in her bath next morning. If only our story could finish here, with Hero and Alistair suitably united, life's victims both, shy academics who could retire into their book-lined world and live happily ever after.

Unfortunately, life wasn't like that, as she had discovered. Alistair represented a phase of her life which was almost gone. Although novels end at a certain point, human existence wanders on indeterminately, and doesn't know where to end. There were no reassuring chapter endings, final paragraphs, conclusions. Hero and Alistair would not voice some meaningful exchange, turn aside, and wait for the credits to roll.

The trouble with real life, Hero realised, was that it needed a good editor.

But she had woken warm and relaxed that morning, with pleasant memories, eager—not anxious—to see Alistair again soon. Making proper breakfast this time, with marmalade and a fried egg, she tuned into a jazz programme and found another apposite song. Husky, world-weary accents intoned an old Dexter Gordon number, and Hero toasted the singer mutely with her mug.

It takes some doin'
Keepin' on goin'
From here to here.

CHAPTER FIVE

'It didn't go s-so badly.'

'I got through somehow.'

'You look marvellously composed, Hero.'

'Of course. That's what the British like.'

Hero and Alistair sat in her flat watching the news coverage of Tom's Memorial Service.

'And you look s-so brave, Hero. Though I thought the s-sermon was dreadful.'

'Yes. Tom never liked all that fire and brimstone stuff. Though I suppose in the circumstances it was appropriate.'

'You look very lonely there—' A long shot of Hero standing, a little bewildered, black hat tilted over her eyes. 'But s-somehow s-strong—'

'Well, that's what people want. The grieving young widow. I'm sure that satisfied the MoD image makers.'

'You're very telegenic, actually.'

'This wasn't the way to find out.'

The camera panned through the crowded Abbey, picking out grim-faced Fitzgeralds and apprehensive Abrahams, swept along rows of dark suits and uniforms. Although she had been at the centre of activity hours previously, Hero found it difficult to believe that she had anything to do with such a public and spectacular event.

'Gilby looked a bit shaken,' remarked Alistair.

'He did, actually. He was very detached at the funeral, but when I've seen him recently he's been—oh, well. I suppose it takes us different ways.'

'Look, there's Carina Villiers.'

'Bloody woman.'

'Hero, she's not important.'

'She acts like she is. Always implying that something—oh, I can't be bothered with her.'

'S-shall I switch it off now?'

'Do. I've had enough.'

'I thought interest would be dying down by now.'

'There's still a lot of mail to get through. It's delivered to Mum's house, and I read a handful of letters occasionally—when I can stand it. Some of them are quite extraordinary. People wanting to *marry* me. You just wouldn't believe it. And I've agreed to do interviews with women's magazines.'

125

'Don't you—mind that s-sort of thing? It's rather intrusive.'

'Well. Gilby pointed out that if I didn't do *any* interviews, the Press would just think I was holding out for more money.'

'Yes—money—of course—'

'Someone even wants to ghost my biography. God knows why, I've never done anything, except marry a martyr. And when the time comes I'd want to write my own bloody biography.'

'The royalties would come in handy.'

'Look, Alistair Urquhart, don't you sneer at me. It's all very well for you to—' Hero was suddenly angry.

'I'm not s-sneering—' Alistair looked up from his glass in bewilderment. They had been friends—for want of a better word—just over a fortnight, and he clearly still found Hero a mass of contradictions. 'What do you mean, s-sneering?'

'Just because you live on a private income, you think I'm being mercenary because—'

'That's not true. I *don't* think you're mercenary—'

'I'm sorry. It's just that—well, any payments I get for interviews do come in useful.'

Putting an arm round her shoulders gingerly, as though placating a cat, he said: 'Of course you're s-still upset. It's not surprising—'

Like a cat, Hero shrugged him off irritably, moved to another chair.

'I'm so angry about the whole thing. It's so *unfair*. There must be masses of people in the Department they could have killed. Why Tom?'

'Hero, if I only knew—'

'There *must* be a way you can find out, surely?'

126

'The security forces are doing all they can. You can't expect to—to succeed where they fail.'

'But you knew him! I'm sure there must have been something about Tom, something special, something you noticed that made him a target—'

'Well, he was Anglo-Irish.'

'But he never served in Northern Ireland. He told me. It would have been tempting disaster.'

'Hero, let it rest. You're tired and unhappy—'

'I can't let it rest.' Hero's tone had become reasonable, but she could not allow the matter to drop, sat worrying at it. 'It's not that I have revenge fantasies—it's curiosity. I feel I owe it him to know who did it, and why.' She paused. 'Though in some ways—'

'What do you mean, in s-some ways?'

'Oh—oh, sorry, Ali. Let's not—'

'I'm interested. What do you mean, some ways?'

'It's awful, actually. I'd rather not.'

'Is it to do with Tom?'

'Yes. Come on, let's go out and have dinner or something. I just—'

'You weren't happy together, towards the end. Were you?'

'How did you know that? Something he told you?'

'I hadn't seen Tom for about six months before he—before it happened. But you weren't happy, and now you feel guilty, because you were relieved when he—when he got killed.'

'How did you *know*?'

'I could see it. You were d-devastated—naturally, anybody would be. But also—'

'I was. There was a terrible sense of relief when Gilby told me what had happened. I felt as if I'd been waiting for it all along. And then I had fits of—well, elation, really.'

'That's more common than you think. I s-suppose it's something to do with knowing one is still alive. S-some very primitive instinct. *Thank God it wasn't me.*'

Hero relaxed in her chair, allowed Alistair to come and sit on the floor at her feet.

'Something's been bothering me for a long time,' she said. 'Tom and I didn't part on good terms. I want to tell you about our last evening together.'

*　　*　　*

Hero wasn't certain of exactly when things began to change between them. Their honeymoon in Sardinia had demanded nothing more than that she eat, drink and lie in the sun like a lizard. When the time came to settle down to real life again, she enjoyed the late summer countryside, the freedom from the prospect of exams, the lazy undemanding days. She made her journeys to libraries, set aside a room in the cottage for studying, and learned to canter.

But by the autumn, her metabolism conditioned to expect a start of term that would never come, she had grown restless. Hero had not expected to feel so isolated (Tom was away frequently) and realised that she only liked to be alone when it was a conscious decision. She missed her friends, the exchanges over cappuccino and Bath buns which once seemed trivial, and were now revealed as the stuff of a comforting social network to which she no longer belonged.

Under protest, Hero attended local dinner

128

parties, and occasionally gave one of her own. The first had been intimidating, and she had catered with military precision. But when she realised that most of Tom's friends were highly intoxicated by the time they sat down to eat, and didn't notice food anyway, Hero was able to relax.

She became a little more poised, but still behaved at gatherings with a stiffness and lack of enthusiasm which irritated Tom.

'I do wish you'd make a little more of an effort, darling,' he commented one chilly March evening as they sat by the fire.

'I do, but I'm so caught up in what I'm doing. I didn't realise researching a book was such hard work, and I've spent the last fortnight trying to read sixteenth-century Russian.'

'I know. But it makes you seem so—arrogant, darling. As if all that really mattered.'

'It *does* matter. It matters to me.'

'I wish sometimes—just for my sake. Still, you went about with such a funny crowd at Cambridge, didn't you? All those girls in cardigans. Real *Guardian* women.'

Hero was actually reclining on the morning's edition of that illustrious paper, which she continued to read in defiance of Tom's comments that it should not enter the house.

'Who was that stringy one? The sort of sludgy blonde?'

'Beth. We used to run together, and go swimming. She got a blue in the end.'

'Yes, well. Girls of that age. Always something a bit strange about female friendships, isn't there?'

'Strange?'

'If you did a lot of sport together, too, well, that

says it all, doesn't it?'

'Says what?'

'Oh, come off it, *I'm* not offended.'

'Offended? What have you got to be offended about?'

'There was obviously something lesbian about your relationship. I've often thought you—you know—you had those tendencies. I don't mind. Actually, it's quite erotic.'

Hero looked at him, puzzled, and said nothing. But she had salted the reference away, in case she could use it on another occasion. The prospect of appearing gay didn't offend her, but what did irritate Hero was the assumption that being lesbian was weird, salacious, and a bit of a turn-on.

'Are you going to get ready for Carina's party soon? What do you plan to wear?'

'Tom—I'm not coming tonight. I did warn you at breakfast.'

'But why not?' Cuddling up to Hero and slipping a coercive arm about her shoulders. 'I want you to come.'

'My lungs are bad at the moment. I don't think sitting up half the night in a room full of smoke would do me any good.'

'But you went for a run this morning. I saw you.'

'It didn't seem too bad then, but it's flared up. And I'm on antibiotics, so I can't drink. I wouldn't have much fun.'

'But we can leave early!'

'We never do.'

'Carina *likes* you. You'll enjoy yourself, Hero. And a little wine won't hurt you. You don't want to turn into a hypochondriac.'

'I'd rather stay here, Tom. Really I would. It

130

means the difference between getting rid of it now, or making it worse and having problems for a week.'

'If you were well enough to run this morning, you're well enough to come up to London.'

'That was this morning.'

'Honestly, Hero, I'd be so pleased if—'

If you really loved me, you'd come to Carina's, interpreted Hero. *And if* you *really loved* me, *you'd let me stay at home and watch telly.*

At that instant the telephone rang, and Tom returned from answering it looking elated. His determination that Hero should accompany him to Ovington Square seemed forgotten.

'Don't worry about tonight, darling. I'll pacify Carina. Don't suppose she'll mind too much having a spare man at table. It's always much worse having too many women.'

'I can imagine.'

'You get plenty of rest, and take care of yourself. We don't want it turning nasty, do we? I won't be late back.'

Hero dug herself into the sofa with relief, covering herself in newspapers and copies of the *London Review Of Books*, the *Spectator*, and *Apollo*, which was big and heavy and kept slipping off. She looked like a literary tramp settling down for the night.

Tom had gone upstairs to change, hair burnished in the firelight, energy crackling like a flame, and his jumper shooting sparks as he pulled it impatiently over his head. When he came back, in evening clothes, it was to kiss her in an obligatory manner, tug on his Barbour, and jingle the keys to the BMW as he turned from the door.

'You look after yourself, darling,' he ordered, as Hero sensed the familiar tension in the atmosphere, the reservations she could not be bothered to define, and the words unspoken. 'I'll be back as soon as possible.'

But he never returned.

★   ★   ★

Spring was far advanced in Hampshire, and Hero felt almost exhilarated as she drove through brilliant green lanes and pools of sunlight. Fresh air whistled through the car—she always drove with her window wide open—and Alistair sneezed frequently as the first pollen spores tickled his nostrils.

It was some days after the Memorial Service, and Alistair had agreed, a little reluctantly, to visit the cottage with Hero. She intended to collect books and clothes—and to search through Tom's papers, in the vague hope that they would provide fresh evidence as to his assassins.

'D-don't expect to find anything, Hero,' he said, anxious that she would be disheartened by a lack of success. 'Tom was a complete professional. He wouldn't leave anything confidential just lying around.'

'I have to know what happened, Ali. I can't concentrate on anything else until I do.'

'I can s-see that Tom has left his mark on your driving,' Alistair commented, as they screeched to a dramatic halt outside the cottage.

'Yes. I'm sorry about that. He taught me a few tricks, and I do love to show off.'

'I still don't think there's any p-point in this. If Tom had any confidential files, they'd be at the

132

Ministry. And they've probably been destroyed by now.'

'Perhaps it wasn't anything to do with the Department. Not officially, I mean.'

'If it was as secret as that, you certainly won't find anything.'

Hero put on lights, opened windows to dispel the damp. *Strange being back here. I keep expecting Tom to appear at any moment, ask what's going on, what we've done with all his stuff—*

*   *   *

During Tom's lifetime, Hero would not have considered going through Tom's wardrobe, opening drawers, dragging suitcases from the tops of cupboards. Even now a certain inhibition remained, an aura of Tom which permeated the cottage and had Hero looking over her shoulder.

'Any luck?' asked Alistair.

'A few back numbers of *Mayfair* in the wardrobe. Just like Tom, really. I think he was happier with two-dimensional women.'

Going to the desk by the sitting-room window, Hero noticed that the middle drawer had been forced open.

'Perhaps Tom did it.'

'I don't remember it if he did. It's quite blatant. Look.' She ran her fingers over the splintered wood. 'They've been here, Ali. The Department's been through the place from top to bottom to see if there was anything—suspect.'

'So I imagine.'

'Well why didn't you tell me?'

'I couldn't have convinced you. It's routine,

Hero. They always ch-check the place over afterwards. They won't have missed anything.'

'But you mean they—they just break in here? I can't believe they actually—it's like a police state—'

'They had to.' Alistair's voice was almost stern. 'For your own protection, as much as anything else. S-suppose that—'

'But how dare they!'

'Look at it this way. They have to p-protect themselves, and you. The Department doesn't want s-some bungling amateur—'

'Well, thanks a lot.'

'I'm only explaining how they operate.'

'And I'm only trying to bloody well find out what happened,' splitting an infinitive in her rage. 'I mean, for Christ's sake, suppose Tom was up to something which had nothing to *do* with the Department. Why did you make such a fuss about Tom having a Beretta?'

'Well—because—because I—'

'Because it's not service issue and it's an Arab gun, that's why. They're popular in the Middle East. I found that out the other day, by ringing Flora's father. He's a pistol-shooting enthusiast. No wonder you were so surprised. What the hell was Tom doing with it?'

'Hero—please—'

'I'm sick of this. I'm sick of being kept in the dark, and not having things explained, and being shut up, and told it's for my own good. I'm sick of having people tapping my telephone, following me in the street, and not telling me anything.'

'Hero—' Alistair made an ill-timed attempt to hold her, but she flounced away angrily.

'And as for you! Retired, indeed! I don't think
134

you're bloody retired. I think they detailed you to keep an eye on me.'

'That's not true.'

'Oh yeah, well why did you pick me up so neatly at the funeral, and take me out, and try and be so lovey-dovey. The whole fucking Department makes me fucking sick.'

'P-please Hero—calm down—'

'I am not going to calm down!' Hero swung at him, wildly, but with effect. Her clenched fist collided with Alistair's jaw, and he was momentarily senseless.

'Good God, you throw a punch, don't you?'

'I'm sorry.' The gesture had restored Hero's senses, and she sat, embarrassed by the outburst.

'It's all right. Nothing's broken.'

Hero looked round the deserted cottage, at the ghostly dust on every surface and the abandoned paperback, broken spined and face down, which Tom never finished reading. Hero let Alistair hold her, bury his head on her shoulder, rock gently back and forth. She was aware that he was crying. After a few moments he raised reddened eyes, took off his glasses and stared earnestly at her.

'Hero—I didn't—keep an eye on you because of the Department. I promise, I don't work for them any longer. I c-can't. After what happened—I feel the s-same way about that organisation as you do. I just wanted to—s-see you through all this, protect you. The Department doesn't come into it—except that I understand the sort of pressure you're under.'

'I appreciate that.'

A chill came over her, here in this sunlit room where she had lain so many times with Tom, so very long ago. Alistair's fears were deeper and

135

stronger than her own. There was despair in him, a need for security which she could never satisfy. She knew that, unless she took great care, he might drag her down into his own haunted kingdom.

They locked up and left soon afterwards, having packed the clothes and books which Hero needed, and drove briefly to the church. The headstone was not yet in place over Tom's grave; only earth, heaving into a mound, and decayed flowers marked the spot. She arranged daffodils quickly, anxious to escape. *Poor dashing romantic foolish Tom, finally copped it once for all. Even you couldn't cheat death. But why did you cop it? What happened? What the hell were you trying to get away with this time?*

* * *

They drove to West Wittering and walked along the shore before lunch. The sea churned relentlessly and one or two intrepid wind-surfers ventured onto its surface, rising and dipping flamboyantly before being swallowed up by waves.

'We used to come here quite often,' she said, clasping Alistair's chilly hand, slithering on pebbles.

'Must be rather pleasant in the s-summer.' Cold air made his stammer worse, he spoke between chattering teeth.

'Summer? We came all year round. Tom used to go out with a board. Another excuse to show off,' she added fondly.

Herring gulls bobbed resiliently on the water, mocking tumbling surfers, as the waves made their endless crash and drag, crash and drag. How wonderful it would be, Hero thought, if she could turn to Alistair, and he would love her forever and take her away, and they would walk along the beach together, as the camera panned out, the soundtrack welled up, and the audience prepared to leave, tears in its eyes. How wonderful, and how unlikely.

'I don't think I'll come here again,' she concluded, sensing Alistair's discomfort, either at her own misery or the chilling air. She clung to him, under the pretext of seeking warmth, but really in search of security. 'Not for a long time.'

CHAPTER SIX

Spring was cold that year. Hero saw daffodils flourish late in Hyde Park, and panicked rabbits scuttle across footpaths as she made her morning run. The air held a chill, as though the sky were a transparent membrane, excluding warmth.

The glacial splinter in her heart remained, visualised now as an oriental dagger with a blade of ice and elaborately decorative handle. Hero wondered whether it would melt eventually, or if some mythic liberator would struggle into her cage and wrench it free.

Meanwhile, this splinter of ice endowed Hero with chilly detachment, a clear cold-eyed view of life. Disciplining her mind, she started work again, welcoming the resumption of an old routine. She read sporadically, following up footnotes and cross-references as she would not have been able to do in the limited time restrictions of a research grant. For recreation, she attempted to read Pushkin and Chekov in the original, deciphering

137

diligently, dictionary to hand, as somebody else would have solved crosswords or played solitaire. She required a task.

Two months after Tom's assassination, the authorities seemed no closer to tracing those responsible. There was still much interest and speculation in the media, questions had been asked in the House, and a grisly reconstruction of events leading to the bombing had been carried out in Ovington Square. This was designed to jog the memories of any witnesses who might have been in South Kensington at three o'clock in the morning. To Hero's surprise, a number of people came forward, and dark-clad figures in para-military dress were said to have been spotted in the area. But so many people dressed like that these days, Hero lamented. How were the spectators to know whether they had seen terrorists, or Imperial College students in army surplus, returning from a party?

Hero suspected that the reasons for Tom's death were more complex than they first appeared. If it were a political assassination, surely the men responsible would have declared themselves by now, applauded it as another blow for freedom, justified the act as one more victory in the armed struggle. That was what usually happened. And it was not as if Tom had been an outstanding figure at the MoD. Certainly, his background was Anglo-Irish, but his family spent most of their time in England, and Tom had never served in Belfast. In any case, the provisional IRA had deplored the action—and the incendiary device which killed Tom did not resemble those used on previous occasions by any Irish activists.

Most of these details Hero had learnt from the newspapers, and from the few details Gilby gave her. So it must be the nature of Tom's life which killed him, she reasoned, if he did not arouse strong antipathies among the Irish. Perhaps he had been involved with the Middle East, the Russians, the Chinese—this was where fiction took over, and she gave up in confusion. Hero had fits of longing for revenge, imagined scenarios in which she gunned down his murderers with the mysterious Beretta; but more often she sank into apathy, convinced that if the Department couldn't find the assassins, she would never be able to. And sometimes she gave up caring: even if they caught those responsible, it wouldn't being him back. *When a man is dead the brains are out.*

There was also a growing anxiety that if she did discover the truth, it might be unpleasant. Hero wasn't certain why that conviction developed, but it was there. The prospect of putting herself in physical danger held no fear: although tormented by sensations of paranoia, death was an intriguing and welcome possibility which she felt adequate to face. In a reinterpretation of the cliché, Hero was quite happy to live each day as though it were her last.

★ ★ ★

Hero was sitting contemplating death, in this detached manner when the telephone rang.

It was ten thirty on a Tuesday morning, and she wasn't expecting any of the few people who knew her number to call. Gilby handled all her contacts with the Press, Alistair would be working on his

139

Georgian grammar over in Mafeking Mansions, Flora had rung the previous evening. She picked up the receiver guardedly.

'Hero! Is that really you? It's me. Stephen. Stephen Lewis.'

*   *   *

Hero had a fixed image of Stephen, frozen at the point three years ago when they said goodbye: black curls, collie-dog eyes and an anorak. It was a shock to open the door, later that morning, to a total stranger.

'Hero—you've changed!'

'You too. I wouldn't have recognised you.'

They stared at each other, Stephen on the threshold, Hero stuffing her hands into the pockets of her electric blue dress and ruining the line. His curls had gone, shorn to a crop. The glasses had been banished, and he wore stylish casuals under what Hero learnt to call a *down vest*.

'Aren't you going to invite me in?'

'Sorry. Never had much in the way of manners.'

The Beckenham intonations were still reassuringly there but he had acquired *Falls*, *go fetchs*, *semesters* and *come visits*. Not surprising really, after three years in the States.

'Jesus Christ, do you live *here*?'

'No, I'm just the cleaner. Of course I live here, idiot.'

'You've turned into—what's the phrase— *something rich and strange*.'

'Strange is right.'

He followed her into the kitchen, staring round, inhibited by the novelty of his surroundings from

140

giving her the old reassuring hug. 'It's difficult to imagine you married, Hero. To a Hooray, I mean. Mum couldn't get over it. She found some pictures in *Tatler*, at the hairdresser's, and sent them over.'

'You could have been there.'

'I would, but I didn't get the letter until it was too late. I've been working on a research project at NASA and—well, I felt pretty bad about not replying, and I kept leaving it, and the longer I left it, the worse it got. And then—this happened. I only found out about *that* recently.'

'So how long have you been back?'

'I came over a few days ago. I got your number from your mother—hope you don't mind.'

'It's good to see you. It really is.'

It really was. Reassuring, comforting, a link with the past. As though the past two years had never happened.

'I've landed an Assistant Professorship at Stanford. To start in the Fall. I reckon I'll be happier teaching.'

'Is research getting tough over there, too?'

'No—but I'm not into space shuttles and star wars, and I've had enough of MIT.'

'Stanford would be nice. Lucky old you.'

'Come visit.'

'Don't be silly.' All she seemed to be doing was telling Stephen how to behave. But he never minded what she said to him, one of his great strengths.

'I really mean it. I want to see you again, and besides—' the real Stephen Lewis was still there, behind the contact lenses and East Coast clothes—'I miss you.'

'That's nice, Stephen. But it was all a long time

141

ago.'

'Really I do. I missed you so much out there. I know I didn't write, but I can't string words together the way you can.'

'Perhaps later this year—'

'What are your plans for the future?'

'That's another American thing you've picked up, isn't it? The future. Having ambitions and knowing what to do. Setting up a goal.'

'You've got to do something, Hero.'

'I thought of registering to do research, either back in Cambridge, or somewhere else.'

'Come and study in the States. I'm sure you could write about Russian art as well there as anywhere.'

'But I don't know what I intend doing yet, Stephen. Teaching, or trying to put a book together, or what. I don't seem able to see more than a few days ahead at the moment.'

'I guess that's natural. But you're still an academic, Hero. You've been working this morning, haven't you?'

'Just trying to read a bit, that's all.'

'Mind you, you don't *look* like an academic.'

'Is that supposed to be a compliment?'

'Supposed to be.' He slid an arm round her waist, and Hero turned to him with the same sensation that accompanied re-reading a well-thumbed novel or settling to watch a much-loved movie.

'What are your immediate plans?' he asked. 'Can you make lunch?'

'I'm supposed to go to the Gay Hussar with Alistair.'

'So he's the new man, is he?'

'Sort of. We're more like—well, he's a bit of a

142

mess, really. We're more like close friends. It isn't very—serious.'

'I didn't think you'd be alone for long, Hero. I know what you're like. Sorry, that isn't very complimentary—'

'You're almost as tactless as me. Must be why we get along so well.'

'So you're too busy to see your oldest conquest?'

'I never said that. Can *you* make dinner?'

*　　*　　*

Stephen hadn't changed much after all, Hero realised, watching him across the candles that evening. Once she grew accustomed to the lack of anorak and spectacles. Life in America had improved him, given him confidence and opened the star-filled eyes. With a little twinge of guilt, Hero slid towards him in bed that night, thinking of Alistair. He knew Hero's oldest flame was in town, had even made some amusing remark about it, but it must hurt him. Somehow one always ended up hurting Alistair. He was that kind of man.

*　　*　　*

'So what do you say?' Stephen concluded, on their last evening together. He had spent the best part of four days with Hero, and was due to fly back the following morning. Stephen had just expounded, logically and concisely, the advantages of Hero following him to the States.

'I don't know.' Hero was as usual confused by the simplicity with which Stephen delineated his theories. It was so obvious to his analytical mind

143

that Hero was available, suited Stephen ideally, and would prosper in the United States. He had explained (and demonstrated) his passion for her, his conviction that they were meant for each other, and the advantages of Hero sharing her life with him.

'It all sounds too easy.'

'But why, Hero? I can't see any problem.'

'I might not like America. I've never been there, and I don't think I'm ready.'

'But you could still study there. And you've got your income from Tom. We could manage.'

'I'm a different person from when we met. I've changed, I realise that now. We might not get on.'

'Of course we'll get on. This is a terrific opportunity for you to make a new life.'

'I've tried that. I started a New Life with Tom, and look what happened.'

'It *can't* be Alistair.'

'It isn't Alistair. We don't expect much of each other. Though I'm very fond of him, Stephen.'

'He sounds like a wimp.'

'He's got a lot of problems. *Prablems*. God, I'm starting to talk like you, now.'

Stephen lay smugly on his back in bed, full of salmon and roast beef and confidence. 'Think about it, Hero. Think of the advantages. You'll change your mind.'

'This isn't an argument, you know. I can't arrive at a logical conclusion by observation and deduction.'

'So let's try observation and seduction.'

* * *

'I'll probably come and visit,' she said later, 'but you've already shown that you're perfectly capable of surviving without me for three years.'

'I had to go, Hero. There just aren't any opportunities for people like me over here. No funding available, you know what it's like. And there was no way you could have gone with me then, halfway through your second year—'

'I know.'

'Anyway, one thing hasn't changed. We still have great sex.'

But it wasn't enough. *Great sex, togetherness,* whatever other fatuous phrases Stephen found to describe their mutual pleasure, it wasn't enough. As they flexed together, as the climax flourished and died, Hero maintained her open-eyed detachment. Even lying clasped beside him afterwards, comforted by Stephen's arms and the yeasty smell of sex, Hero still felt frozen currents run through her veins, as the waters of a northern sea are chilled by the motion of vast icebergs shifting slowly from the Pole.

★   ★   ★

'But you'll think about it? Promise?'

'Promise. Especially if the weather goes on being as bad as this.'

Rain streaked the windows of Heathrow, as they watched forlorn planes, strangely small at this distance, manoeuvre across grey tarmac.

'You will come over?'

'Yes. I'll need a holiday.'

'What have you got in mind? Are you planning on something?'

145

'Oh, one or two things. Nothing—special.'

'Take care of yourself, now. I don't want *you* going the same way as—'

'I won't.'

Hero had told Stephen nothing of the facts surrounding Tom's death, or her doubts about the Department. But he was extremely perceptive, capable of working out for himself what was going through her mind.

'If you ever want a break, call me and I'll arrange the whole thing. Tickets, the lot. If you suddenly decide you've had enough, just come. And it'll be okay.'

The last call for the flight to Boston was announced. Stephen picked up his leather grip, kissed her quickly, with passionate deftness, and rushed away, the bag bouncing against his legs as he departed.

Hero watched from the airport windows, as the plane taxied into the rain, slid down the runway and took off. She wondered whether to rush to Grosvenor Square now, get a visa, and follow immediately.

But it was too soon. It was too easy. And she still had responsibilities.

$$\star \qquad \star \qquad \star$$

'Mrs Fitzgerald! Whatever are you doing here?'

Anticipating a brush with the Press or some unwanted admirer, Hero turned warily to see Alex Gilby, white and grim in the chilly light of the lounge.

'Seeing off an old friend.' Sounding more mournful than she had intended. *All that warmth,*

146

she thought, *all that genuine kindness and affection. Stephen is turning into one of those nice dependable men other women marry.*

'I've been doing the same thing myself.'

'Really?' Hero was hostile. She couldn't believe anyone in the Department *had* friends.

'I'm glad we bumped into each other like this. Would you like a drink? Or some coffee, perhaps?'

'Thanks, I have to get back to London.'

She didn't, there was nothing to hurry for, but Hero wanted to avoid Gilby's company.

'Let me give you a lift. I'm going back to town now myself. No—' taking her arm. 'I insist.' Although there was no pressure, Hero interpreted it as a coercive gesture. 'I've been meaning to telephone you for some time.'

'Is that a fact?'

'I was going to ask you to lunch.'

Oh no, not another one. Even the solicitor rang the other morning to invite me to a drinks party. Will nobody leave me alone? Why is it that as soon as you're back on the market they're all over you? Why do they imagine I'm so desperate to get someone else? I'm just getting used to being on my own again.

Gilby handed her into the blue Volvo graciously, and it did not even occur to Hero to make a run for it. Why should she? Why entertain such paranoid thoughts? This was just that nice Commander Gilby, Tom's good friend, giving her a lift home from Heathrow and possibly inviting her to lunch so that he could offer further moral support. Nothing wrong with that. He was probably worried about her, nothing more. He had a wife and three sons tucked away in Hampshire, and wasn't likely to make advances. Surely? And there were no other

147

dangers involved. Were there?

They drove for over twenty minutes without exchanging a word. Finally, Gilby said: 'I spoke to Colonel Fitz yesterday. He's very well—' as though Hero had spoken '—considering the pressures he's been under, and hopes that you are recovering. We discussed you, in fact.'

'So that's why my ears have been burning.'

'We both thought you put up a considerable show at the Memorial Service.'

'Thanks. Glad I fulfilled the brief.'

'You were very impressive, Mrs Fitzgerald. Very good indeed.'

'Think I'll get a BAFTA nomination?'

Gilby ignored her, and drove scrupulously, with constant reference to mirrors and dials, as though at the controls of a destroyer.

'We thought the tension was beginning to tell a little, now. Just a little. Perhaps you need a break.'

'Is that so?'

'I bumped into Alistair Urquhart yesterday afternoon. He seemed a little concerned about you.'

'Bumped into him? Where?'

'Oh, in the street—literally, in Gower Street. Alistair told me that he'd just come from the British Library. I understand that you're quite good friends, these days.'

'You could put it that way.'

'Well, I'm very glad. It struck me that poor old Alistair needed a helping hand. He's had rather a time, you know.'

'Him and me both.'

Incapable of anything other than acid little comments, Hero felt like the feed in a comic dialogue. Except it wasn't funny.

'Alistair thought that maybe you were—under a little too much pressure.'

'What sort of pressure, for God's sake? What have you all decided is wrong with me?' Goaded into outrage.

'We think that you need a total change. A break from everything which you associate with Tom. Do you know anyone in particular with whom you could go and stay?'

'Not offhand, no. I've just waved one friend goodbye.'

'Ah yes. Mr Lewis. He seems to be a pleasant enough young man, though not known to us.'

'Thank God for that. He's had a lucky escape.'

'We do try to keep an eye on your friends and acquaintances, you know. It's for your own benefit.'

'People always say that about things I don't like.'

Hero glowered at herself in the mirror. Pale morning made her skin whiter than ever, the eyebrows livid above blue irises, ringed with black. *I do look a little manic. But who wouldn't be?*

'Alistair also mentioned that you were— unhappy—about the progress of the investigation into your husband's death.'

'I'm pretty pissed off about it, yes.'

'I don't think you appreciate the fashion in which the—investigation—is carried out.'

'Nobody's doing anything, as far as I can see. There's been nothing in the Press, nobody's told me what—'

'Details of our activities seldom appear in the papers. You should know that by now. The task is not approached like a straightforward murder hunt.'

149

'Perhaps you'd get more results that way if it was. There doesn't seem to have been *any* progress.'

'So you decided to take matters into your own hands.'

'What do you mean?'

'I believe you've been making some attempts to discover the nature of the events leading to—'

'I've been wondering, that's all. As far as I know, I'm legally entitled to—'

'Mrs Fitzgerald, I can't emphasise enough the dangers which surround amateurs who attempt to—participate in these activities. You are putting yourself at a great disadvantage in your wholly laudable attempts to discover your husband's killers.'

'I'm not bothered.'

'I think you should be. I applaud your instincts, but to go around behaving like a cross between Modesty Blaise and Calamity Jane is not advisable.'

'What are you talking about?'

'It was mentioned that you still have your husband's collection of firearms.'

'Huh. I suppose Alistair—anyway, I don't carry it round in my handbag, if that's what you're thinking. And I've got a permit. I joined a club when Tom taught me to shoot.'

'I remember one widow before. Wife of an officer in Belfast. Tragic, in fact, they had been married less time than you and Tom. After he was shot by one of the para-military organisations, she took it upon herself to trace his killers. She succeeded in getting herself knee-capped.'

'Really?' Hero sounded unmoved.

'A sportswoman, like yourself. And an excellent event rider. Terrible shame.'

150

'Where is she now?'

'In a private nursing home. And likely to remain there for some time.'

'Why are you so anxious to scare me off?'

'I'm not anxious in the slightest. But I am at pains to assure you that there are questions better left unasked. Leave it to the people who are professionally competent to find out. They are paid well to take risks. I—we—admire your spirit, but your fervour is misdirected.'

'What are you so afraid of? What do you think I'll find?'

Gilby did not reply, and Hero sat rebelliously, staring out at West Cromwell Road. He did not speak again until they were pulling up outside the flat in Hans Place.

'Take a break. Have a few weeks in the sunshine somewhere. Try to forget about everything that's happened.'

'Just like you?'

'I've told you about my reservations. And I must warn you, Mrs Fitzgerald, that if you do find yourself in some sort of—trouble—as a result of your activities, you can expect no help from the Department.' *Just like the movies!*

'So if I go off my head and start shooting people in Harrods, you'll disown me?'

'That's a rather sensational way of putting it. But you do have the right idea.'

'Well, thanks so much for all your advice.' Hero slammed out of the car so violently that passers-by turned to stare. 'I didn't expect much help from you. Now I'm not getting any, and it doesn't surprise me.'

'We will continue to make arrangements for your

151

safety, Mrs Fitzgerald. But if you take it into your head to do something erratic there is no guarantee that we will protect you.'

*   *   *

Hero slammed further doors. The doors of the mansion block, the doors of the lift, the door of her flat as she thumped inside and threw her coat angrily over a chair.

Everything was still in chaos, legacy of Stephen's meteoric visit, the bedclothes rumpled and stained. Ripping off sheets and stuffing them into the washing machine, banging cups into the sink and shoving rubbish down the disposal chute, Hero lost herself for twenty minutes in a frenzy of activity, before sinking onto the sofa with a mug of coffee and a deep sigh.

In this cold May light—when would summer come, *when?*—the room was chilly and grim, its restrained good taste insipid and dreary. She had done nothing to change the furniture, remove the engravings of huntsmen, take down the equestrian-featured ancestors. It was still Tom's flat, and Tom's presence hovered round, inhibiting and restraining her. Suddenly she was sick of the sight of it, and longed to be gone.

*   *   *

Hero was forced to admit that Gilby was right. Nothing but danger could come from her attempts to locate Tom's killers. A man—or woman—who had not scrupled to blow up a car with Tom inside it would scarcely treat Hero any better. And there

152

would be so many ways in which her death could be disguised, as the grief-stricken reaction of a young widow. She might fall from a window, take an overdose. There was more than one way of killing a suspicious wife. She remembered the story of the unfortunate Aileen Philby who, after her husband's defection, ran around wildly gabbling of agents and attempts on her life before dying conveniently of an overdose. Hero could sympathise: in the circumstances, her reaction had been perfectly normal.

'If only I knew where to start,' she said aloud, into a silence punctuated by traffic noise and the thump of the washing machine. 'What were you playing at, Tom? And how the fuck will I ever find out?'

CHAPTER SEVEN

Hero did not have to wait long for an answer. Sitting in her armchair, back to the window and coffee in one hand, she froze at the familiar rattle and tumble of the locks in the front door. With horror she imagined remnants of Tom battering for entry, as in *The Monkey's Paw*, and sat transfixed. She could see straight through the hall to the front door, but was too frightened, after Gilby's warnings, to call out or move to the bedroom where the Beretta waited under its pillow.

There was another thump and heave, whoever it was showing unfamiliarity with the sticky locks. I *should have bolted it*. But Hero had got out of the habit, with Alistair and Stephen coming and going.

Her fears had subsided. *And there's a security man outside. Somebody must have seen—*

The front door swung open and a tall, apprehensive girl, younger than Hero, stood on the threshold, keys dangling from her hands. She wore baggy leather trousers and a crushed shirt, as though she had dressed in a hurry.

'What are *you* doing here?' she asked.

'I live here,' replied Hero, getting up. The sensation of fear gave way to one of outrage, but she had the classic military advantage of surprise. 'And I could ask you the same question.'

'You must be Hero.'

'Ten out of ten.'

'Oh shit.'

'Don't stand out there. You may as well come in.'

Hero found it hard to believe that she was confronting a potential assassin, or the agent of a foreign power. The girl, who could only be about twenty, had a distinctive upper-class accent, a gawky, crane-like walk, and dark rings under grey eyes. She looked devastated by Hero's presence, and Hero almost felt sorry for her.

'Is that all right? You don't—mind—do you?'

'Mind? Why should I mind? You've got a key, so you obviously know your way around. I'll get you some coffee,' she added, as the girl shed her leather jacket with an overpowering waft of scent and sat edgily on the sofa. She reminded Hero of somebody, but she could not think who.

'Did you come in to water the plants or something?' Hero asked, bringing in a tray.

The girl looked up between eyelashes encrusted with last night's mascara, twisted the rings on her slender fingers. She gave the impression of

154

displaying her awkward charms to please Hero, which irritated the latter out of all proportion. The girl shuffled her expensively booted but scuffed feet and said at last: 'I'm Nerissa, you know. Tom's girlfriend.'

Tom's girlfriend.

Hero did a double-take. Yes, how obvious. How in character. How inevitable, that Tom would have a mistress. And how conceited, how optimistic, how bloody naïve, to imagine he wouldn't.

'Tom's friend,' Hero amended, 'of course. He didn't actually mention you by name—but I assumed there was someone.'

'Oh—' Nerissa was confused and apprehensive. Blinking appealingly, she added: 'Tom said you knew—about us. And that you didn't mind. I used to come here—during the week. While you were in the country.'

'There's nothing here for you now. I've been living here for over two months, and there aren't any clothes of yours.'

'I—I know that. I—someone fetched them for me. The day after it happened.'

'Anyone I know?' enquired Hero airily. Poised against the mantelshelf, coffee-mug in one hand, she wished she had a Cowardian cigarette-holder.

'Someone who worked with Tom. Gilby, that was his name. He went round for my things the following morning.'

'Good of him.'

'I wouldn't have dreamt of coming here if it hadn't been for—I thought you were out, you see. I didn't want to disturb you—'

'Well, I'm disturbed now. Very disturbed,' she added, giving the word its full implication. Hero felt surprisingly composed and cool, the way she hoped she'd be when she reached thirty-five.

'So what do you do, Nerissa? Don't tell me you worked with Tom as well?'

'Gosh, no. I'm not a career girl. Just a temp. I've been trying to get my modelling career off the ground, but I have a thyroid problem. That's why I'm so tall. And it means I don't have much energy.'

Nerissa did possess a torpid quality, which Hero knew must have appealed to Tom.

'And where did you meet my husband?' *My husband.* It was still odd calling him that.

'We met *ages* ago. Then we sort of drifted apart. Then we bumped into each other again—at a party. Just before Christmas. It was at Carina Villiers' house.'

'Carina Villiers had to be behind all this.'

'Well, apparently. Tom had seen me somewhere else—but Carina actually—got us back together, you know?'

'I know. I can imagine only too well.'

'But I never thought—I mean—oh dear—'

Nerissa was embarrassed, and Hero felt sorry for her. She realised that there were certain resemblances between them, the white skin, awkward air, spindly limbs. But Hero was powerful now, and she knew it. She had developed strength and determination because of—or in spite of—her life with Tom. She remembered a line by Nietzsche which Alistair was given to quoting ironically: *If it doesn't actually kill you, it makes you strong.* The observation was a good account of Hero's marriage.

'Just out of interest, what basis was your relationship founded on? Did Tom seriously intend

156

to leave me and marry you?' *This shouldn't be happening*. At twenty-four it is difficult to adjust to being deserted for a younger woman.

Nerissa looked appalled.

'No. No, of course not. That isn't what—it wasn't like that. Tom told me that he loved you very much, and couldn't imagine what life would be like without you. I think he would have fallen apart if *you'd* left *him*. He admired you and used to say how clever you were. I'm not a bit clever. But—there was the problem—shit, I don't quite know how to say this—'

'Try. I'm intrigued.'

'Tom told me that you—that you didn't like sex. Or, well, what he said was that you wouldn't sleep with him any more because you were a lesbian, and he was getting frustrated.'

'How original.' Hero gave an exasperated laugh. 'How amusing.'

'You mean it isn't true?'

'I'm afraid not. How many people have—I mean, did he put this story about, or just save it as an explanation for you?'

'I think, I think he and Carina discussed it once or twice.'

'No wonder she kept giving me funny looks. Well I'm sorry, but I'm going to have to disappoint you. I hope you didn't come here to try your charms on me.'

'No!' Nerissa sounded horrified. 'But why would Tom say something like that? Why would he say something that wasn't true?'

'I don't know. I suppose—he was a curious man. The more I find out about my late husband, the more strange I realise he was. He *seemed* so—'

'Reassuring. He seemed very straight. You always thought you could trust him with— anything.'

'But underneath. I don't know. I can't imagine why Tom made up that story. Perhaps he believed it.' She sighed, putting down her mug. Somehow the outrage wasn't there, her gorge didn't rise and her words didn't choke, but she visualised her heart coated with icy crystals like sheeps' lights in a coldstore. 'Did you ever see *Citizen Kane?*' she asked.

Nerissa shook her lank blonde curls.

'That's who Tom begins to remind me of. They try to find out about a man— he's dead when the film begins—and the more they try to find out about him, the more confusing this one person turns out to be.'

'That sounds like Tom. Look, have you got a drink—or something? I'm feeling a bit wired.'

Hero fetched a bottle of Glenfiddich. 'I still don't know what you're doing here,' she commented.

'I left some stuff. Something I couldn't ask Gilby to collect for me.'

'Well, I haven't found anything out of the ordinary.'

'You wouldn't have done. Look, Hero—you won't get me into trouble, will you?'

'That depends.'

'Let's make a bargain. I haven't seen you, if you haven't seen me.'

'What are you so afraid of?'

Without reply, Nerissa stood up and pulled one of the cushions off the sofa seat. Her movements were surprisingly deft. Unzipping the chintz cover, she fumbled in the stuffing and produced a small

158

bottle which had once held vitamin supplements. The gelatine capsules were still visible inside, but held another substance now. 'Still there, thank God.'

'What's that?' Hero had already guessed.

'Smack. I put it in these empty capsules, and left it here. Seemed like the safest place.'

'But—' It was Hero's turn to be astonished. 'I don't know much about drugs, but there must be enough—you must have a small fortune there.'

'Not a *fortune*. Enough to keep me going for a week or two. I use most of it myself. I stored it there for a rainy day.'

'You're welcome to it. Is there any more about?'

'Tom was very careful about that. Never kept it on him, unless it was necessary. He had guys working for him mostly—you know.'

'Just a minute—'

'These top pushers are all the same. Wouldn't be caught dead with the stuff, but Tom being in a government job—the security—well, I mean—'

'You're telling me I've been sitting on a goldmine for the last two months? And Tom was a *dealer*?'

'Well of course.' Nerissa was briefly superior. 'What do you think? He didn't get an income like *that* from the Ministry of Defence—I say,' suddenly concerned, 'didn't you know?'

'There's a lot of things, I didn't know,' Hero realised.

'Look, I'm most awfully sorry I barged in the way I did, but I was desperate. And I do—I do miss Tom. I do know how you feel.'

'You can't possibly know how I feel,' Hero replied with grim authority.

She watched Nerissa languidly drag on her

jacket, as if the weight would prove too much, and shake free her hair. As she slipped the inoffensive-looking bottle into her bag, Hero reflected: *Me with my automatic, Nerissa with her heroin, there are a lot of dangerous women walking around London. And nobody knows how dangerous we are.*

'Tell me something,' she asked, seeing Nerissa to the door as if she were an old friend who had popped in for coffee before tackling Harvey Nicks. 'Were you there—at the last dinner party?'

'At Carina's? The night it happened? Why, yes, I was as a matter of fact. Because you didn't come. Tom offered me a lift, but I thought he was too pissed, so I called a cab. I'd left before—before it happened.'

'And you called him that night in Hampshire, to say you were coming?'

'Carina did. Apparently it worked out very well, since I'd just got back from a shoot—awful assignment, in Belgium—and you didn't want to come, so I got to go instead. You can imagine how I felt when I heard his car had gone up.'

'Vividly.'

'You've been very good about all this. You could easily grass on me now, couldn't you? Why don't you?'

'What good would it do?' she asked, closing the lift door after Nerissa, seeing the girl's pale face through the bars. 'What difference would it make?'

*   *   *

Hero went back inside as the telephone rang, picked it up anxiously wishing illogically that it would be Stephen, who was now halfway across the Atlantic. Stephen, with his starlit collie-dog eyes. But it was almost as good. Alistair, tense and anxious, interrupted her cautious hello.

'Hero? Are you all right? What's g-going on over there? S-someone was seen entering the flat.'

'No. No. I'm not all right. I feel terrible, really terrible. Please come. Come now.'

★   ★   ★

Alistair had arrived immediately, coatless and running up the stairs with surprising speed. Tense and alert, he took one look at Hero, and removed his glasses.

'You can't see anything.'

'I can see more than you think. I hide behind these things.'

'Like Clark Kent.'

'I'm not in the Superman class.'

'Funny you should say that. I've been thinking about Nietzsche just now—*Man and Superman*—you know what he said about things that don't kill you making you strong, well—' Hero was gabbling helplessly.

Alistair shut the front door and steered her into the drawing room, arm about her shoulders.

'I thought something like this would happen.'

'I'm not any stronger, Ali.'

'Hero, don't try to talk now. Just sit down and—'

'I'm going, Ali. You're losing me.'

'Don't talk like that.' He was sharp, dismayed by what he saw happening to Hero, but she misinterpreted his tone.

'You don't know. You can't. *They've* won,

161

Alistair. They've got me at last. They've won.'

'Have you had any Scotch? No?'

'Help yourself, Ali. Help yourself. If only I could help myself!'

'Listen, you must tell me what happened, Hero. Who's been here?'

'Nobody.'

'Someone has, haven't they? You must tell me.'

Alistair seemed to talk from outside a goldfish bowl. Hero saw his lips move but scarcely heard his words. Everything was freezing over now, and she would be trapped beneath the ice, until her mouth, face and eyes had been invaded by the crystal kingdom. Nothing could save her now.

'Hero, who's been here? For God's sake, say something!'

Hero noticed his stammer had gone. This observation retarded her own disintegration for some moments, so that she could say: 'Why—you've stopped—'

'I do sometimes. When I've got better things to think about. It's not important. For God's sake, Hero, don't try to protect anybody. Just tell me what's been going on.'

'Give me some of that.' She pointed to the whisky bottle and Alistair poured a measure. 'Tom had a girlfriend. A *mistress*. Why did you lie to me? I thought I could trust you.'

'Believe me, Hero, I didn't know that. Not until Gilby put me in the picture the other day.'

'They sent you to keep an eye on me, didn't they? You don't care about me at all really, do you? Nobody does.'

'I took you on because I wanted to, Hero. I don't work for the Department any more, but I did know

162

the position you were in. And I wanted to help.'

'Tell that to the Marines. Or the Russians. Or the Chinese.'

'I'm getting you out of here now. I'm taking you to my flat.'

'You've come to take me away from all this, have you?' Hero laughed wretchedly, and finished the glass. Whisky burned in her throat, but could not undo the invading ice crystals, the frozen particles which already pierced her flesh. She visualised her ribs literally thick ribbed with ice, her lungs seizing up like a motor on a frosty night. 'Well, it's too late. *They've* won.'

'What are you talking about?'

'I know what I'm talking about. For once. Tom. Great wonderful heroic Tom, Tom the captain of the cricket XI, Tom "Richard Hannay" Fitzgerald. He was just a fucking pusher.'

'Hero—'

She couldn't prevent herself laughing hysterically now, at the fine joke of it all. 'This little cow came round, she'd got a load of heroin stashed in our sofa, and I didn't even bloody know—'

'Hero—I've been trying to protect you from this—'

'You mean you've been trying to protect the Department. You didn't know what sort of a fuss I'd have made once I found our Tom didn't die heroically at the hands of the Provos. I guess he just got too greedy with the drugs barons and they decided to cut him off at source.'

'Oh Christ.' Alistair subsided onto the sofa, appalled at this recital.

'I'm right, aren't I?'

'I may as well tell you what I know.'

163

'It's about bloody time.'

'We—the Department had known for some time that Tom was abusing diplomatic privileges. It's extraordinarily easy for someone in his position to evade security checks and get substances through airports which ordinary travellers would never dare carry. He had the VIP treatment all the way, plenty of trips abroad, scheduled and unscheduled—part of the reason he was away a lot—and he had the sort of social contacts who would pay for whatever he got.'

'No wonder he was so popular.'

'You know that many of the terrorist organisations finance themselves through narcotics.'

'So Tom just turned a blind eye in return for a couple of kilos?'

'That's about it. He had a very well organised network and some very sophisticated ways of disposing of his stock.'

'So *that's* where the money came from. I thought he had a good income.'

'The capital left from Tom's little enterprise is in a separate bank account.'

'Swiss, I suppose?'

'Spanish, actually. I've no doubt the Department will lay their hands on it eventually.'

'I suppose he got too greedy. Or too careless.'

'Something like that. His suppliers regarded his attitude as a little too cavalier and arranged a surprise for him. It was also intended as a demonstration of their powers to anyone else who knew Tom's real occupation.'

'But—but the Department let him! They let him go on with it! They condoned it!'

'That's their way. Can you imagine the scandal if

a fairly high-ranking member of the Ministry of Defence—and of the security services—was convicted of drug smuggling? There'd be even more egg on their faces than usual. Especially in view of all the recent Intelligence scandals.'

'But people died as a result of what Tom sold them!'

'Do you think that they, in their infinite wisdom, care about that?'

They. The Department. Tom's family. Tom's friends. Tom himself. They had destroyed lives and were destroying Hero.

'He lied to me. They all did. They lied to me and wouldn't tell me what was going on. You knew all the time. Gilby knew. Even Colonel Fitz probably knew. And none of you even gave a fuck.'

They. Alistair, Flora, Carina, Villiers, Gilby, everyone except Stephen Lewis seemed to have conspired to bring Hero to this pass. She felt her heart constrict as she froze, straining under the effort of rejecting all this knowledge, the icy dagger in her heart numbing her into denial.

'Tom would still be alive today if you'd done something to stop him!'

'*I* wasn't responsible!' It was the first time she had heard Alistair angry. Again, his voice seemed to come from far away. Hero felt a little spring of flame kindle at last, as though her natural defences made some headway with the ice. 'I've had my life *ruined* by the Department. I didn't want to see them destroy you too. I've been trying to protect you, Hero.'

They gained on her now, she felt her limbs heavy and dull, but she must somehow stagger to her feet. She must react, burst from this carcass of frozen

165

tears and unspoken words. Hero had enough strength to stand up, moving as if in the grip of one of those jungle poisons that paralyses the respiratory system.

She saw Alistair approach, his gesture wholly benevolent, his intention being to catch her and calm her before telephoning medical help. But she must escape, she was trapped and confined, memories of some old phrase buzzing in what remained of her brain. *The body is the prison of the soul*. If only she could break out of this freezing armour of constricting limbs and tissue. She didn't realise, but Hero screamed now, yelling for help as though trapped in a mineshaft or lost in a crevasse. She had a vision of herself ripping away her ribs, like the bars of a cage, somehow stepping out of her own body and discarding it like a spacesuit, tearing off a costume of flesh. It seemed so logical to reach out with failing energy and smash the whisky bottle with the panache of a pub-brawler, grasp it by the neck and turn it towards her right arm. Before Alistair could seize her left hand, Hero had raised the bottle high and with an immense, primitive satisfaction slashed her wrist with the jagged glass, gasping with relief and struggling in his arms as she saw the jet of blood arch upwards and splatter the restrained grey ceiling like a field of poppies.

PART FOUR

CHAPTER ONE

Why am I here? Perhaps it was just another part of the dream. Hero turned and turned again in the crackling white sheets, burrowed into a pillow and slept once more. When she opened her eyes again the room was darker, but she was still surrounded by an expanse of starched fabric. It was like lying between sheets of crisp A4 bond. Empty and curiously spartan, the place reminded Hero of hotels and college rooms. A brilliant splash of roses caught her eye, but presently she sank again into the undemanding regions of sleep, where her dreams were vague and magical. She saw red roses bloom from bloodspots fallen onto snow.

★　　　★　　　★

Hero stirred again among the cool white and looked around. Sunlight filtered through venetian blinds, patterning the white rug on the white floor. Trying to sit up, she glanced round for something reassuring in this unfamiliar room. There were roses again, mop-headed country blooms in a clinical vase, and yet she could hear no birdsong, no familiar outdoor sound, no distant roar of traffic. She pushed aside the covers and discovered someone had dressed her in her old silk pyjamas. But the effort of movement tired her, and inertia overcame her as she sank back on the pillows again, wondering what would happen now.

★　　　★　　　★

Next time she opened her eyes, it was to see a young woman in a white overall standing watching her. Sunlight threw a louvre design through the blinds and across the opposite wall, and from its mellow quality Hero guessed it must be afternoon.

'So you're awake, are you?' The women's voice was detached but not unkind.

Hero nodded, trying not to ask the obvious question.

'Who are you?' she said instead. Her voice sounded husky and strange.

'Nurse Watkins. Call me Sue. How do you feel?'

'Strange.' Hero couldn't really tell. The effort of speech exhausted her, and she had no inclination to form words. When she looked again, Sue had gone. And the room was dark once more.

*   *   *

Hero woke with the light, thirsty and suddenly revived. She propped herself on one elbow, drank the tepid water from beside her bed, and found that she could sit up without feeling too giddy. Swinging her legs down to the floor, she thought that they seemed thinner than usual. The pyjamas swam round her ankles (they had always been too big) and when she bent to adjust the drawstring, Hero fell over. *Don't tell me I've got to learn to walk all over again, as well as everything else.* Pulling herself up by the windowsill, she parted the louvres of the blind with one finger, and looked out.

The scene was reminiscent of a college quadrangle. A green, surrounded by gothic-windowed buildings, shone with the tonsured quality of grass which has been tended for generations. Beneath a tree, a boy dressed only in shorts lay with a Walkman clamped over his ears, and two girls walked past carrying tennis racquets. Hero knew that although it was early, some people had already started their day.

As she turned from the heavily glazed window, the right sleeve of her pyjama jacket slid back, and she gazed at her arm curiously, wondering what to expect. There was no vivid mark, but only a thin scar, pale now as if it had been inflicted years ago, crossing her right forearm. A line reminiscent of a crooked vapour trail, or the track of a bicycle ridden erratically across wet sand. She was interested to note that it crossed a vein. Surely that must have caused a lot of bloodletting? It was hard to imagine so much blood, in such a white room.

For a second Hero saw the drawing room at Hans Place, Alistair's appalled expression, a fountain of scarlet cascading from a naked arm. Her arm. Arching like a burst water main, falling in vermilion rain over the sofa.

The image faded, and she stumbled into the bathroom and drank glass after glass of cold water.

★　　　★　　　★

When Sue Watkins appeared half an hour later, Hero risked the obvious and asked where she was.

'This is Ash Grove. It's a nursing home.'

'How long have I been here? I feel a bit strange.'

'You've been resting. You needed to, you know.'

'Tranquillised, you mean? Drugged?'

'Not drugged. You've simply been catching up on your sleep.'

171

'Do you think—do you think I could have some tea, or something? And a bath? I don't think I want to sleep any longer.'

Hero had to be helped into the bath, but was pleased to see that someone had provided all her make-up, and the familiar bottle of *Eau Sauvage* bought by Alistair years ago, or so it seemed. Glimpsing herself in the mirror, she was astonished by how much weight she had contrived to lose by lying in bed. Her clothes would seem bigger than ever now. Letting her head fall back into the water, she watched dark red streamers of hair float alongside her. Hero's nails were longer now, too.

'Are you up to seeing anyone yet?' Sue asked, helping her into fresh pyjamas.

'Seeing somebody? I suppose that depends on who it is.' Hero sat on the bed, struggling with buttons. She allowed Sue to towel her hair, then lay back nonchalantly. In the past few minutes she had realised why people became confirmed invalids. This was a confortable existence. 'All right,' she said. 'I'll see Somebody.'

★   ★   ★

Dark, almost sallow, amid the clinical white, Alistair loped in apprehensively. In his blue striped shirt and disreputable cords, he seemed out of place in the spartan decorum of Hero's room.

'Hero! H-how are you? Any better?'

'Better than what?' She saw a shadow cross his face at this gnomic statement, and amended it. 'I mean, what's been happening? Why am I here? Why aren't I at home?'

'S-so—you don't remember what happened?'

'I remember this.' She stretched out her arm, the scar clearly visible in the golden light which slanted in through the windows.

Alistair was unable to speak. He had been standing in the middle of the room, staring at her anxiously, but now he came over and embraced her. She stared bewildered over his right shoulder as he crushed her against him, inhaling his scent of dust, petrol fumes and whisky: the smell of the outside world.

'What about my cat?' she asked prosaically. 'When I came here—what happened to Cat?'

'Your cat's fine.' Lapsing with relief into mundane concerns. 'She's at your mother's house.'

'Are we far from Oxford?'

'We're in Dorset.'

'Dorset! What on earth for?'

'Ash Grove is—'

'Jesus, it's a funny farm, isn't it? The nuthouse. An asylum.' The last word had Gothic connotations for her.

'Not at all. It's simply a nursing home. All s-sorts of people stay here, Hero. Addicts, overworked executives, actors—anyone who can't cope with life and needs a break from reality for a while.'

'And casualties from the Department?'

'I had hoped you weren't going to mention that.

'You mean you hoped I'd forgotten.'

'I s-stayed here. They were very good to me, Hero. After what happened—I got you in here as s-soon as I could. I wanted you to be able to recover in a place which had no bad associations.'

'But how soon after? I mean, I couldn't have come straight here.'

'If you really want to know—but it's p-painful

talking about it.'

'I don't mind.'

'Well, I do,' helping himself to mineral water, and pouring Hero a second glass. She lay back and let the bubbles explode on her tongue, the sensation reviving but almost painful.

'After you—after what happened, I patched you up until the ambulance arrived and they got you s-straight round to St Stephen's. I came with you in the ambulance. You were out of it by this time—sh-shock, I suppose. You needed stitches, transfusions. I hope you'll never do anything like this again.'

'That makes two of us. Go on.'

'As soon as I could, I got you down here. You spent most of the time asleep. Just asleep. No drugs, or anything. But they told me that grief takes some s-strange forms, sometimes.'

'And how long ago *was* this? I mean, how long have I been here?'

Alistair sat close to her on the bed, so that she could see his face in lean and leathery detail. She felt elated, wanted to show him she was well and unharmed, but couldn't find words.

'Three or four weeks. Almost a month.'

★　　★　　★

Hero's tears surprised them both, but she mopped her face with the edge of the sheet and leant against Alistair's bony shoulder.

'I'm sorry—I suppose I still don't know what's happening to me. When will they let me out of this place?'

'Whenever you like. This isn't a psychiatric

174

hospital, you know. S-sometimes people come here to convalesce when they've had more radical treatment, but there's nothing to keep you here. You c-could leave now, but I'd like you to wait until you're fully recovered.'

'So what do I do? Just lie around and read?'

'Read, go swimming, play croquet, feed the ducks—the place is run like a country house. I'm sure you'll be happy here for a few weeks. I'll come and see you every day. If you want me to.'

'Of course I want you to.' She hugged him, the only reminder of another life in this sterile room.

'I think your nurse will see me on my way shortly. We've t-talked quite a bit, you know, for your first day.'

'Will you come back? Later?'

'I'll look in at tea-time. I've been every day, you know, just to look at you. But you've always been asleep.'

'I was dreaming about roses. You bought those great shaggy ones, didn't you?'

'That's nothing. I—I want you so much to recover, Hero. I need you.'

Hero nodded. She had heard this before, and the prospect of being needed rather dismayed her. But Alistair was good and kind, and he had saved her life.

*   *   *

'I suppose they'll want me to see a shrink?' she asked him next day, as Alistair sat on her bed. Hero had passed the previous evening watching television, reading a historical romance from the library and—surprisingly—sleeping. The habit of

175

convalescence—she had not been seriously ill for years, and had never been in hospital—gradually returned to her.

'It's what usually happens when s-someone tries to kill herself. It wouldn't do you any harm. I'd hoped I could persuade you to talk to the Resident Psychiatrist—'

'I don't mind. Though I think that after everything I've been through, he'll say I was justified in going over the top.'

'Possibly. But just talking things through with an understanding s-stranger. Things you couldn't talk to me about, or your mother.'

'What no-one seems to understand is that I wasn't trying to kill myself—I didn't want to die. It's just that I felt I had to get away from myself. I felt as if I was freezing myself to death, turning into a human glacier. I just don't know if I can ever make anyone understand that.'

'Do you still feel that way?' he asked sharply.

'No. No, I think a bit of me died back there—I've left myself behind. I'm sorry if I'm speaking in cyphers. Perhaps it's losing all that blood. Someone else's blood is keeping me going now. I wonder whose it was?'

'I'm sure whoever it was wouldn't begrudge it,' Alistair replied, hot eyes brimming. 'I'm just so appalled that I couldn't help you. That I let it happen.'

'You didn't have much chance. You couldn't have stopped me. At least you were there.'

He kissed her with a passion which was almost aggressive, then hastily looked away, as though embarrassed. 'Last time s-something like this happened to me, I didn't get there in time.'

176

'You mean?'

'When I was with the Department. I let s-somebody die because I didn't answer their call quickly enough.'

'You can't blame yourself for what happened. Maybe the Department wanted it that way. You can never tell, with them.'

Alistair sighed. 'I hope that this in s-some way makes up for what happened then. And I nearly let you become one of their victims, too.' He clutched her. 'I'm s-sorry. I'm upsetting you.'

'Don't worry. I can imagine—it might have been worse to watch than to do. Look, Alistair—' adroitly changing the subject '—who's paying for all this?'

'You haven't realised?'

'It's the Department, isn't it?'

'Hero, I haven't been entirely straight with you.'

'I don't know whether I can stand much more of this.'

'No, listen. It's nothing to do with the Department. There's s-something I haven't told you. I'm paying, and I don't begrudge a penny of it. Whatever it costs to get you back to normal—'

'But you *can't*! You can't afford it!'

'Of course I can. Just as I've also been able to afford to take a cottage in the Isle of Purbeck, s-so that I can visit you every day. And so that I can get on with some writing.'

'Writing? I didn't realise Georgian grammars were so lucrative.'

'I make quite a good income from writing. Another sort of writing.'

'An exposé of the Department for the *Sunday Times*? Will the MoD let you?'

'No. In the past, I've tried to keep quiet about it, but I do exploit my knowledge, and it pays well.'

'You're a Russian agent.'

'Can't you ever be serious?'

'After the last few months, I doubt if I shall ever be serious about anything again.'

'I'm—well, my other name is Mungo Parke.'

'Mungo Parke? Wasn't he some sort of explorer? Ages ago? Some sort of writer?'

'Some sort of writer is just about it. You see before you the author of *Sands Of Time* and *The Secret Configuration*.' Alistair had picked up some of Hero's flippancy.

'Oh, but I've read you! Tom bought me *Sands Of Time* last year when I was stuck indoors with bronchitis!'

'Was it all right?' with authentic authorial anxiety.

'Great. Couldn't put it down. And it certainly sold well.'

'But it wasn't what you might call literary. Not the kind of thing that a fellow of the Royal S-society of Literature might care to be associated with.'

'No, but I bet you got a lot for the film rights.'

'You're a child of your time, Hero. There you are, lying among your pillows like Camille, and talking like a publishing executive. You haven't changed much after all.'

'And aren't you glad? But I think it's great that you're writing successful adventure stories. Anyway, don't you want me to be enthusiastic? After the last few months?'

'It's wonderful to have you back. The Real Hero. The Hero I didn't know before.' And he kissed her again.

178

CHAPTER TWO

The following weeks passed like a gentle holiday. Ash Grove, its smooth lawns tinted chartreuse green by sunlight, had a storybook air. Everywhere seemed touched by an enchantment which suffused the patients with lotus eaters' calm, and the silence was broken only by birdsong and the occasional screech of five peacocks, which picked their way fastidiously across the lawns.

After a few days, she was allowed outside, and soon after that, was assisted to the swimming pool and managed a game of croquet with some other patients. The climate, neither too hot nor too cold, seemed specifically programmed to aid recovery, and she spent afternoons wandering happily among the kitchen gardens, watching strawberries ripen under their net, while drunken bees bumbled over the foxgloves.

Ash Grove did not correspond to Hero's sensational concept of a psychiatric hospital or addiction clinic. There were no desperate figures chained to walls, no padded cells or cold-turkey rantings. As Alistair said, the Grove was a rest home, and indistinguishable from a country house hotel. Over the next few weeks Hero came to know a celebrated actress, three men from the Foreign and Commonwealth Office, and a fifteen-year-old boy with a Double First in Mathematics and, until recently, a cocaine habit. She was also introduced to an astonishingly beautiful model who was recovering from an attempt to 'cure' her lesbian tendencies by getting married. Hero could have walked past any of these people in the street without considering them to be potential psychiatric patients.

*   *   *

Soon after Hero's return to consciousness, she had a visit from her mother. Maeve, chastened and quiet, seemed uncharacteristically lost for words, in some way diminished.

'Why did you not tell me how you felt?' she demanded, sitting at her bedside and staring at Hero, as at a specimen in the zoo.

'But I didn't *know* how I felt,' Hero replied. 'I didn't feel anything. That was the point.'

'I could have done *something*.' Maeve's voice was mournful. 'I should never have allowed you to stay at that flat on your own. It was quite wrong. I blame myself. Perhaps I have not given you enough attention, perhaps I've been neglecting you—'

'That's crazy! Whoops, I shouldn't use words like that in here. I mean, that's ridiculous. I never wanted to be fussed over.'

'That was the trouble. You drove us away. And everyone else who tried to take charge of you. That poor Alistair said the same thing.'

'You've met Ali then?'

'Of course. He seems devoted to you, Hero. And more your sort than Tom *ever* was. I always had my doubts about poor Tom—' 'poor' was Maeve's favourite adjective '—he said you wouldn't admit you needed help. You always were so bloody-minded, Hero.'

'I didn't think about needing help. I just wanted to be left alone.'

180

'I've always encouraged you to think for yourself. Perhaps I should have been a little more domineering—'

'Do we need to go in for these post-mortems?'

'Well thank God it is *not* a post-mortem! Hero!' Maeve's anger revived her, and her hair bristled. 'Why do you blame yourself? Nobody's to blame. Except perhaps the bloody Department.'

Hero sank back on her pillows dramatically, but with real exhaustion. Curious that she should have slept for so long, yet tired after a few minutes' conversation. The doctors had warned her about over-exertion, pointing out that the world would seem a strange and noisy place when she left the confines of Ash Grove. Even here, other people, their feelings and thoughts and words, seemed to intrude and batter her thin new skin. Like a snake which had sloughed off its old armour-plating. Hero was supple and vulnerable to every emotional wind that blew. At one moment she would feel tears stand on the threshold of her eyelids: at another, wild elation and fine amusement at her present situation lifted her high as that helium-filled balloon which had escaped at Henley.

'But you are feeling more yourself?' Maeve asked anxiously. She looked old suddenly, her face skinny and creased, as if she had suffered more than Hero. She probably had.

'More myself,' Hero agreed. 'I don't think I was ever myself during that whole thing with Tom.'

'Will you agree to treatment—if it's considered necessary?' For someone with such pronounced liberal attitudes, Mrs Abrahams made psychiatric help sound shameful as a visit to the VD clinic.

'Why not? Can't do any harm.'

181

'Cassie wants to come up this weekend. She'd like you to meet her new boyfriend.'

'A boyfriend? Cassandra?' Maeve was visibly relieved by the sound of Hero's laughter. 'I don't *believe* it! What on earth is he like?'

'He's a trainee stockbroker, who managed to get himself thrown out of Sandhurst for failing the written tests, and his name's Douglas. He's one of poor Tom's cousins.'

Hero giggled so much at this news that Maeve looked doubtful, until she had recovered sufficiently to reassure her mother.

'Cassie and Douglas!' she said. *'Plus ça change—'*

* * *

Alistair joined them soon afterwards bringing another bunch of cottage roses wrapped in the *Observer*. However tediously reliable he had been in London, Hero found herself looking forward to his daily visits now, and was always glad to see him. She touched the soft petals, and arranged them in her water jug. An earwig dropped from one flower and sped across the bedside cabinet, and Alistair rescued it tenderly, putting it through the window where it landed softly on the grass below.

'Gone off to t-terrorise the basement,' he commented.

'It didn't frighten me. You could have left it here.'

'They can give one a nasty nip. Besides, I wanted to protect you from it.' Maeve beamed approval, and said that she must be leaving.

'You're very sweet, Alistair. And very kind,' Hero said later. In fact, she sometimes wished he

182

wasn't quite so sweet and kind. 'I don't know how I'm ever going to pay you back for all this. It must be costing you a fortune.'

'There's nothing else I would rather s-spend it on. I hope s-soon you'll be well enough to come and stay at the cottage. I'd like you to be there for a while. Just until you decide what to do. Will you come?'

'Of course I will,' Hero said confidently. But she watched him leave, wondering wistfully if she would ever feel the way about Alistair that he evidently felt about her.

*   *   *

In addition to keeping her at Ash Grove, Alistair literally showered Hero with presents. He brought newspapers, paperbacks and magazines, a video recorder with tapes of her favourite films, and a cassette recorder with a catholic selection of singers. Unexpectedly, he had turned out to be something of an authority on rock, an interest which Hero would never have predicted. He gave her several new novels, including his own, and a copy of *The Little Drummer Girl*, which didn't do much for her peace of mind but had an admirable authenticity. Hero sat among her presents, turning the pages of a magazine as her headphones buzzed, feeling like a sick princess surrounded by tributes.

*   *   *

Hero's first outing, some weeks later, was an ordeal. She sat in her room gazing out at the golden evening, fiddling with her engagement ring and wondering again whether to continue wearing it. The emerald was heavy, and threatened to slip off her finger.

For all the rest, Hero was gaunt, as though she had spent weeks getting stoned in nightclubs. The white cotton trousers and shirt, worn last on her honeymoon in Italy, were baggy on her thin frame. Hero's eyesockets were hollow as her cheeks, and the freckles stared, like spatters from a gold-tipped paintbrush.

She had attempted to put on make-up, but the colours seemed artificial against her indoor skin, the lipstick harsh around that pallid mouth. She scrubbed her face with soap and water, and combed her hair, shocked as ever by its crude brightness in the subdued room. Red looked so unnatural, so bold and forward, that she felt distinguished and extinguished. *Perhaps I am a little mad. Split personality. A brazen bolshy redhead with a shy personality. Like the way I always seem to be involved in extraordinary events when all I want to do is get away and read a book. I don't think I'm ever going to be allowed a quiet life.*

Down in the courtyard Lorraine, the former model, lay under a bosky chestnut, reading Lisa Alther and chewing an apple. She had told Hero the previous evening of her own spectacular collapse—jumping, coked to the eyeballs, off Chelsea Bridge—which made Hero's experience pedestrian by comparison. Now, she lay peacefully, elegant as a gazelle, suffused with sunlight. The comparison brought Yeats to mind: *The innocent and the beautiful have no enemy but time.*

At least she's found out what she is. Who she is. And now she's leaving, happy, and some friend from the old

184

days will look after her, and they'll be settled, running their dress shop in Harrogate, at least for the time being. If only I could suddenly find out that I had an organic disease, or a chemical imbalance, or was really gay. I've often wondered if I might be. Except I don't fancy women very much.

Hero's reflections were interrupted by the arrival of Alistair, who took her hand and led her softly through carpeted corridors to the lobby, where flowers were arranged freshly every day, and the statue of a neo-classical sylph smiled to herself beneath irisless eyes, standing forever in the well of the stairs as though waiting patiently for someone who would never arrive. *Smiling at grief*, thought Hero, as Alistair discussed plans for the evening.

Alistair never drove in London, and Hero was surprised when his car turned out to be a little green MG, and not the Morris Minor she had expected.

'I thought we'd go to my local,' he said, climbing in beside her. 'It s-should be fairly quiet at this time of the evening, though people tend to pile in later.'

'I didn't expect a sports car, Ali. But then I didn't expect you to listen to the Pogues, either.'

'You know enough of my world to realise that people are s-seldom what they s-seem. Don't you?'

'I'm getting used to it.'

Hero fiddled with the radio, but was distracted by the wind whipping through her hair, the dipping green hills and roads curving unexpectedly. Though it was almost seven, sun was bright on her eyes, and she put on her Reactolites, shocked by so many smells, sounds and sensations. Alistair glanced sideways to see her taut and rigid in the seat beside him, and pulled up beside a gate.

185

'Are you all right?'

'I feel a bit—peculiar. I can't take it all in.'

'It's always like that when you first come outside.'

'Christ, what's it like for people who've spent years in gaol? I don't think I can handle it.'

'S-shall I take you back?'

'No. I can't spend the rest of my life inside. And besides, I want to get to the pub.'

'I'll take care of you. Any time you feel—unhappy, tell me, and we'll go back to the Grove. It'll t-take a bit of time for you to get used to it—'

'To being alive again. I realise that.' She pushed the glasses back onto the bridge of her nose, nervously, as the world pressed in on her.

Alistair started the car again, and they drove off, poised at the top of a hill before dipping down among fields of vivid green and vast empty skies. Sweeping curves of pasture, and the distant vista of cliffs dropping into nothing impressed and disturbed her. It was a dream landscape, in which she could run forever without growing tired, and fall through blue air into fathoms. *A sea-change, into something rich and strange—*

'What was that, Hero?'

'Did I say something? Sorry. Must have been talking out loud.'

She lowered her head in embarrassment, fiddling again with the radio knobs. Among the crackle and phase Hero suddenly heard a few familiar bars. *All day through*, someone sang faintly, as though at great distance, before the words were drowned in white noise, *no-one else will do—*

'Oh, listen! Listen, it's that! Ali—'

186

Alistair flicked the tuner and the sad ballad wafted through the evening air.

> *All day through*
> *I miss*
> *I miss*
> *I miss you*

'I don't know who recorded that, or who wrote it, or anything about it. But there's something about those words and that tune which makes the hair stand up on the back of my neck. It's moving, but somehow a bit creepy and spine-chilling too.'

The music died away to be replaced by a second, dissimilar track. Alistair glanced across.

'You liked that?'

'Yes. It touches a nerve.'

'That's interesting,' he said, almost as though the incident had confirmed some private suspicion of his own. 'I'll have to s-see if I can trace it for you.'

*　　　*　　　*

There were one or two locals in the bar, and a raucous young woman in riding kit who reminded Hero of the old days with Tom.

'Let's sit out,' she suggested, irritated by smoke in her nostrils and the girl's brash, uninhibited laughter.

They settled on a wooden bench, glasses of dark warm beer on the table beside them, the sky gathering itself up for a Mediterranean-style sunset. Green shoulders of land rose above the sea, and they could hear the far-off smash and drag of waves below.

'That'll be better than any gin and tonic,' Alistair told her, as she drank the dark beer speculatively.

'I'm allowed to drink. I'm not on tranquillisers or anything.'

'Nothing at all?'

'They don't seem to think it's necessary.' Hero set down her glass, trying to fit it into the wet ring it had already made on the wooden tabletop, remembering Tom's initial shock when she had asked for her habitual pint (she and Stephen had drunk nothing else) and his attempts to convert her to more ladylike drinks. Alistair possessed no such anxieties about her femininity. He seemed softened by the evening glow, his features relaxed and less strained, eyes vulnerable without the protective glasses. 'Contact lenses,' he had said, when she remarked on the absence of spectacles. It was a great improvement.

'All the business with Tom seems so long ago now,' Hero said, allowing him to fold her hands in his, drawing closer to Alistair as though in comfort. Even the birdsong, and the faint rush of cars on the B road seemed loud and unfamiliar.

'P-perhaps you can put it in perspective now.'

'I found an article about me. In one of the magazines you sent.'

'Oh—I should have vetted it. Was it—did you—?'

'I'd forgotten all about it. It was an interview I gave shortly before—before what happened. It seems to be about another person.'

'It upset you?'

'Not as much as I thought it would. There was a double-page spread, with a picture of our wedding, and the car in Ovington Square, and me getting my degree at the Senate House. Quite a nice woman came round, it was one afternoon back in April. And a photographer. All the same, it's a strange way to get famous.'

'I want to try and protect you from all that. N-nothing's got into the Press, you know. About what happened to you. Gilby s-saw to that. And the tail has been taken off. No-one will shadow you now.'

'I suppose the Department has realised by now that I knew nothing about it. That I wasn't involved in Tom's—business.'

'That's for certain. And s-soon—well, I hope you'll be able to forget all about it.'

'I intend to. I don't plan on spending the next forty years as Superwidow. Particularly now I know what Tom was really like.'

'Aren't you being a little hard?'

Hero glanced down at her hands, which were twisted in his. She clenched her fingers slowly, felt her eyes watering. *Oh hell, let the tears fall if they will. What's so great about controlling your feelings anyway? What's so great about being cool?*

'Yes. He *was* a bastard, and he lied and cheated and I'm glad he's dead. But I still miss him. I wish it hadn't happened. I pity the poor sod.'

'Hero—' He lifted his hand, stroked her hair as it swung forward to cover her moist face. 'I wish I c-could make it up to you.'

'That's kind.' She shook herself free of him though, taking up her glass and smoothing her hair where he had touched it, just as a cat, ineptly stroked, will lick its ruffled dignity back into place.

'I know you were going to see the psychiatrist at Ash Grove. D-did you—has—'

189

'Yes. We've spoken a couple of times. It went quite well.'

'But did you find it helpful?'

'I suppose so. I mean, we didn't seem to talk about much in particular. It was rather like a supervision, only I was the subject, and I didn't have to write an essay.'

'But did you talk about Tom?'

'A bit. And well, nothing dramatic happened. I didn't lie on a couch and think myself back into the womb. Nothing like that. But he made a few suggestions, about how my grief over Tom was mixed up with my feelings when Dad died, and we talked about why I was so competitive. He seemed interested in that. And about what it was like growing up in Oxford.'

'Will you s-see him again?'

'I think so. Dr Berridge is a very easy man to talk to. He doesn't pass judgement, he just listens, most of the time. Rather like going to Confession, but without the consequences. He's suggested I continue to have psychotherapy when I leave, but I don't know if I'll bother. We talked a lot about changing my circumstances, and I think I'll try to do that.'

Drifts of grey shadow gained on the sky over the last traces of a spectacular marine sunset. Other drinkers arrived, and there came the comforting burr of rural accents, only occasionally adulterated by London laughs from weekenders.

'I'm putting the Hans Place flat on the market. I can't go back there, and I could use the money. And I think I'll probably sell the cottage, too. Might go back to Oxford.'

'You've obviously been doing a lot of thinking

recently. But would it be wise to go to Oxford? It doesn't s-seem—'

Hero shrugged. 'I'll register for research, either there or in Cambridge, do a bit of travelling, maybe buy somewhere when I know where I'm going to live. I don't fancy going back to London.'

'C-can I get you another pint?'

Hero nodded, and watched Alistair slip away into the darkness, a shadow on the move. She still felt weak, disproportionately emotional, and his sudden departure left her at a loss. It would be very easy to become dependent on Alistair. And not unpleasant, for a time. When he returned, Hero was already prepared to answer the question he had not yet asked.

'I was wondering—perhaps when you come to s-stay—if you'd like to make it more than a week or two? In fact, as long as you like. Until you know what you're r-really doing.'

Hero smiled, watching his eyes light up as she replied. How easy it was to please Alistair. And how manipulative she had become.

'I'd love to stay, Alistair. You're so kind.'

He hugged her, warm with relief, arms tight about her thin frame, face buried in her hair, as Hero experienced a twinge of guilt before accepting her role as one of life's takers.

CHAPTER THREE

Being an invalid was an undemanding activity, and Hero understood why so many Victorian women took to it assiduously. She sat in the cottage garden,

191

listlessly reading paperbacks and absorbing sunshine, the headphones of the Walkman insulating her against unwelcome thoughts. When not listening to music she concentrated on birdsong and was able to distinguish martins and yellowhammers with new-developed proficiency.

Hero was malingering and she would have been the first to admit it. Alistair loved to wrap and protect her, shroud her in tartan rugs and bring glasses of Perrier water, allowing complete freedom to his paternal instincts. And Hero accepted his care, as she would never have done six months ago.

Their relationship resembled Hero's life with Tom, but the crucial difference was Alistair's presence. He wrote in the mornings; afternoons and evenings were spent together. His patience and concern seemed inexhaustible, and Hero was sometimes paradoxically worn out by the intensity of his care for her.

'Perhaps I *can't* love anybody again,' she suggested, as they sat listening to the birds' last chorus and watching the sunset one evening. 'Perhaps I'm basically very selfish. Some people are.'

'I doubt it very much, Hero. Anyway, it doesn't m-matter, does it? You like, I think you're f-fond of me. That's enough.'

'But it doesn't seem fair to you.'

'I want you to s-stay with me. That's all. I'll try not to be too upset if you want to s-see other people. I don't own you. But I hope that you'll be able to s-spare some time for me.'

'Of course I will. But please—don't expect too much. I don't want anyone to expect anything from me, ever again.'

'That was part of the trouble, wasn't it?'

'Part of it. Dr Berridge said I had—what was it—unrealistic expectations. I always wanted to win and to succeed so people would love me, which is what made me so competitive. At least, that was his idea.'

'Perhaps when you're better you can get back to your running. That s-seemed to help. Once you've recovered your st-stamina.'

'Stamina! Huh! Look at me! I've been living on Guinness and chocolate, and I haven't put on an ounce.'

'Well, think of how many women would envy you. Private income, thin figure, st-stunning hair. You're very well off.'

'It's strange that being told to count your blessings is no source of consolation.'

'You console me. I'm the one who's better off. Here you are, living with me, s-sleeping in my bed, being there when I wake up in the morning. More than I ever expected.'

'You *are* sweet.'

★   ★   ★

He *was* sweet, and that was just the trouble. Next day Hero stalked about the garden rerunning that conversation in her head, and realising that though she loved Alistair, she was not *in love* with him. He worshipped Hero like a barbarian goddess, She Who Must Be Obeyed, but his slavish devotion made her a little uneasy.

'He'd marry you tomorrow,' Flora commented some days later, on a visit. 'He's absolutely besotted.'

'I *know*. It's a shame really. He could be giving all this to somebody else. Somebody who really deserved it.'

'What makes you think you don't? You're beginning to sound like all those people with titles or private incomes who go around feeling guilty because they're more fortunate than the rest of the world.'

'I *have* got a private income.'

'Yes, but you aren't going to get rid of it, are you?' replied Flora pertinently. 'It's all carefully invested now, not to mention the mint you'll get when you sell the flat.'

'I suppose you're right.'

'If you've got any sense, you'll take Alistair at his word. I know he's a bit—sensitive—but he's so fond of you, Hero, and he's a very successful author. You'd never think he wrote those sort of books to look at him though, would you?'

Hero poured Flora another glass of Lambrusco bianco, for which she had developed a recent passion. Alistair deplored her taste, and complained that it was like drinking lemonade. They sat and listened in reverential silence to his word processor pecking from an upstairs window.

'Honestly Hero, if I was in your position, I know what I'd do.'

'I'm in no hurry to marry again. But it's funny how many proposals—and propositions—I've had since I've been free, so to speak. The most unlikely people make passes at me. Even my solicitor and the accountant.'

'I've heard of that before,' agreed Flora. 'The same thing happened to my aunt. She's only about ten years older than me—gorgeous—and when her husband died there were men queuing round the block to console her. And now look at me!'

'But you've always got someone! Lots of people!'

'Want to bet? I haven't met any suitable men for ages. Lots of unsuitable ones, though. All this business with Roger is getting me down.'

Roger was Flora's managing director, with whom she was conducting an affair.

'He's so charismatic, Hero. And powerful. He came up the hard way. He has these exciting, gritty, working-class attitudes—'

'And an exciting, gritty, working-class wife and four kids.'

'Yes, I know. But every time I see him—and we've been involved for three months now—I really think we could—'

'How often *do* you see him? Apart from at the bank?'

'About once a week. He comes round, or we go out to dinner. But we have to be careful about being spotted together in public.'

'And I suppose he spends his weekends at home?'

'Why do you think I'm down here? I get so much free time now, I don't know what to do with myself.'

'I think you're daft. Have another glass?'

'I've got to drive back soon.'

'What for?'

'Good point.' Flora stretched in her deckchair. 'Fantastic weather you've got down here. Up in London the summer's virtually over. I've been buying winter clothes.'

She was vivid as ever in turquoise green, her favourite colour, and a fashionable one that year. Flora's complexion glowed goldly, the product of expensive sessions on a sunbed and occasional exposure to the changeable elements of Clapham Common. Despite her name, Flora presented a metropolitan glamour to the world. 'I wish I could sit around here all day and behave like a poor little rich girl,' she remarked, somewhat pointedly.

Hero sat up. 'Me? Poor little rich girl?'

'Well, you aren't exactly putting yourself out, are you?'

'I'm still getting over it all.'

'I know, Hero, and I do understand. Honestly. But you should be doing *something*. You're not even preparing stuff for your research, are you?'

Hero admitted that most of her reading consisted of thrillers and expensive magazines, though she kept up with the weeklies.

'I think you should train for something.'

'Such as?'

'Anything. Become a secretary or a librarian. Go to law school—you'd make a fantastic barrister. Do a *cordon bleu* course or work for the Samaritans. Something, Hero. You'll just vegetate, otherwise.'

'But plenty of people just do nothing.'

'Not intelligent people. Don't kid yourself. The idle rich are mostly busy hanging on to it. And you've got talents to make use of, Hero. Remember all those funny, quirky essays you used to write for the school paper before you started getting serious.'

'I know you're right.' Hero huddled Alistair's jumper protectively about her shoulders. 'But I just can't seem to get round to it. And I can't concentrate.'

'Well, do at least give it a bit of thought. There's so many things you could be doing. I'm not just saying all this because I envy your life of idleness.'

Hero smiled at her and stood up. The word processor had ceased, and they could hear Alistair treading lightly down the wooden stairs. 'Come and have lunch,' she suggested. 'And don't give Alistair the slightest hint that we've been talking about him.'

★   ★   ★

And Flora was perfectly right, Hero admitted, lying in bed one night, sleepless beside Alistair. She really must do something. But the days flowed idly into one another, effortless and undemanding. They woke and embraced, having slept tangled in one another's limbs, drank coffee and showered, sometimes together. After breakfast Alistair went upstairs to write, and Hero wandered down to the shore. Their cottage was on a large estate, and had a private beach. Alistair rewarded his creative exertions with a huge lunch, which they cooked together, and afternoons were given over to making love or driving to a safer beach, up the coast, where they swam. At tea-time, they shared a bottle of wine as Alistair read over the day's work, and drifted into evening together, sharing another bottle, building up the dusty logfire in the sitting-room grate, sometimes going down to the pub for supper and a pint.

'I wish we could always live like this,' he said one night. They had been lying in bed listening to rare rain patter on the windows. 'I could buy a place round here, if you w-wanted.'

'Perhaps.' Hero sounded unenthusiastic.

'Are you—is it because I s-sometimes—because s-sometimes things get me down?'

'Of course not.' Although perhaps that was one of the reasons. Occasionally and without warning, Alistair hit a reef of profound depression. Sometimes this was brought about by a technical difficulty in his novel, at other times Hero's refusal to commit herself was the cause. Moods of fantastic sadness possessed him: glooms which even Hero never knew induced Alistair to hit the bottle and drink himself into oblivion. He was never objectionable on these occasions. Hero was relieved that he did not stagger, vomit and beat her up when the affliction struck, or demonstrate other anti-social tendencies. He just sat in his chair with the whisky at his side, growing sadder and sadder and drunker and drunker, until he passed out. On these occasions—it had happened three times since Hero arrived at the cottage—Hero propped him up so that he would not choke, covered him with a blanket, and crept alone to bed. In the morning he would be haggard, sickly and contrite.

'But why do you do it?' she asked him, as they lay listening to the rain. It was August now, summer on the wane.

'*Every now and then I fall apart.*' He shrugged. 'It c-comes from working for the Department. And it hasn't happened for a while. Has it?'

'No.' Which probably meant it was going to, very soon.

'We'll look after each other, won't we, Hero? We've got each other, and that's all that matters.'

Hero did not reply, kissing him instead. Whenever possible, she substituted physical affection for words, so that she didn't have to lie all the time.

But she was fond of him. After Alistair had fallen asleep, rolled like a caterpillar in the blue duvet, she gazed thoughtfully at the spider activity on the ceiling. Perhaps she did love him. How could one know for sure?

Hero had reached some hard-won plateau of detachment, and could look down now upon the buttes and mesas of the past months. She had arrived here after a long journey, lungs adapting gradually to the altitude, the air a little thin perhaps, but exhilarating all the same. Hero almost experienced spiritual vertigo, inducing her to leap back to the depths of despair, embrace the familiar darkness rather than face a demanding future.

She would stumble on, trekking across emotional latitudes like an explorer, meeting new friends and discovering strange customs, learning novel behaviour and adapting to unexpected conditions. And then suddenly the land would rise steeply before her, another outcrop throw its shadow across her path so that she would be forced to stop, test her ropes, check her equipment, and prepare for the next assault.

Of course she was still in the foothills, faced not with one insuperable obstacle but with a mountain range. She remembered from fell-walking days that no sooner has one got to the top of one ridge, than there is another with a more fascinating view beyond it. She would have no choice but to go on.

Hero had abandoned the idea that someone would save her, fly to her with confidence and skill, transport her to a spiritual recovery station like the object of an emotional air-sea rescue operation. She was on her own now. And Alistair was the last person to rely on for comfort in these challenging wastes, being so much in need of help himself.

What a contrast he was to Tom, especially viewed now, snoring slightly, oblivious to the fact that he had pinned her arm under his bony shoulder. He reminded her of an orphaned colt once seen at a stable owned by Tom's friends. It had been nursed all night by a lad, bottle at the ready, and its thin legs stirred in its sleep as it ran imaginary races.

Hero made herself comfortable, as best she could without disturbing Alistair. For someone with no discernible bulk, he contrived to have a great deal of weight to throw around when he chose. Abandoning any attempt to sleep, and because restless nights were too familiar to be a discomfort any longer, Hero settled down to think.

Hero had come to welcome these vast wastes of night as times to evaluate all that had happened both during the day and over the past months. Her body still ran on the finely charged, electric impulses that govern the nervous systems of shocked people. She found great reserves of energy when necessary, but could be exhausted by a simple task. There had been occasions when she outdid Alistair in nervous energy, and other times when an evening before the television left her wanting to sleep out a week. *Viewed with detachment, I am not what they call a Together Lady. At least not at present. Neither of us are what you might call all there.*

Some lines of a song, which had haunted her ever since she overheard them in a pub recently, wove in and out of her mind. *We both know that I'm not what you need*, the song had lamented, but had gone on to plead in mitigation, *you know that I still love*

200

you-ou-ou.

All this talk of love. Since her recent introduction to popular music (Maeve had always kept the tuner firmly on Radio 3) Hero had reflected on just how many songs dealt with the subject. Love won, lost, unrequited, discovered, hidden, secret. What an awful lot of it there was about: or what a lot of awful people there were deluding themselves that it existed.

Still, lying in semi-darkness, listening to the rain and holding the warm body of a man had a certain reassurance. His presence brought some consolation. Alistair twitched in his sleep, turned over, and threw an arm about Hero, just as Tom had done, light years away. She allowed him to curl closer, letting herself be folded in. After all, he did provide tenderness, a devotion which she would not easily forget.

Whatever happened.

CHAPTER FOUR

Towards the end of October, winter gales massed the waves higher on the shore, and the last of the summer visitors had gone. Hero and Alistair stayed on in their cottage, but despite their idyll Alistair, his novel almost completed, had begun to talk about the advantages of wintering in London. Yet Hero enjoyed the bleak dramatic countryside, seeing it as an outward sign of her inward turbulence.

She walked on the damp beach every morning, the tartan blanket flapping about her shoulders.

Red hair streamed in the wind; it had grown during her incarceration at Ash Grove. Wildly romantic, headphones pulsating with Walton, Williams and Jean Michel Jarre, she watched the eternal movements of the waves, and traced the patterns of distant clouds. With Alistair's binoculars she spied on seabirds, able to identify different varieties now. Gulls haunted the shore, driven inland by oncoming winter and rough weather.

*   *   *

A few weeks earlier Alistair, overhearing Hero think aloud in her customary allusive style, suggested she commit her thoughts to paper.

'As therapy. Or s-simply for fun.'

'What, write something, you mean?'

'Don't try to keep to a framework. Discard any s-sort of idea that someone else will read it—criticise it—just do it for yourself. That's what I do.'

'You're probably a better writer than I am. I'm not the creative type. I'm analytical. My father always told me so.'

'Forget what type you are. Try to pretend you're writing a letter—to yourself or s-someone you know. It doesn't matter who.'

'What are you up to, Ali? Looking for an apprentice?'

But Hero settled down after lunch with a glass of wine, a felt-tip and a loose-leaf pad. She was self-conscious, and though Alistair was in Swanage, she felt as if someone might look over her shoulder, and criticise what she had done. The words came wooden and stiff, but she persevered, and after a few days thoughts and images emerged and took form on the paper. Gradually, these resolved themselves into some semblance of poetry. She found it easier to write in short lines, and her epigrammatic observations were better suited to verse, although it was not what Hero herself would have called poetry, had someone presented her with it. The sentiments expressed had more in common with rock lyrics, and she enjoyed manipulating clichés and catchphrases, turning the familiar small change of conversation into something rich and strange. Within a month Hero had amassed three complete poems, with which she was reasonably satisfied. The rest were discarded, to be picked over like refuse tips which might yield useful phrases. Alistair was more impressed than Hero, but she felt she had done something at last, if it was only to contribute *Not All There, By The Time You Read This* and *Like There's No Tomorrow* to the heritage of English poetry.

Writing—even putting together what she considered might make suitable lyrics for the B side of a single—was exhausting. She came to realise why Alistair needed his isolation. But there was relief in putting pen to paper, it became a compulsive activity, and Hero felt that at last she had provided an excuse for her long period of inactivity. She needed no justification. She was a Poet.

*   *   *

Now Hero wandered by the shore, a self-confessed Writer and more than a little mad, tasting sticky brine on her lips and feeling the heavy lift and slap

203

of her damp hair. She remembered someone saying that the disadvantage of real life was its lack of a soundtrack. Now she even had that, melancholy rhythms humming softly through her headphones to complement the grey waves and turbulent skies. After listening to Alistair's extensive record collection, Hero had formed a taste for electronic music and New York art bands. That day she was accompanied by *On Some Faraway Beach*.

Restless romanticism was preferable to the realms of ice, the crystal kingdom which once threatened to claim her for its own. Since waking in Ash Grove, Hero had not been troubled by that frozen dagger in her heart. She had been sad, pessimistic and angry, but had experienced the sensations acutely: the numbness wore off like an anaesthetic.

Hero thought of Tom constantly these days, in an almost academic way, puzzling out his behaviour and motives as she had once studied the life of Justinian.

Poor Tom. Strange, I never thought I'd ever call him that. What did go wrong, anyway? I keep thinking of him, not as just another pusher creeping round London with a loaded automatic but as he should have been, wielding not a gun but a cricket bat, the hero of a Hotspur *strip, dazzling in his whites against the greensward of Lords or Trent Bridge. Why did he get mixed up in it all?*

Obvious, I suppose. He needed the money for a life he could no longer afford but which he thought he deserved, and drugs was an easy way to get it. He's like the man in the Sherlock Holmes story—The Empty House—*who seemed the perfect officer and gentleman until without warning, he went to the bad, started to twist like a diseased tree, instead of growing tall. He went off at a tangent. He went crook, as the Australians say. Tom was greedy, vain and immature. Though it's easy for me to say so now.*

Even having a girlfriend when he was still married to me. To him that was perfectly respectable. He had to have it all. Nerissa was necessary—to massage his ego, which wasn't a service I could perform. It wasn't a criticism of me. I'm prepared to bet he cared about me—in his fashion.

And all those nightmares I used to have—all those doubts. There was something strange about him, after all. Something wrong with him all the time. He really belonged to darkness.

The memory of another poor Tom came to her then, though the song's narrator seemed to have more in common with Hero than with her dead husband:

With an host of furious fancies
Whereof I am commander
With a burning spear, and a horse of air
To the wilderness I wander
By a knight of ghosts and shadows
I summoned am to tourney
Ten leagues beyond the wide world's end
Methinks it is no journey.

Tom O' Bedlam. Poor Tom. Mad Tom. Major Tom's A Junkie. Or in this instance, Major Tom's A Pusher.
Suddenly Hero realised she was not alone.

★   ★   ★

Fear tingled down her spine. Switching off the cassette, she pushed the headphones onto her neck
205

and turned to see who might be watching. It was a lonely beach, awkward and inaccessible. The estate had an efficient security system (one of its attractions for Alistair, so that Hero would be shielded from the Press). Reaching the beach involved a slither down a pebble-strewn path and a final leap onto the shingle. Scrambling up was frequently undignified.

A dark figure stood at the top of the cliff, gazing out to sea. From this distance Hero could not tell whether the dishevelled hair and flapping black overcoat belonged to a man or woman. Although the figure's eyes seemed fixed on the horizon, Hero sensed that until that moment she had been the object of observation.

With a justifiable return of the old paranoia Hero quickened her pace. If she walked on for two miles, and scrambled over some rocks visible at high tide, she would be able to scale another cliff path. It was a tiresome journey, but she wanted to avoid the stranger, whoever it was. She wasn't in the mood for conversation. Presumably Whoever It Was had been staying on the estate.

As she hurried off, the distinct sounds of someone moving over the pebbles could be heard, a slither as the figure made its way down the path and crossed the limestone ledges leading to the beach. Against better judgement, Hero turned round.

It was a man, thin and perhaps younger-looking than he actually was. His clothes, commonplace in London, were at once incongruous and appropriate. Instead of sensible shoes and a cagoule, he wore black which matched the cliffs and lent him a spectral air. The dark suede boots were encrusted with soil and seawater. He stopped three yards short of Hero and stared at her unblinkingly. Hero stared back. Although she wasn't frightened, something about the young man produced an antagonistic air, charging the atmosphere not with menace but—she suddenly realised—with a sensation of excitement.

He seemed familiar, but perhaps that was the red disordered hair, so like her own. It looked unnatural, but then so did Hero's. Neither spoke. They were creatures of the same rare species meeting in the wild.

At last he broke the silence.

'I think I've seen a ghost. My ghost.'

'So do I.'

'How did you get here?'

She tried analysing his accent, but it was impossible. The tones were flattened and neutral, though Hero could detect the faintest trace of South London.

'Same way as you,' she replied, in her old accent, before Tom got at her for running words together and droppin' Gs.

'How did you get in? Who are you?'

He was anxious, defensive—almost afraid.

'I could ask you the same question.'

The young man—not so very young, perhaps Alistair's age, but curiously white-faced, as though he had been shut indoors—backed off a little.

'Don't you know who I am?'

'Haven't the faintest,' Hero replied.

Relieved, he dropped his shoulders and put his hands in his pockets. Hero noticed a pale white mark over the left cheekbone, reminiscent of a duelling scar. It added to his rakish appearance.

'You're trespassing,' he said, in a slightly softer

voice.

'No, I'm not. What's it got to do with you, anyhow?'

'I own this beach.'

Hero was incredulous. She had met a selection of the landed gentry, but found it unlikely that this sad young man possessed a stretch of the Dorset coastline. Unlikely, but not impossible.

'You're kidding.'

'And you're on my land. I'm going to have to ask you to leave, and not to come here again.'

'Who do you think you are?'

The not-so-young man seemed to find this amusing. Half smiling to himself he gave a melancholy shrug.

'So you're staying on the estate?'

'Of course. I'm a guest of Alistair Urquhart. I believe he rented the cottage from Moonsleaze House.'

'That's right.' Again with that rather eerie half-smile. 'He rented it from me.'

'I don't believe you.'

'Suit yourself.' Having warned her off, and ascertained a reasonable degree of anonymity, he came across and stood beside Hero as they both gazed out to sea. She was astonished by a sudden buzz of sexuality across the space between them.

'I've been away.' As it if explained everything. 'For months. I'm always glad to get back here again.'

'Where've you been?'

'London, Paris, Milan, Rome, Venice, Vienna, Hamburg, Amsterdam, New York, Chicago, LA, Tokyo, to name but a few. You did ask.'

'Did you enjoy it?'

'It was hard work.'

'So that's how you come to own this beach?'

'And the house. I don't sleep out here, nights.' His voice was deadpan. 'So what about you? Where do you fit in?'

'Fit in? I don't fit in anywhere.'

'Sounds as if *you* don't know who you are, either.'

Having asserted her right to the beach, Hero now felt it was time to get back for lunch. The wind chilled, and she had grown tired of the drab blue-grey vistas, the black rocks. Though it would be a shame to leave this fascinating apparition.

'I've got to be going.' She turned aside and headed for the cliffs. It would be ignoble to be seen scrabbling up that path, and she hoped he would not turn round.

'*Must you go?*' Suddenly all courtesy.

Hero nodded, gathering folds of Black Watch about her, pushing hair, whipped into long red ribbons by the wind, out of her eyes.

For the first time he smiled fully, showing irregular teeth, and Hero was startled by the resemblance to herself. Given that both had an androgynous quality, she could have been looking in a mirror.

'Listen—' Sure of his audience, he paused for a second, letting her stand attentive in the wind. 'You can come back. If you want. *I* don't mind.' So this was a momentary glimpse of the charm which had compelled them in Venice, Vienna and Tokyo. It was quite devasting but Hero felt obliged to hold out.

'Well, *thank you*.'

'I don't mean to be patronising. This is strictly

my beach, but I don't mind you being here. That's all.'

Hero felt guilty. Perhaps she had over-reacted. This sad young man, whoever he was, certainly wanted to ensure his privacy. 'I'm sorry.' Attempting to inject a little normality. 'See you around.'

He nodded, turning back to the sea, and stared at the bleak expanse of water as though consulting an oracle. Hero scrambled quickly up the cliff, hoping he had not seen her ungainly progress. When she turned at the top, he was still standing there on the shore, dark-clad and mysterious, gazing out to sea.

*　　*　　*

Hero took the long way back to the cottage. For some reason she was in no hurry to be on time. The autumn sun had disappeared behind a leaden cloudbank, occasionally shooting Blakean rays to highlight moody hills. Regretting that she wore no more than an old pair of Levi's and Alistair's aran sweater, she pulled the tartan rug closer, fingers whitening in the cold.

Ali'll think it's amusing. I met this amazing guy on the beach. Really thin and romantic. Like Byron the morning after. I think we were terrified of each other. He says he owns this place, but he doesn't look the type. More like someone on the way home from a costume ball. Bit spooky, too. Like some of the junkies I met in the Grove. I think he lives in a world of his own.

But this wasn't what Alistair would hear. Bright amusing London-scene speak would not suit the uneasy ambience of their meeting. Something about the self-conscious not-so-young young man,

,alternately confident and afraid, filled her with recognition. Whoever it was didn't just look like her. He shared Hero's ambivalent attitude to the rest of the world. Hero had been brought up sharply: it was like turning a dark corner and walking into her own reflection in a mirror. She remembered those old legends of the *fetch*, the supernatural look-alike who assists mortals from this life to the next, and almost caught herself glancing over her shoulder. She was fascinated and slightly disturbed by that strange young man.

A powerful engine distracted Hero as she was a mile from the cottage, and she stood aside, knee-deep in nettles, to let the vehicle overtake. A long, unfamiliar American car swept along the narrow country road, smoked windows and black bodywork glistening like a hearse. Wondering vaguely who drove around the Isle of Purbeck in such incongruous style, Hero went home, trying to concentrate on the prospect of poached salmon and blackcurrant crumble, and forget that strange meeting.

★   ★   ★

She wasn't really surprised to find the black limousine outside the cottage, though the burly driver polishing the windscreen was a bit of a shock. Assuming someone from the Department had called to visit Alistair, or that they were being honoured with a visit from the local gentry, Hero walked confidently inside. Her shyness had diminished recently, and new people did not alarm her as in the past.

'Ali! I'm back! You there?' She tossed the bunch

211

of wild grasses onto a chair, seizing a hairbrush to give herself a swift grooming before Alistair appeared. This was a recent habit, too.

'Hero! I wondered where you'd got to!' Alistair appeared from the sitting room, flushed and genial, so that she wondered who on earth had shown up. Alistair was normally drained and grim after a morning over the terminal. 'Come in here. There's s-someone I'd like you to meet.'

She wasn't really surprised. In fact Hero could already predict—with a certain comforting fatalism—the direction events would take. Seated languidly, mug in hand, hair tousled stiff by salt sea air, was the man from the beach.

* * *

'Hero, this is John. John's just popped over for a drink.'

He got politely if unsteadily to his feet, and they shook hands. His palm was cold and dry, the fingers clenching with unexpected vigour. They stared at each other like two cats before making conventional salutations, and the same current ran between them as before. It reminded Hero of a childhood incident where she and her friends held hands in a circle while a charge of electricity coursed through them, and she wondered how Alistair could possibly miss the galvanic implications of the contact.

It seemed he could.

'Hero, John Fane's a very good f-friend of mine.' Alistair was busy at the drinks tray, his back turned as they subsided into their respective chairs. Fane continued to stare unsmilingly, and Hero stared

212

right back. She wondered if he would make some reference to their previous encounter, and guessed he would not. It was as if they had already entered a secret pact excluding Alistair—and everyone else.

Interpreting the silence as mutual shyness, Alistair said: 'John's just got back to England. After quite s-some time. Nearly six months, I believe.'

'Five months. Felt like longer.'

'Where have you been?' she asked, as if she didn't already know. Alistair settled close on the sofa, draping a long arm round her shoulders.

'John's been on tour. Europe and the States as well as Australia and the Far East. Quite a marathon by the s-sound of it.'

'What do you do?' Hero's ingenuousness was genuine. 'Are you something to do with the music business?'

Fane smiled, as if to himself, but Alistair burst out laughing.

'Oh Hero, you're p-p-priceless! S-something in the music business! Don't you know who this is?'

'No.' Hero smiled blankly, and could see that her ignorance had found its mark. But far from being dismayed that his fame had not preceded him, John Fane smiled back.

'Perhaps I'm slipping. Or maybe I'm just a little before Hero's time.'

He turned to Alistair, who looked embarrassed, and back to Hero. 'I'm almost flattered. Makes me feel *ordinary*.'

'Why would you want to feel ordinary?' Hero asked, going through her mental card-index for references to Fane, John. Associations began to come back.

He didn't reply, simply gave the slightly

irritating shrug again. Finally, he said: 'I have to be off. Sorry I can't make lunch.'

'Not at all.' Alistair was understanding. 'You must st-still be jetlagged. We'll meet again soon.'

'I don't see that many people when I'm down here. But you and Hero must come over for dinner one night.'

'Sorry about the *faux pas*,' said Hero.

'Forget it.' With another unsmiling stare he allowed Alistair to see him out. Hero heard them talking in the passageway, and a few minutes later the limousine started outside. Hero glanced through the window to see it slide off, sleek and black among rotting hedgerows and banks of tawny fern.

'Pity you weren't back earlier,' said Alistair, stretching luxuriously and reaching for his glass. 'You two could have got to know each other better.'

'Really?' Hero succeeded in sounding more than a little bored.

'I can't believe you didn't recognise John Fane.'

'Well, who is he, anyway? You know I'm not at all well up in rock music.'

'He's more of a composer these days, really. What they call egghead rock. He's got a home st-studio down here, and does a lot of experimental, electronic stuff. The kind of thing you quite like, actually. He st-still does concerts, but that was his first world tour for about three years. Used to be more of a performer.'

'I think it must have been before my time,' said Hero, mischievously.

'I'm afraid you're probably right. He must be—what—my age? Mid-thirties, anyway.'

'Over the hill.'

'Speak for yourself.'

214

'So what was *he* up to while I was still taking my "O" levels?'

'Oh, John Fane was one of the st-stylists. Back in the glitter-encrusted s-seventies with Ferry and Bowie. He's worked with everyone. Lou Reed, John Cale, Eno, you name it. Used to have a fantastic band called the Livin' Daylights. It all s-seemed rather shocking, in those days. And then he went into his hermit phase and did the music for that s-science fiction film, *Tender Alien*. I've got it here somewhere.'

Hero shrugged, trying to seem uninterested.

'So what's he doing down here? How did you meet?'

'Oh—around here. John *owns* Moonsleaze House. This land all belongs to him. He bought the place off the old family, lock, stock, and barrel. And he's kept it just as it was. The place is a m-museum, and the man's a recluse.'

'Isn't he rather young to be a recluse?'

'John's had a lot of difficulties in the past. And I s-suppose the pressures, that sort of thing—it would rather make one want to s-spend a lot of time on one's own.'

'I can understand that.'

'It'll be a real blow to his ego, your not recognising him.'

'Oh, I'm sure you can make excuses for me. Say I was brought up in an ivory tower. My mum only likes classical music, however trendy she looks.'

'I'll s-sort out some albums for you. There's a particularly good one called *Land Of Cockayne*—about drugs, obviously. Do you know, I rather s-suspect that you made a big impression on John. Cool, you know. Unimpressed. I sh-should

215

think women find him very attractive. Though I wouldn't know, not being that way inclined.'

Hero laughed, already practising dissimulation.

CHAPTER FIVE

The following day brought heavy rain and a third letter from Stephen Lewis.

'Why not visit him in the States?' enquired Alistair, pouring the acrid Italian coffee that was his only concession to breakfast.

'Sometime I will.'

'A holiday might do you good.'

'But I'd have to leave you, Ali.'

'Perhaps you need a holiday from me.'

'I'd like to get away from this climate,' she agreed, buttering a slice of toast. 'But I don't want to start all that up again. I don't want to be another Faculty wife.'

'He s-seems to be very attached to you. And the pay's probably s-so much better over there. I'm sure you'd both be happy—'

'I don't have to worry about money, do I? And the thing is, I'm a different person now. I keep wishing I was that same old Hero, head in the clouds, cycling round Cambridge and planning research schemes, but I'm not. I never will be. I'm certainly not the same girl Stephen went out with, and I don't think he's the same old Stephen Lewis from Beckenham either—Ali, what's wrong?' Suddenly noticing Alistair's head bowed with over-emphatic concentration over *The Times*.

'Oh—nothing.' He raised his eyes, and she

216

noticed an expression she could not interpret before his normal, slightly sad gaze returned. 'I was just hoping that we'd always s-stay in touch, too. Whatever happened.'

'Why should anything happen?'

'Oh—well, can't expect this to last forever.'

Hero wondered if he suspected anything. Not that there *was* anything to suspect, nothing but a secret fascination.

'Forgive me. I've been working too hard. Which reminds me, Hero. I've s-some publicity coming up, and I have to be in London for the launch of *Silent Night*. I thought—because the weather's so bad now—perhaps you'd like to join me?'

'Go to London you mean?' she asked, stupidly. 'Leave here?'

'For a couple of months. And then, at Christmas—we'll decide what we want to do next.'

London offered escape, Hero realised, and the opportunity to forget what threatened to be a foolish enchantment. She remembered Flora's words, and knew if she had any sense, she would stay with Alistair. Although Flora had never seen him desperate and inconsolable beside an empty whisky bottle.

'Would you like to do that, Hero?' He looked at her speculatively along his nose, head slightly to one side. The long narrow face with its flop of black hair and brown, appraising eyes reminded Hero irresistibly of a horse. She got up and patted his neck.

'I'm not sure,' she said, slipping her arm around his shoulders where he sat. 'I don't know *what* I want. How's It going—up there?' with an apprehensive glance at the ceiling, indicating

217

Alistair's study as though acknowledging the temple of some despotic deity.

'It's all right,' he replied, in similarly reverential tones. 'But I'll be glad when It's finished. It's been a real s-sod, this one.'

'What's wrong with It?'

'Oh, I'll sort It out.' Alistair never discussed work in progress, and was dismissive of his considerable commercial success, as though it were in bad taste to make a good income from writing. 'We'll have a real celebration when It's over.' Standing up. 'Oh, by the way, I s-sorted out an album for you. One of John's. See if you like it. I'm sure you'll recognise a few s-songs when you listen to them.'

'Thanks.' Hero's attempt to sound indifferent was successful. 'See you at lunchtime. If this rain gives over, I'll go for a walk.'

*   *   *

But it rained for three days, and Hero was too overcome to venture near the beach, though she kept her feelings to herself. Playing the album for the first time after breakfast that morning, she had been surprised by the number of tracks she already knew. But one song in particular, *Tender Alien*, about a pair of literally star-crossed lovers from different planets, touched Hero with a shiver of recognition:

> *All day through*
> *No-one else will do*
> *I miss*
> *I miss*
> *I miss you*

It stopped raining on the third afternoon. Pearl-grey clouds were still suspended over the horizon, and gulls wheeled petulantly inland, but Hero ventured out in wellingtons, cords, and the Black Watch rug to which she now attributed talismanic properties. Binoculars around her neck, she wandered into a wild wet world.

As if I'd do anything as predictable as fall for Fane. Just because there's something about his song which strikes a chord. Happens all the time. I wouldn't give him the satisfaction of behaving like another conquest, and I've had enough of dashing, attractive men. Alistair's the one who really looks after me. I'm just not right in the head at the moment. That's all. Still a little crazy. Can't eat, can't sleep, don't know what's the matter with me. If I go on like this I'll end up back in hospital. Maybe it's a good thing that we're going to London.

Don't kid yourself, said another voice suddenly. It was a long time since she'd heard from Other Hero, but her super-ego was obviously in a patient mood. *Who are you trying to fool? You wouldn't be human if you didn't fall for someone new now and again. It's not so terrible. Things aren't all that terrific with Ali, now are they? Who's looking after who?*

But I don't need it, replied Hero. *I bet this John Fane is a complete bastard. Has to be, to be so successful. Probably a hundred times worse than Tom, and I'm sure I've heard some pretty nasty things about him. Sunday papers gossip. Sex and drugs and under-age girls and boys and black magic. All the things you associate with rock stars. I can do without that.*

Don't believe everything you read in the papers. Other Hero was encouraging, for once. Patient,

219

sympathetic, a bit like her brother Philip on a good day.

Hero had anticipated the disappointment when, after spending an hour at the beach, she remained alone. But that did not make it any easier to bear.

Walking back to the cottage, she made a conscious attempt to control her emotions. *I'll get tea ready when I go back, and buy some of those hand-hewn biscuits he likes from the tourist shop in the village, and get him to talk about the publicity for* Silent Night. *Then there'll be packing, and I must write to Stephen and—*

Hero came out of the shop with her biscuits just as the black limousine drove down the high street. Ignoring it, she threw the tartan rug across her shoulders in a passable imitation of a wild Celt and began to walk home.

But the limousine overtook her on the solitary road, slowing to a halt yards ahead. Hero kept walking, head up, hair streaming in the wind, and the door opened like a wing at her approach.

'What do you think you're doing? Kerb crawling?'

Fane looked slightly hurt, and, she thought, slightly ill, sitting there in the back all on his own.

'I was trying to offer you a ride.'

'My mother said I shouldn't take lifts from strange men.'

'That rules *me* out.'

Hero got into the car and sank back into the leathery shadows.

'On your way to a funeral?' she asked. *Why the hell am I being so rude to him?*

'The car does have sinister connotations.'

'Bit like King Cophetua and the Beggar Maid, this.'

'Except you're no beggar.'

Hero shrugged. Talking to Fane was at once very easy and very hard. If she responded intuitively, the psychic crackle sped between them like messages across an invisible wire. Once she allowed rationality and common sense to prevail, all communication was lost, and they became a pair of near strangers.

'You don't drive, then?'

'I used to.' He sighed, and Hero sensed that it would be wise not to pursue the issue. 'There can be security problems.'

'I know all about those.'

'Yeah. Alistair told me about you. In fact, I recognised you. That time on the beach.' He spoke in neutral tones, but allowed a tinge of feeling: 'Must have been tough.'

'It was. Tough.' Hero looked out of the window, keeping over to her side of the car as much as possible. Something about Fane still intimidated her.

'Listen, we never got much chance to talk, did we?'

'Talk about what?' Emulating his tonelessness, unconvincingly.

'Come back for a coffee?'

This was such a prosaic suggestion from a sinister celebrity that Hero laughed out loud.

'What, now you mean?'

'If you can spare the time.'

It sounded almost pathetic, as if he expected her to have better things to do, and Hero recognised in

221

Fane her own insecurity.

'Yes—all right then.' Maybe he wanted to discuss the rent, fix a date for dinner, show her his studio. It was bound to be something very mundane.

But she hoped it wasn't.

*   *   *

By the time they reached the wrought-iron gates of Moonsleaze House, the atmosphere inside the car was one of tension. Hero had abandoned attempts at smalltalk, and restricted herself to occasional glances at Fane's profile.

A light mist wafted through the deserted parkland, and the sunless day had turned to dim blue dusk. Ferns and trees burnt with the infernal red of Fane's hair, and moisture beads hung like crystal on nearby branches. Hero shivered in the warm car and pulled the rug closer.

Moonsleaze House rose elegantly in Augustan proportions, and, though immaculate, had an air of loneliness and desertion. She was shown into a musty hall with a tessellated floor like a chessboard, and a staircase which wound upwards round an atrium, culminating in a glass dome through which the last of daylight was faintly visible. Fane led her down a long corridor with wrinkled carpets, and she was aware of moth-eaten brocades, shadowy alcoves with oversized marble heads, whose sculpted eyes appeared to turn and follow her.

The salon was no different from many country house drawing rooms Hero had visited with Tom. If anything, cleaner. The bleached chintz, dusty gilt, and expanses of leaded looking-glass were almost homely and reassuring.

222

'You don't seem surprised by it all,' Fane commented.

'It seems quite normal.'

'I suppose you're used to Stately Homes.'

'Only the ones I pay to visit.'

'We came here to shoot a video two years ago. One of my researchers found it. Old Sir William was happy to sell up and retire to Jersey, so I bought the place. Funny, I find it homely myself. Kind of cosy. You wouldn't think so, would you?'

'Why not?'

'It isn't what I was brought up to.'

'I suppose you're a working-class hero.'

'My mother would *hate* you saying that. If you really want to know, I'm a dentist's son from Croydon.'

'So *that's* it. That's why I find your accent so reassuring. You sound like Stephen Lewis. Someone I used to go out with.'

'Lucky Stephen Lewis.'

Hero had difficulty in adjusting to Fane's sudden changes of mood. At one moment he was silent and intimidating, at the next charming and flirtatious.

'What are you looking for?' he asked, seeing Hero turning round.

'I don't know. I suppose I expected—people. Groupies, PR officers, go-fors. Hangers-on, you know. All looking a bit like the cast of *The Rocky Horror Show*.'

'I'm sorry to disillusion you. All the admin's done from London, and as to the rest—I'm a bit of a loner. I'm here to *work* and not much else.'

Despite the romantically shambolic decor and air of decay, there was an ineradicable atmosphere of order and professionalism. Hero imagined Fane as a lonely workaholic, retreating to his studio for weeks on end, working, sleeping and working.

'So it's just you?' Hero knew nothing of his personal life.

'There's Harry my driver. He's in charge of security. Used to be a Para. And a Spanish couple who do practically everything. I don't entertain much.'

The female half of the Spanish couple appeared, carrying a tray.

'Just coffee or Perrier. I'm afraid I don't drink these days,' he added, in a more approachable voice. Hero began to feel that at least six John Fanes inhabited one body, and she couldn't tell which would speak next.

'Or smoke,' he added. 'I used to be on heroin, and the thing about the cure I took is you have to avoid addictive substances. No tobacco, no alcohol. I'm pretty irreproachable, these days.'

'Is that tough?'

'Not any more. I don't even serve wine if people come over for dinner.'

'That won't do Ali any harm.' As soon as she'd spoken, Hero realised the comment was disloyal.

'Alistair having problems, is he?' Fane's face had reverted from animation to gravity, but Hero was getting used to that now. In repose, he looked like the death mask of Keats. Apart from that scar on the cheekbone.

'Look, I must be getting back. Ali will wonder where I am. He'll be worried about me.'

'Of course. But you still haven't answered my question.'

'It's none of your business.'

'How do you think I met Alistair?'

224

'I don't know. Around.'

'We don't exactly move in similar circles.'

'Well, I suppose I thought he got to know you through the entertainment world. Or a mutual friend. I hadn't given it much thought.'

'I met Alistair when I was taking the cure. I'd come off drugs and was getting myself together in the Grove. They were trying to dry *him* out.'

'I see—I didn't—'

'He's a great guy. Kind, open-minded, generous—but he still hits the bottle, doesn't he?'

'Look, I really must be going.' Feeling treacherous.

'Harry can drive you back.'

'Why do you want to know? Why are you so interested in me and Alistair?'

His answer was almost rude in its simplicity.

'Why do you think?'

*   *   *

As they stood, as though in freeze-frame, Hero could see their reflections in the dim blue looking-glass and marvel again at their similarity. They were more like brother and sister than—than what? She reined in her imagination.

'I want you to come here again.'

'Tough shit. Don't try ordering me about.'

'I didn't mean that to sound the way it did.'

'I'm not one of your groupies.'

Surprisingly, he laughed quietly to himself, and turned aside. The tension was broken. 'That was the last thing I had in mind.'

'Then what did you mean?'

'I like having you around. I like to look at you.

225

That's all. Nothing for Alistair to worry about.' He stepped over and tugged a faded bell-pull. 'I'll be in touch. Pehaps I'll see you both next week.'

'We're leaving. We're going to London.' Even as she spoke, the mournful phrase reminded her of some poor little rich girl, life dictated by nomadic shifts from one fashionable place to another.

'Maybe I'll see you in London. I have a house in Hampstead.'

Harry appeared, driver's hat under one arm, and Hero turned to the door.

'You forgot this,' said Fane, picking up the Black Watch rug which had fallen to the floor. Standing behind Hero, he draped it carefully. 'You'll be home before dark,' he added, an Erl-King guaranteeing her safe passage through a world of ghosts and shadows. His hands lingered on her shoulders, and they both stared into the long looking-glass above the fireplace. Hero was relieved to find Fane actually *had* a reflection, he seemed so vampiric.

'There's an amazing resemblance,' he agreed, watching their images. 'Don't you think?'

Hero nodded, past speech.

'Is your hair really that colour?' he enquired, sounding more normal. Hero nodded again. 'Mine too. Most people think it's dyed. Irish origins, of course. You too, I guess. Makes us terrible charmers, so I'm told.' Resting his chin on her hair, preventing Hero from a third nod. 'You're so cool, Hero. You're really quite scary.'

'I have to go.'

'But I don't want you to go.' He dropped his hands and turned aside, suddenly private again. The whole episode was an elaborate charade, an

226

outlandish courting ritual. Hero got herself to the door, where Harry stood impassive, as if unconscious of the whole performance. But perhaps he was used to it. Fane demonstrated a lack of self-consciousness in front of servants which reminded Hero of the old rich.

'They used to say red hair was infernal,' Fane continued, as if delivering a lecture. 'The mark of the devil. Did you know that?' Hero didn't reply. 'Talking of which—I'm going to be in a Dracula movie. Did Alistair tell you? We're shooting at Twickenham after Christmas. It's more like a rock promo than a horror movie. Be some location work in London. So I'll be around, while you're doing the Season.'

'That's nice.' Hero couldn't have come up with a more uninspired comment if she had tried. 'What's it called?'

'*The Prince of Darkness Is A Gentleman.*'

★   ★   ★

Luxuriating in the back of Fane's limousine, Hero replayed the scene compulsively in her mind's eye, realising how strange the afternoon had been. Fane's changeable nature. If this was how he was now, what must he have been like on drugs? The mysterious old house, full of cobwebs and passageways, like an English *Sunset Boulevard*. The unpredictable current of sexual electricity which flowed between them. The strange elaborate ritual characterising their mutual fascination.

Wait till I tell Alistair. But she wouldn't tell Alistair, or no more than a sketch. Hero looked out in the twilight as the dark park slid past, then saw

227

the lights of Alistair's cottage twinkling in the distance. As she had done earlier that day, before the limousine appeared, Hero tried to love Alistair, to summon up the same apprehensive excitement Fane induced, but the feeling was not there to command. She could entertain no stronger sentiment than affection, and some compassion. And also, because he had saved her life, a strong sensation of guilt.

The haunting lines drifted into her head again, and Hero found herself in tears. *It'll come to grief*, she thought, as though despair were a destination. *It'll come to nothing*. For a few minutes she felt as helpless and doomed as the star-crossed Venusian heroine of *Tender Alien*. Why it all seemed so impossible, she couldn't understand. But, speeding alone in the darkness, Hero already felt she had left half herself behind, and she missed, she missed him.

CHAPTER SIX

Hero walked alone through Kensington Gardens, during a dusky twilight in the New Year. Branches dripped grey mist, and birds pattered forlornly by the Round Pond. Other solitaries, accompanied by their dogs, worked off the torpor of Sunday lunch.

Wandering aimlessly, Hero often paused to gaze down blankly. Earlier, a man in a tracksuit appeared, face furrowed with anxiety, as she stood staring at a patch of sodden grass.

'Looking for something? Have you lost something?'

228

Hero glanced up, watching the concern in his face turn to wariness, as though undergoing a chemical change.

'You could say that.' Flatly, conscious that her appearance these days gave cause for alarm. 'Except I don't know what it is.'

The plump man made excuses and backed off. Hero watched him jog away with a certain degree of satisfaction. Although her external appearance was not unusual, Hero had recently acquired an intimidatingly aloof air. Men usually found her threatening, and no-one ever whistled at Hero in the street or tried to pick her up. The majority treated her with the apprehensive deference accorded to more violent prisoners in gaol.

Though Hero was far from dangerous. It was her very restraint most people found intimidating. She was surrounded by an aura of self-sufficiency. Alistair never feared for Hero when she went out alone.

A few acquaintances judged her insane, pointing to Tom's death and her subsequent grief as causes. Others assumed she took drugs.

Only Hero could have told them the truth.

*   *   *

The heart of ice had become a heart of darkness, past sorrows mingling with present so that, tormented, she moved like night from street to street. Her aimless journeys were an attempt to exercise (and exorcise) her inner pain. The poetry, although providing release, had become more obscure, and Alistair read it with appreciative concern. 'I don't know what you're trying to s-say half the time. I think you must be one of those very clever people who are close to madness.'

Hero sometimes thought he was right.

*   *   *

Wandering, looking for something or somebody, she had paced the sinister dank subway at Hyde Park Corner, and the darkening park. Last riders thudded past on the tanbark track; cropped Americans sprinted through the trees. There would be no sunset as there had been no discernible sunrise; it was one of those days with no real distinction between morning and night, a perpetual twilight, *entre chien et loup*.

They were closing the gates as she left Kensington Gardens, and stepped out into the dark chasm of private road between the palace and the embassies. Discreet cars, reminiscent of Fane's limousine, were drawn up outside bolted windows, meshes, grills. Embassy life must be like a superior form of prison. No wonder poor Alistair went stir crazy.

Kensington Palace Gardens was illuminated by green gaslight, which cast a sad romantic ambience across the deserted road. At the barrier where cars were checked, the guard stared at Hero as she walked by, something she had become used to. Recently, Hero had been stopped by customs on the cross-channel ferry, and again when she accompanied Alistair to Galway for a fishing trip. 'You look the type,' they had explained, once Hero's identity had been verified and she was released with apologies. 'You've got what's called the terrorist profile.' Hero never knew if this referred to her physiognomy or her air of single-minded determination, but the somewhat dubious tribute had not perturbed her. *Must be because I look a desperate woman. I* am *a desperate woman.*

The High Street was quiet, and she walked past Barkers', where dummies stared out from a world of towels and aluminium pans. Hero wondered where so many objects came from, who bought them, why so many inanimate things were stacked up behind the glass. A group of Arab women, heavily veiled, moved about the grocery shops, and a clutch of foreign students passed, laughing loudly at some secret joke. Unwilling to go home yet, Hero turned down Earl's Court Road, looked at arbitrary arrangements of old books and broken lamps in junk shops, and walked past silent houses, their eyes downcast along the windswept pavement, their rooms filled with other people's lives.

Even at tea-time on Sunday, the end of Earls Court Road buzzed with sleazy vivacity. After silent streets Hero's senses were bombarded by sounds, smells, neon signs and representatives of every colour, creed and gender shoving past. Exotic frying reminded Hero she was hungry and she began to make her way reluctantly to Kenway Road, towards the flat Alistair had taken in Abingdon Villas.

Walking past oriental grocery stores and straggling assemblies of Australians and South Africans, she was soon back in the black and white restraint of Kensington. Through the distinctive melancholy of a London night, windows glowed like warning beacons. *The hour of dog and wolf, when ghosts walk. I'm almost a phantom myself now.*

She walked up Marloes Road, through Stratford Villas, along Allen Street. Domesticity was visible at this hour, before the curtains had been drawn; she looked down into warm basement kitchens, watched families hand round teacups as they sat before the television set. Out here in the cold street Hero was an alien, a lost stranger returned from her battle with the knight of ghosts and shadows, finding all changed, the old life gone.

As Hero turned into Abingdon Villas, a figure appeared in one third-floor window. Tall and thin, it was recognisable even at this distance as Alistair. Silhouetted by lamplight he stared into the darkness for a moment, and Hero wondered if he had seen her. She stood looking up, feeling as though they inhabited separate worlds, that the shadows had already claimed her. *Is this what it's like to be a ghost?*

Alistair stared unseeing for another second, then swept the curtains together. Hero stood looking at the dark window where, a second before, he had been illuminated. Not a single ray of light now spilled out onto the pavement.

She stood alone in the empty street, whistling in the dark, preparing herself before she went inside.

★   ★   ★

It hadn't been an Unfestive Season. Hero was treated like an emotional invalid by her family, a veteran correspondent fresh from covering Hades, with scars to prove it. They had told her at Ash Grove that she would never lose that mark; it remained on her arm, a white diagram of death, but it did not disturb her.

232

Alistair continued to be good to her. They left Dorset and moved to a flat in Abingdon Villas, W8, as Mafeking Mansions was not big enough for two. Alistair continued to go over there to write. He lavished affection on Hero, dressed her in expensive clothes, took her proudly to literary parties and book launches, where she met his friends. Alistair's companions were well disposed, if a little quaint: given to deliberate eccentricities of dress, passions for obscure operas and minor poets, traditional values and even more traditional political opinions. Hero found them individually kind but collectively inhibiting.

Christmas had been spent with Hero's family in Oxford. On Christmas Eve, Hero and Alistair sat together long after everyone else had gone to bed, surveying the usual domestic carnage of empty glasses, overflowing ashtrays, crumpled gift-wrappings and flapping cards.

'It's strange being back here,' she commented. 'I feel as if I've never been away. I've only spent one Christmas anywhere else.'

'I was amused by Cassandra.'

'Yes, wasn't that funny! I expected *her* to change—come home all Gucci loafers and headscarves. But it's Douglas who's different.'

'I know.' Alistair yawned. 'Joining CND. I wonder what Colonel Fitz makes of that.'

'Colonel Fitz is a more complex person than you imagine. We had lunch recently—it was a bit strange.'

'How are the family coping?'

'Oh, you know. They're still Tom's Family, and I'm not. I never did quite belong, and we've got nothing in common now. But Colonel Fitz—we did manage to get along, at a certain level. I'll miss him.'

'What do you mean?'

'This sounds horrible, but I want to avoid the family in future. I don't see much point in our meeting. What have we got to talk about?'

She looked at Alistair, tracing the deep lines which ran from cheek to jaw with her finger, trying to conjure up more than affection as that melancholy, equine gaze rested on her.

'It's curious John hasn't been in touch,' he remarked.

'Maybe he's busy.' Hero sounded uninterested.

'Perhaps we hurt his feelings by leaving Dorset without visiting Moonsleaze House.'

'He mentioned something about working hard.'

'He's always working hard. And I read s-somewhere that he's involved in some charity campaign. A s-series of rehabilitation centres for addicts. There's to be a concert, and an album.'

'Sounds very worthy.'

'It's s-such a pity you two didn't take to each other. I thought you'd like him.'

'He was all right. You know.'

'I really hoped that you two would hit it off. You're s-so alike.'

'Perhaps we're *too* alike.'

*   *   *

Hero concealed her obsession well, for it *was* an obsession, secreting copies of *New Musical Express* in her desk, playing Fane tracks only while Alistair was out, slipping off to old concert movies in the cinema clubs of W1. She already felt as though she

234

were being unfaithful. Fane was no teenage idol these days, but his distinctive features appeared regularly enough on the covers of magazines to make her stop with a start whenever she passed a bookstall. The black and red poster, where Fane's idealised features and black hat indeed bore an uncanny resemblance to Hero's own, confronted her every time she went past Athena. It was disconcerting to care so much for someone who was common property.

After weeks of trying not to think about Fane, she had finally agreed with Other Hero's analysis. Hero could remember the moment perfectly: she had been lying in front of the television, watching a thriller and trying to concentrate on the plot. Suddenly, Other Hero announced: *Admit it. You're in love with the man.*

It was a rage which would pass. No doubt there were several psychological explanations for her sudden access of romantic passion, discontent with Alistair being only one of them. If the fascination had been limited to Hero, she could have laughed away her infatuation. It was the fact that strong emotion obviously existed on both sides which drove her to alternating exhilaration and despair. Fane made no attempt to contact her, and Hero suspected that she knew the reason. He probably believed that his friendship with Alistair, and Hero's own position effectively ruled out any involvement. While in theory Hero thought such scruples admirable, she wished that Fane—who, according to the Sunday papers, was a master of decadence—had not turned out to be so unexpectedly ethical.

'Perhaps we'll s-spend *next* Christmas together,' Alistair was saying. 'Unless you're in the States, with Stephen.'

Hero shook her head.

'There's no going back. I'm not plain Hero Abrahams any more. I wish I could be.' She remembered days, long ago, when she sat upstairs wishing that something dramatic would happen. Now it all had: and she wished it hadn't, longing desperately for those uneventful years.

'Hero?' Alistair's voice was faint and far away. 'I know what you're thinking.'

'What do you mean?'

'You're wondering if I'm ever going to finish this drink so that we can get upstairs to bed.'

*   *   *

Hero stood outside in the darkness now, remembering that evening, the household full of guests and relations. Hero and Alistair shared a bed, courtesy of progressive Maeve, though Hero would have preferred a quiet night in her own little attic room. Then there had been the journey to Scotland for New Year, the overnight sleeper and Alistair's long tall family. Intimidating at first, they had emerged as patrician, haphazard and surprisingly tolerant. They drank phenomenal quantities, presumably as protection against the stone-flagged castle's icy cold.

'It's very romantic. Don't you agree?' Alistair asked, as they watched the sunset over the loch.

'Very appealing,' agreed Hero, trying to stop her

236

teeth chattering. 'I don't *mind* the Celtic Twilight, but does it have to be so cold?'

'You'll get used to it.'

'Get used to it? Never.'

'I was—I wondered—how you might feel about coming to live here?'

'I—er—well—'

'My family are very impressed. Especially my mother. She keeps s-saying that you're a woman of character. And that you have great s-spirit.'

'That's very kind.' Hero had never declined a proposal of marriage before and had no training in this archaic practice. 'But my background and everything. I'd never fit in. You need one of those nice girls in cashmere sweaters, who can walk ten miles before tea and know what to give an alsatian for fits.'

'That's a quote from Wodehouse.'

'This is rather a Wodehousian environment.'

'What has your background to do with it, Hero?'

'Well, I'm not exactly the lady of the manor, am I?'

'If you're worried about—prejudice—our nearest neighbours are Jewish. A banking family, been here almost a century now.'

'I'm not Scottish. Aren't you all terribly keen on keeping your Gaelic identity?'

'Scots, not Scottish. Anyway, at least you're half Irish. That's the next best thing. It isn't as if you were *English*, for God's s-sake.'

'It's very sweet of you—I really don't know what to—can I think about it?'

'Certainly. It was just a s-suggestion. I was trying to be practical. We could both work up here just as well as we work in London. Perhaps better, without

237

the distractions. And I know you like the open-air life. And I s-suppose it would be nice to make things official. It isn't as if there's anyone else, is it?'

'No.' Hero looked out over the loch, at the wild romantic landscape which was extravagantly beautiful in this silver light. It would be a better life than she had known in Hampshire. And an even quieter one. Hero already missed the febrile buzz of London. *I must be mad, turning all this down.* She wanted Other Hero's help, but her alter ego had deserted her. The old restlessness tingled in her veins, a constant desire for change which made her wonder if she had gypsy blood.

'What are you thinking about?'

'Ages ago, when I was still at school in Oxford, I used to wander around the countryside pretending to be the Scholar Gypsy. I know what it sounds like. Preposterous. Like Elfine in *Cold Comfort Farm*. But I still feel like that, sometimes. An outsider. As if I don't really belong.'

'You'd like it here. They're good people, and I've known everyone all my life.'

'They don't take kindly to strangers though, do they?'

'You're one of us.'

'Maybe I don't *want* to fit in. Maybe I'm too selfish to try.'

'It'll always be here.' As he gestured to the wild shore, shimmering sheet of water and distant horizon, Hero felt her eyes brim. 'It doesn't really matter what happens between you and me, does it? I mean—s-suppose there *was* somebody else, you'd still be welcome here. We'd always be friends.'

Hero was in tears. She buried her head in the oily

wool of Alistair's jumper, and wept desolately. It was as if having acknowledged the prospect of their inevitable separation, she now regretted it.

★   ★   ★

That was three weeks ago. Now Alistair waited, patient and fond, in the warm flat with the coal fire, yellow walls, dishevelled Sunday papers. He bought the qualities and two tabloids, claiming to gain inspiration from news stories. Hero knew he would be sitting there, notebook on one knee, making comments and outlines for his next book. Alistair worked prolifically, turning out one novel a year. He seemed always to be finishing one manuscript, proof-reading another, plotting a third.

Hero went indoors, walked slowly upstairs, avoiding the old lift with its gaping cage and creaking cables. As she put her key in the lock, Alistair opened the door, swung Hero off her feet into an embrace, happy as ever to have her back.

But it wasn't enough.

When she had disengaged herself, taken off Alistair's Barbour and accepted a cup of tea, he announced: 'I had a call from John Fane today.'

'Really?' Trying to keep all excitement out of her voice.

'He apologised for not being in touch. He's been working through most of Christmas.'

'That so?'

'To compensate for his neglect, he's invited us over to Hampstead. For s-supper.'

'When?'

'Wednesday night.'

'That's a bit short notice.'

'Oh Hero, don't be so hard on the poor man!'

'Sorry. Did you say Wednesday?'

'I thought you'd be a bit more excited. It isn't everybody who gets invited to dinner with a rock star.'

'Er—yes. You're right. It could be interesting.' *A born liar. No wonder Tom thought I'd be good in Intelligence.*

'Unfortunately, I sh-shan't be able to come with you.'

Hero's cup rattled on its saucer. 'What do you mean?'

'I've got a previous engagement. Jim's just got back from Kabul—he was out there for the *Observer*. We're having a party for him over at Peter's.'

Jim was a foreign correspondent, one of Alistair's invaluable sources.

'A piss-up, you mean.'

'Put like that—'

'Oh well.' Hero sounded reluctant. 'I suppose I'll have to go on my own. But I thought it was *you* Fane wanted to see.'

Alistair smiled, consigning a colour supplement to the corner of the room with abandon. 'You'll just have to represent me.'

★   ★   ★

Hero agonised about Wednesday night like an adolescent on her first date. But the day came round inexorably, like the morning of an exam, and Hero got up and tried on every garment in her wardrobe. She wore long dresses these days, to please Alistair, and milk-maid petticoats. She had even taken to

240

pushing back her hair in a black velvet Alice band. Putting the flounces and tasteful, flower prints aside, she decided eventually on an old black jacket and trousers, her black hat, Alistair's piqué dress shirt and his bow tie. Alistair, writing all day at Mafeking Mansions, was not available for comment on her appearance.

If Alistair had been anyone else, Hero would have become suspicious of his long absences. But he rang three times a day, and produced a visible alibi in the form of a fat typescript which put on weight week after week. If only he *had* indulged in other activities, Hero would not have felt so guilty. Shooting her cuffs, buffing Alistair's gold links, Hero wondered why she was always wearing other people's clothes.

Now, in her gangster trilby and dramatic black, she could be Fane's double. It was a sincere form of flattery, and at least she couldn't be accused of trying to look sexy. Though in a paradoxical sense, she looked more like a girl, dressed as a boy.

*   *   *

Fane had told Alistair that the limousine would collect Hero at seven fifteen. Hero was ready by six o'clock. She had passed the time in agitation, trying to concentrate on news programmes and a recent Talking Heads video. But it was impossible to sit still, impossible to eat, impossible to watch television for more than five minutes without getting up and walking about, like a cat in stormy weather.

When the car arrived, she placed the hat over her shiny red hair and remembered for a moment that

241

other evening, two years earlier, when she had prepared for her first party with Tom. There had been the same anxiety, apprehension, combined with bolshiness: it had all seemed so important then. Now there was the added dimension of fear: fear of disappointment, humiliation, loss.

'Harry, ma'am,' said the voice on the intercom.

Ma'am, indeed. For a second she missed the old days in Cambridge, sitting in her room with coffee and digestive biscuits, waiting for Stephen.

'I'll be right down.' Harry treated her with the gruff deference accorded to army wives. Holding the door, making certain she was installed before pulling away. Harry remained taciturn. He consigned her to a certain role as though marriage to Tom had left a military stamp on Hero's forehead. Young wife, officer for the use of. Now she was army surplus.

Hero often bantered with taxi-drivers, but was grateful for Harry's lack of smalltalk. She wanted to relish every moment of the journey.

It was a sleek London evening, traffic lights glinting beneath a glossy sky. Great houses with dark windows ranked Notting Hill, and Regent's Park was a ghostly lost domain. Hero always found London infinitely mysterious and slightly sad at this time of night.

She would have preferred this journey never to end: *it is better to travel hopefully than to arrive.*

As they passed the Heath, sinister beneath a full moon, Hero almost asked Harry to turn back. It would be so easy to manufacture an excuse, telephone afterwards and apologise. She opened her mouth to speak, but closed it once more.

Fane's house was a vast gothic creation,

242

stair-gabled and spired. One window shone high above the street, like the warning beam of a lighthouse across the windswept expanses of Hampstead Heath. Harry operated an electronic device on the dashboard, and the high wrought-iron gates swung open, closing swiftly after the car passed through. Hero felt as if she were in the first reel of a horror movie.

Summoning up her courage, Hero asked: 'Where are the other guests? I can't see any cars.'

'There are no other guests, ma'am.'

CHAPTER SEVEN

The Spanish manservant from Moonsleaze House greeted Hero at the front door, and ushered her through a dim entrance hall into a shadowy room lit by old silver candelabra.

An ancient gilt pier-glass over the mantelshelf intensified the light, and Hero saw that the room contained little furniture. She was looking about her with curiosity, inspecting her appearance in the speckled depths of the mirror, when she saw the reflection of Fane, standing in the doorway.

He leant against the lintel, pale and fine drawn in his loose white shirt and trousers, looking more like someone answering the telephone in the middle of the night than a potential host.

'I'm sorry. I was asleep. I hope you don't mind being dragged out like this.'

'Of course not.' She came forward, extending a sociable hand as Tom and Alistair had taught her. He seized her fingers in the expected-unexpected

243

strong grip. 'I like the suit. Looks good. You also look like my little brother, but who cares. Come on through.'

Fane led her by the hand into another low dark room. The outlines of lacquered cabinets and rococo Chinese furniture were visible through penumbral candlelight.

'Do you *have* a little brother?' Hero was always literal.

'No, just one of me. *A lonely only*, as my gran used to say. I invented companions, though.'

'So did I. Mine are still around.' Hero sat gingerly on a satin divan, which yielded beneath her slight weight, pitching her backwards. She struggled to a sitting position and reflected that such furniture must facilitate seduction.

'I hadn't expected you to be here alone,' Hero said, taking a fruit drink from the tray proffered by Fane's housekeeper. 'I thought it would be a dinner party, with lots of guests.'

Fane shook his head, pushing a lock impatiently back from his face. But the hair, which had grown since autumn, persisted on tumbling forward into his eyes.

'I'm not a great party giver. Or a party goer, for that matter. Now I'm filming I've got a great excuse to stay home.'

'I hate parties too,' Hero blurted out, regretting it. Impulse and sobriety were still at war in her soul, and for all Other Hero's imperatives to *Go For It*, she was still terrified of saying the wrong thing.

'You look the type.'

'I thought I hid it pretty well.' Hero was a little angry now, hating to be consigned to any category.

Fane seemed almost embarrassed by the

244

impertinence of his remark.

'What I meant was—you have a reflective quality. Sort of reclusive. I like that.'

'How's the film going?' she asked hastily, anxious to move away from the personal. 'Are you enjoying it?'

'I'm not *enjoying* it, but we don't have that bad a time. It's an art movie, of course, so it won't gross much. But it could do quite well, and it's been a pet project of the director's for a long time now. We've been meaning to do it for years, but with my commitments and his, and me being out of the country, it's been difficult.'

'So it's not like a horror film?' Hero was relieved to turn the discussion towards Fane's professional life.

'No, though there's lots of references to them—quotes, if you like. The idea is to present this anguished, existentialist vampire, a sort of self-destructive outsider who can't break his addiction to human blood. It's the only way he can stay alive. Bit like being a junkie, in fact.'

'So you'll be the cool ghoul.'

'Or the camp vamp. We could use that, Hero. Ever thought of writing screenplays?'

Hero laughed, unconvincingly. As he rearranged himself on the sofa opposite, she wondered if he shared any of the anti-social characteristics of his vampire role. She was at once at ease and intimidated: felt as though they had been friends for years, and as though the wrong nod or cough might despatch her to outer darkness and a swift trip back to W8. She wished Maeve was there, with her tales of houseboats in Chelsea and dating musicians in the 1960s.

'You're worried about all those candles, right?'

'Er—oh no—er—yes. Yes, I *was* thinking about the candles. There must have been a lot of fires in the days before electricity.'

'Don't worry about it. There's a sprinkler system fitted. And you're quite safe. Besides, candlelight's easier on the eyes after a day in the studio. Restful.'

'You could wear dark glasses.'

'I wouldn't be able to see you properly then, would I?'

*　　*　　*

They dined in a parquet floored room with french windows and midnight blue walls. It was a vegetarian meal, vaguely oriental, and Hero wondered if Fane had consulted Alistair about her tastes. She still couldn't look at meat without thinking of charred human flesh. Albina served them, and Fane revived after the first course, entertaining as though conscious of his duties as a host. He was diffident, almost shy, not the compulsive namedropper Hero had half expected. With reluctance, he told her anecdotes about other musicians, but his aim seemed to be to amuse Hero rather than show who he knew.

As Hero peeled her second peach, he asked: 'So what about you, now? What are you doing?'

'Doing?'

'I heard from Alistair you'd been writing. Lyrics, or something.'

'Just a bit of poetry. But I don't show it to anybody. It's not really that good.'

'How can you tell?'

'I'm not arty, really. I've never written much

246

before, and everything that everyone else writes seems so much better.'

'Sounds like healthy self-criticism to me. Why don't you do something with it?'

'Well, what I'm trying to write isn't exactly Faber and Faber. And people might be nasty about it. I don't want to face that.'

'So what? I've had to cope with people being nasty ever since I got up on a stage ten years ago.'

'Yes, but you're *good*. And anyway, I'm supposed to go back to Cambridge next year, and do my PhD.'

'And what will you do till then?'

'Time slips by. I read a lot, go running. See people for lunch. Alistair's there in the evenings, or we go and see his friends. That kind of thing.'

'Aren't you ever restless, Hero? A little bored?'

'Sometimes.' She turned her eyes away from his, which were as blue and disconcertingly penetrating as her own. However languid and ethereal Fane liked to appear, he possessed a strong instinct for survival and a sound business sense. She was more and more conscious that he was actually the sensible dentist's son from Croydon, and not the mysterious alien he liked to appear.

'I think you're wasting your time.'

★   ★   ★

'Look, Hero, I asked you here for a reason. Well, a couple of reasons, really.' He smiled briefly. 'You know I'm trying to set up some rehabilitation clinics for users?'

'Alistair mentioned it.'

'Everyone I know, and a few I don't, is going to

contribute. There'll be an album, a video, all the usual spin-offs. There's already a lot of public interest. The money's going towards three clinics in inner-city areas.'

'But there's a lot of drug-abuse clinics already.'

'If Mummy and Daddy can afford it, there are. These are designed for street-level victims. The kids who are on smack because there's sod all else for them.'

'That sounds very worthwhile. You must be working very hard on it.'

'Yeah, I am. But there's something else. You're famous, Hero.'

'In a way—I mean I suppose—'

'People know who you are. They've seen you on TV. I saw you last year. After the assassination. You were interviewed a few times, and you really came across. Yes, I *know* the circumstances were appalling, but forget that for a minute. You've got a very—compelling—air, and I think we could use that.'

'Use it how?'

'I'm not saying you're about to become a megastar or something, but there are some people who come across on television, some who don't. And you're one of those who do. I don't know what it is you've got, but we can use it.'

'Well, thanks.'

'Don't thank me. Hasn't anyone else mentioned it?'

'Well—I believe that the MoD were satisfied with my appearance at Tom's Memorial Service—'

'Hero, I need someone to help me co-ordinate all this. I can't do it on my own. I'm going to *use* you, Hero. To be honest. But it's in a good cause. You

248

can be really effective on the promotional side, telling people why we're doing it, talking about the kids on the dole who get to be users—I'm not interested in the *Tatler* crowd, and I'm not interested in any Government-led anti-drug campaigns—all those do are to hit the small-time pushers who need help like all the other junkies. You can write press releases, and I'll sort you out with my PR team. You can put words together, and you sound more educated than me. So what do you say?'

'I never expected this.' Hero reflected ironically on Tom's major source of revenue. 'I've never thought of doing anything like this before.'

'It's better than moping around with Alistair. Hero, you've got so much energy and promise. And it's going nowhere. You might as well be useful.'

'So we'd be working together?'

'It's a team effort, not an excuse for self-promotion. Though there'll be the usual cynical comments. We'd be thrown together pretty often. Does that bother you?'

Hero sighed, looked grave.

'When do I start?'

★   ★   ★

The next three hours were spent discussing the project. The campaign had already been in the planning stages for some time and the album was to be recorded next month, released prior to the concert in March. Detailing programmes and schedules, outlining budgets and describing personalities, Fane was animated and enthusiastic, a different person from the languid wraith who had greeted Hero before dinner.

As Fane described his PR team, Hero yawned inadvertently.

'Tired? We haven't even *begun*.'

'Where do you get all your energy from?'

'Nerves, I suppose. Do you fancy some fresh air?'

★ ★ ★

They stepped into an old-fashioned gilded cage of a lift, and emerged on the roof. Above their heads, the sky held a tapestry of stars.

'I come up here a lot. Whenever I want to be alone.'

'But you're on your own all the time, aren't you? I mean, you're practically a recluse?'

'I wish I was. But something's always going on, some distraction or other.'

'Alistair says you're a sort of musical Howard Hughes.'

'I should be so lucky. *Something* is *always* going on. The idea of living like this is that it's supposed to conserve my energy. But it doesn't seem to help.'

'Don't you ever do anything except work?'

'Not now.'

He had pulled on a black jumper as they stepped out into the roof garden, and now seemed dark and remote again, surrounded by a tangible aura of loneliness, which almost defied Hero's attempts to break through.

'I'm glad you're joining us, Hero. I think it'll be good for you. Starting a charity campaign in the middle of shooting a movie has to be crazy, but I couldn't put it off any longer. I like to do

250

everything at once. Makes life more exciting.'

'Your life is really so lacking in excitement?'

'I bore easily.'

'It all *sounds* exciting. I'm a bit surprised I never thought of anything like it before.'

'Yeah. I thought all you debby types went in for charities. Still, you'll be able to boast to your friends about all the celebs you meet. Though you probably know quite a few already.'

'Scarcely. A few drunken journalists Ali hangs out with, the odd Hon. I'm not a deb, anyway. I'm very ordinary.'

'But you move in those sort of upper-class circles.'

'Only because I married in. I've got more in common with you than you think.'

'Oh well, I had to think of *some* excuse to see you again.'

Hero couldn't believe her ears.

'You know, when I first met you, Hero, I was really scared of you. Frightened, even.'

'Come off it.'

'You were so classy and aloof. Terrifying.'

'I was scared, too.'

'The thing was, at first I thought you might be a fan. They get in, sometimes. It can be embarrassing, sometimes frightening. I seem to attract some real nutcases.'

'You should see the letters I got when Tom was killed.'

'I've been meaning to ask you, Hero. How did you get that scar on your wrist?'

'Didn't Alistair say?'

'I knew you had some kind of breakdown.'

'I tried to kill myself. How did you get yours?

251

Was it when—'

Fane touched his cheekbone, as if the mark still hurt.

'Yeah. When Carmel died.'

'I read about that. I'm sorry.'

Hero knew that Fane's wife had died in a car crash, and that he had been driving, but the details were vague.

'It was when we were living in LA. The reason I crashed was that I was coked out of my skull. And afterwards, I needed more and more just to ease the pain. It wasn't until my manager virtually locked me away that I came off the stuff. And it took some doing. I suppose I'd be dead by now, if it wasn't for him.'

'You too.'

'What do you mean?'

'Well, doesn't it ever give you the jitters? The fact that by all reasonable expectations, we should be dead? It's happened to me twice now. Once, by not going to a party with Tom, when he was killed. And once when I freaked out and opened my vein, and Alistair was there to save me. It seems weird that I'm here at all.'

'You know, you're a spooky girl. But I think I like that.'

'You can't still be frightened of me!'

'You are frightening. Just because you've survived so much.'

★   ★   ★

They stood side by side and gazed up at the stars together, just as Hero used to with Stephen. Fane knew the names of all the constellations, pointed

252

out planets.

'I'd be a physics teacher now, if I hadn't got side-tracked,' Fane commented. 'I used to be obsessed with science fiction. Got a whole library of videos downstairs.'

'Even those old Quatermass films?' Hero shared his passion for those grainy, cosy excursions into the extra-terrestrial.

'Even those. I did a year at Imperial College, but even then I spent all my time playing in a band. The authorities drew the line when I failed my exams because I'd be at gigs instead of revising.'

'I thought rock stars were all supposed to go to art school.'

'Not with my father the way he was. He wanted me to do something sensible.'

'He must be pleased now.'

'He still asks me when I'm going to get a proper job.'

'It didn't matter in the end though, did it? Think how many physics teachers would like to be in your place.'

'Especially right now.'

Fane's flirtatious remarks were so disconcerting, almost out of character, that Hero could not think how to respond. Instead she commented: 'It's strange, you and Ali being friends.'

'Oh, we've got plenty in common. Apart from you, that is.'

'What's the time?'

'After midnight.'

'I must get back, John.' It was the first time she had used his Christian name, and it sounded odd.

'Harry will drive you. And I'll be in touch about the campaign. I really meant what I said, Hero. I

253

want you to come and join us.'

'I'm very flattered.'

'I'm not flattering you. In fact, I'm being quite ruthless where this business is concerned. I know you've got some sort of talent. Even if I'm not sure what it's a talent for.'

*   *   *

As they stepped out of the lift, Fane said quietly: 'Stop a minute.'

Hero stopped. Flickering candlelight illuminated tenebral recesses and looming shapes of furniture.

'What's the matter?' Hero turned round, and in reply he placed his hands on her shoulders and kissed her. Fane was tentative but unblinking, so that she could see his apprehensive eyes in close-up. Hero was simultaneously devastated, and overwhelmed with relief. After the initial impact, their proximity had a familiar quality: as though they had performed this action a thousand times.

'You'd better go. You'll be late.'

'That doesn't matter.' She was hoping he would do it again.

'Alistair will be worried. And I'm supposed to be at Twickenham by five tomorrow morning—this morning.'

'I wish I didn't have to go.'

'So do I. But perhaps—'

Hero looked anxious, so he kissed her again before guiding her to the door. Outside the sky was deep above the uncanny no-man's-land of the Heath.

'You really do look like my other half,' he commented, as she got into the car. 'My better

254

half.' He squeezed her hand companionably, before closing the door. 'I'll see you on Friday.'

The limousine drew away into the night, and Hero turned in her seat to stare through the rear window. The impression of his mouth lingered on her lips, curiously forceful in such dreamlike conditions. Fane stood alone in a glow from the open door, as though in a spotlight, until the car turned a corner, and he disappeared from view.

CHAPTER EIGHT

From having time hang heavy on her hands, Hero suddenly found she had no time at all. She was surrounded by activity, whirling from receptions to press conferences and back again, with barely enough space in between to snatch a few hours' sleep and have her hair fixed before attending another interview. As Fane had predicted Hero's decision to use her unwelcome celebrity as a means of generating media attention for the campaign was a brilliant promotional move, particularly as Fane's campaign coincided neatly with the first anniversary of Tom's death. Remorselessly convinced that Tom owed her something, Hero exploited her fame, and found the Press more than willing to co-operate. She appeared on chat shows, was interviewed by women's magazines, had a profile in the *Guardian* with the predictable headline *Anti-Heroine*. Hero had little opportunity to worry or think. She woke early, bound for Fane's house in Hampstead or for a meeting with the PR team and the advertising agency handling the campaign account; she arrived home late, frequently after Alistair had gone to bed, and fell asleep effortlessly. Often, she had to cancel outings with Alistair's friends, and was too tired to attend dinner parties.

As a stranger to the music business, Hero had been astonished by the problems involved with recording sessions, the artists who refused to appear with each other on political grounds, the performers who were too drunk, unpunctual or—ironically—stoned to play, the raging egos. The human element, in fact, which tested the organisational abilities and diplomatic skills of the most experienced managers. Hero frequently found it hard to believe that everyone was supposed to be supporting a common cause, but by some miracle the album was recorded, the concert venue confirmed, the running order and lengths of sets agreed without actual bloodshed. The album, *Beating the Dragon*, was released in February, and charted quickly, before the actual concert, scheduled for March. Tickets sold out fast.

During these weeks Hero led a double life. Superficially, she worked with Fane, the publicity team, and the satellites surrounding them. On a day-to-day basis she was astonished by how easily she and Fane communicated. Once she restrained her fears of rejection and personal disaster, and treated Fane as he treated her, they worked together successfully. She suppressed the physical symptoms brought about by his presence or even the mention of his name, and was surprised, watching herself on the rushes for a recorded broadcast, by how cool she seemed, sitting at his side in the studio.

Hero was perplexed by Fane's remote kindness,

his professionalism and energy. As she watched him at work, the less appropriate did his gothic tags and scary reputation seem. Perhaps he was simply a gifted musician with a misleadingly ethereal, lantern-jawed appearance. Perhaps when age and fat had done their work in a few years' time, he would cease to be physically remarkable. Perhaps the haunted alien and the dentist's son would merge to form one coherent human being. They spent whole days together, watching the production team edit videos, scripting talks, attending meetings, giving lunches: and they never more than kissed. Perplexed, Hero ran compulsively through the indications of this restraint, discarding homosexuality, misogyny and the phantom of Aids as reasons. Eventually she decided that perverse loyalty to Alistair must be the cause. Hero admired Fane even more for this. But she dreaded what would happen when the campaign was over, and they no longer had any excuse to see each other.

*   *   *

At first Alistair had been pleased by Hero's new occupation, seeing it as evidence of her recovery. He did not begrudge her rushed exits in the morning, her absence in the afternoons, the arrangements for dinner altered or the invitations declined. But as the weeks passed he became less tolerant, and Hero ceased describing the day's activities to him as they settled into bed at night. Partly because he was so often asleep before she returned.

'What the hell do you do all the time?' he burst out, as Hero arrived home long after midnight for

257

the fourth time in one week. 'That's *all* I want to know. I'm s-sure you can't be working!'

'But we are!' Hero was shocked by this unfamiliar angry Alistair who had waited up and opened the door as she slipped her key softly in the lock.

'You're never here, I can never get hold of you, I s-see more of you on television than I do in my own bed. I'm having an answering machine put in s-so that I can catch your few messages on the rare occasions when you condescend to telephone—'

'Ali, I can't be on the phone to you all the time. Not if I'm in an interview, or at a meeting, or something. Now can I?'

'I took this flat—s-so that we could be together. S-so that I could look after you. We were s-so happy here.'

'You were happy. I was surviving.'

Alistair looked hurt, but Hero found she didn't care any more. In fact, she despised his dependence.

'I'm so fond of you, Hero. I want you to be happy—it's just that I can't s-stand by and—I didn't mean—' His words were drowned in an explosion of stammering.

'I thought you wanted me to be friends with John. You virtually threw us at each other. What did you expect? I can't waste the rest of my life moping around. What *did* you expect?'

'I wanted you to be friends. I d-did.' His face was wretched and strained and Hero, wondering if her vision had become distorted by tiredness, or was it the tears, seemed to see a second face emerge from behind the features which Alistair normally presented to the world. It was an agonised, twisted face, terrifying in its inadequacy, like some tormented figure in the *Inferno*. It seemed as though he had been flayed. Hero blinked, and the (almost) normal Alistair returned, as though a mask had been replaced.

'I'm s-sorry,' he was saying, tears scoring his cheeks. Hero watched fascinated as the drops raced down his face, wondering which would arrive at his chin first. Alistair caught her staring.

'What's the matter? Why are you looking at me? Haven't you ever seen a man cry before? I'd have thought it was a familiar sight.'

'Please believe me. It's not what you think, John and me. We're just two of a kind, that's all. He's never tried anything. For all I know he doesn't even fancy me. He could be gay.'

'Not with his reputation. Are you trying to tell me you two never get up to anything?'

'Ali, we don't have the time! We've been under so much pressure trying to get this campaign going, it's all been happening so fast—it's bloody hard work, Alistair!'

'I've lost you though, haven't I?'

'I never belonged to you to begin with. You don't own me, Alistair. No-one does, and they never will.'

'Brave words. Until the next time you slash your wrists.'

'Who can tell? But I'm fucked if I'll give a man the satisfaction of dying for him. It's just not worth it.'

'You're so *tough*.'

'And what's wrong with that?'

Alistair sat weakly, and Hero noticed the empty bottle beside his chair.

'Was that a fresh bottle? Tonight?'

Alistair nodded.

'I'm surprised you're not unconscious.'

'I've got a head like a rock.'

As if to prove this, Alistair stood up and went to the cupboard for another bottle.

As she watched him, without premeditation and without having realised what she was going to do, Hero said: 'We're through.'

Alistair turned, bottle in one hand, glass in the other.

'What did you s-say?'

For the first time in her life, Hero was frightened of him. She had grown accustomed to his height, the hidden strength in the wiry arms and broad shoulders, and had never before regarded him as a threat. Now, drunk and desperate and angry, he could be dangerous. It was so difficult to reconcile him with kindly anxious Ali, who had bought her over-blown roses and saved her life.

But she stood her ground.

'I'm off.'

Alistair put down the glass—but not the bottle—doing everything in slow motion as the impact of her words sank in.

'What?'

Hero's mind, which seemed to work as rapidly now as in the days when she studied art history, was already busy. She would take nothing but go, now, into the darkness. You could always pick up a cab on Kensington High Street, even at this hour. And there was only one place to seek refuge. Already she was pulling on her coat and picking up her shoulder bag.

A stab of guilt pierced her heart, that heart which

was now almost whole again, not frozen with grief or haunted by shadows. She remembered another Alistair, looking out over the loch, and felt momentary remorse.

But it was time to save her own life now, and she was already half through the door when he cried out. The bottle, which she had anticipated as a missile, smashed harmlessly on the opposite wall. *Poor Alistair*, she thought, trying to ignore her fears as she ran downstairs and into the darkened lobby. He always was wide of the mark. The bottle had not been meant for her. It was just another desperate gesture.

*   *   *

Fane did not seem surprised when Hero arrived at three in the morning. She picked up a cab outside the Tara hotel and scrambled hastily inside, as though Alistair might give pursuit. It was an unlikely contingency. Constant sounding of horn outside Fane's house brought Harry to the gates, and he too seemed far from astonished by Hero's dramatic appearance. Fane, draped in a scarlet kimono, looked at her enquiringly for a moment, then led Hero into the Chinese room as though he received runaway women every night of the week. Perhaps he did.

'I think we'll break the rules,' he said, as though to himself. 'Harry, get Hero a glass of something strong, would you? There must be spirits somewhere.'

Harry returned quickly with brandy, which Hero swallowed rapidly, holding out her glass for a refill. Then she asked for a pot of tea.

261

'I don't need to tell you, do I?'

Fane made a tutting noise, sighed volubly.

'Hit the bottle again?'

'Except this time the bottle nearly hit me.'

'Poor old Alistair. We'll have to do something about him.'

'Lock him up, for instance.'

'I'll talk to him. Oh—' putting up a hand '—not right away. When he's had time to recover. Perhaps the fact you've walked out on him will bring him to his senses. He'll realise what he's doing to himself.'

'He's basically very kind. But there's something lacking. He doesn't just have feelings of inadequacy. He *is* inadequate.'

'I expect working in Intelligence screwed him up.' Fane poured tea. 'Anyway. You did the right thing, coming to me.'

'Are you sure? There weren't many places. My sister's only got a tiny room in Stockwell, and my best friend Flora's gone to New York and let her flat out.'

'You're very welcome. There's plenty of space here.'

'I'll have to go and get my stuff back. Though most of it's technically his. All the books and clothes Ali bought me.'

'We can talk about all that later. Until then, you'd better get some sleep. We've got that band arriving from LA in the morning, don't forget.'

'I *had* forgotten.'

'Well, let's get to bed.' He stood up, looking green around the gills, as Maeve would have said. For once Hero had not been paying a great deal of attention to Fane's appearance, but now she noticed how gaunt he looked. The cheekbones, always pronounced, seemed to push out through the white skin, and there were rings round his eyes.

'You look *awful*.'

'Thanks a lot!'

'I mean, I know you always look deadly, but really, John. You've been overdoing it.'

'I'm tired, that's all. I'll get Albina to air a room for you. Or you could share with me, if you like. Perhaps you could do with a bit of company.'

'You don't waste much time, do you?'

'Well, if poor old Ali's going to be suspicious, we might as well give him something to be suspicious about.'

'But—'

It shouldn't be like this, she thought indignantly. *I'm not ready for it. I'm not in the right mood, and besides I planned to be wearing that black dress when this happened. And shouldn't it all be more romantic?*

Get your act together, Other Hero retorted. *When are you going to learn? This is real life, Hero. You have to take what you can get.*

Fane put an arm loosely round her shoulders.

'Don't worry. I was talking about sleeping, not anything else. You've got nothing to worry about.'

★   ★   ★

'Why is there nothing to worry about?' enquired Hero, worrying, as she lay in the great shadowy bed, wearing a pair of Fane's pyjamas. Chinese Chippendale loomed against ghostly silk wallpaper, so that the room reminded her of a haunted country house she had once visited with Tom. Fane had waited for her to change before coming into the bedroom, and now slid under the covers as though they had been married for years. Hero found it extremely disconcerting. Even lying beside her he possessed an insubstantial quality. It was like preparing to spend the night with a friendly phantom. Or a tender alien.

'Well—' propping himself on one elbow, so that she could make out his dim form in the darkness. 'I've got a confession to make. Suppose I tell you now, so you've got the chance to leave me, too?'

'You *are* gay? Even though you were married?'

'No. Though there was a stage when I tried virtually everything. Not gay. Sad, if anything. I'm harmless. Or useless, which is a better way of putting it. Ever since the accident, though it's nothing physical.'

'How awful.'

'It is at times. And weird, when you get a great big screaming crowd of fans and know you couldn't satisfy a single one. And it's bad at times like this.'

'Perhaps you'll get over it—'

'I didn't want to get too close to you, Hero. I knew this would happen. I didn't want it to. I used to think I'd got like this because everyone wanted a piece of me, and this is one piece nobody's going to have. But that isn't true now. I'd really like to—'

'It doesn't matter.'

'Really?'

'I'm not that interested. Not right now. It's the last thing I need at the moment.'

'I'd like you to stay. I mean just stay around.' He chose his words carefully, and reminded her a little of Alistair in his tentativeness. 'I wouldn't mind—or at least I'd try not to mind—if you saw other guys. You know what I mean.'

'I don't want to see other guys. I'm too busy to
264

see *anyone* at the moment. Except of course, you.'

'And you don't mind?'

'Not really. Or at least not at the moment. There are lots of ways we can—'

'That's such a relief. My last girlfriend said she'd be better off sleeping with a woman. Wouldn't it seem like that to you?'

'Not really. There's more to making love than screwing. And perhaps I'd *like* to feel as if I was in bed with another woman. Tom always reckoned I must be lesbian. I think it's just that I like androgynous men.'

'I don't care what you are, what you do, who you do it to. But I do want you to stay.'

Curiously reassured by Fane's ineptitude, Hero reached out to hold the body which was so like her own. Somehow his marble shoulders and alabaster back were more disturbingly erotic than any sunburnt biceps.

CHAPTER NINE

Hero stepped into the gilt chill of a September evening, air cool and sharp as wine. Trees opposite Clare were flushed with russet, and the beginning of an elaborate sunset was visible in the blue fenland sky. Vapour trails and cirrus clouds stretched infinitely, and she half expected to see scantily-clad deities disport themselves against this classical scene.

She unshackled her bicycle with a practised gesture, but was too absorbed to ride. Instead, Hero walked towards Sidgewick Avenue, abstracted but safe in the knowledge that there was little threat of traffic. Michaelmas Term was three weeks away, summer language students were long gone and only the bemused regulars haunted the library.

Tonight there would be mist, and by the time she arrived at the modest cottage in Grantchester, river damp would have risen through the water meadows, and soaked the apples still suspended from the trees in her back garden. Indoors the soup and Chablis waited, left ready that morning, and Cat, a swift adaptor to new routines, would flex and come to meet her. Hero wondered why the traditional consolations of spinsterhood should be a source of mockery. The reassuring solitude, the cat's uncritical warmth, the evening free to read and dream, appealed as they had done so long ago, before Tom arrived to tell Hero that her life was boring.

Hero didn't want excitement these days. Though only twenty-five now, she felt like one of those soldierly old dons, an almost extinct breed by this time, who retreated into the mysteries of the Peloponnesian War or Bilabial Fricatives after tense, dangerous years in wartime Intelligence. The undergraduates of the previous summer, and the fresh-faced virgins attending college interviews, seemed not another generation but another species. These days, she was a tough and wary tigress, a little scarred about the nose but with a good coat, roaming the groves of academe and possessed of a presence which intimidated and brought respect before she even spoke.

Though Hero would have been surprised to learn that, superficially, she had not changed much during the course of her adventures. Despite her air

266

of self-possession, she looked no older than she had done when she met Tom: and several times during the coming Term, she was to be mistaken for a Fresher.

*   *   *

Adjusting to Cambridge in 1986 after an afternoon of mediaeval Russian, Hero got on her bicycle and rode towards Maid's Causeway. She had grown accustomed to her solitary habits in the short months since she left London, and enjoyed returning to the empty house, resuming a book left open at breakfast time, going upstairs to a bed without anyone else's imprint on the mattress, free from the shreds of someone else's nightmares. Gilby had told her that many people from her world came to live like this: solitude and routine governed their lives, replacing the secrecy and ritual of the Intelligence world. Hero had lived as an agent without even realising it.

Hero's cat ran forward with her familiar chirrup, and there were messages on the Ansafone. Alistair's latest novel, which had arrived that morning, still lay in its Jiffybag on the kitchen table. He was back in Scotland now, and likely to remain there, apparently content to be alone with rod and gun and word processor, though Hero had no way of knowing. She was often saddened by the callous method with which she had destroyed their friendship, that love in adversity which had flared suddenly like a flame, and which she had just as suddenly extinguished. Occasionally John Fane mentioned him. The new novel held a polite inscription. They never spoke, but read about each

267

other in grossly inaccurate articles, in fashionable magazines.

★   ★   ★

Hero opened a bottle of wine and looked round her with pleasure, tinged with a not unpleasant sense of elegy. Here were her books, and her pictures, and her cat, and her orderly life. The thesis, on which she had done so much sporadic work, was at last getting itself written. She would have enough poetry for a collection soon, and though she knew it would be published for notoriety value—her fame as a widow still preceded her—Hero was enough of an artist to seek publication at any price. Unlike her fellow research students, she need have no anxiety about her future. Tom's money absolved her from the need to make a living as an academic. She was to start a little supervising later next Term. Tom's money had also made it possible to come back to Cambridge: she had seen and bought the cottage within weeks, almost as soon as she knew that she must escape. Back in Cambridge, back in this Lewis Carroll city of dreams, Hero felt almost at home.

And she had needed to escape. It seemed a dramatic move, last May, when she packed her bags and left the house in Hampstead, but it had been inevitable. She couldn't say for sure when the old fear had gripped her, the bubble of hysteria begun to swell. During their first weeks together, as the campaign successfully raised funds to start the rehabilitation centre, as they were fêted and photographed, Hero had thought she felt entirely happy. During the weeks of love, when Fane's trust and Hero's patience had eventually overcome his impotence, they had behaved like besotted and rapturous teenagers, spending every free moment in bed—or not necessarily in bed. But that old fear returned: it had haunted her behind the shuttered windows and electronic locks, the glimpses of crowds seen through car windows on the way to some studio, the occasional attack in magazines. They seemed to live in a protected world, like exotic animals.

And, like an exotic animal, Hero felt trapped.

★   ★   ★

Fane had been astonished by her desire to leave, but assumed it to be some temporary aberration, legacy of her grief. He telephoned regularly, was driven to Cambridge to see her, never reproached her, and never mentioned other companions in his life. Hero knew that there were none: he was involved now with an Anti-Apartheid campaign, and spent much of his time on this new cause; he was less of a recluse than he had been, and was always cited as one of the great unspoilt survivors of rock. He always mentioned Hero's influence on such occasions.

There were dark moments and dark nights when she remembered Fane, exclaimed aloud at her own stupidity in leaving him. And moments when, unrecognised as she stood alone in Sainsbury's, Hero knew that to have stayed in Fane's world would have brought about personal extinction. She would leave him to save the world: Hero was still engaged in trying to save herself.

This was by no means the end of the story. If

269

Hero had possessed editorial control over her own life, she would have married John Fane, reformed Alistair, written poetry, and lived Happily Ever After. Unfortunately, there were likely to be another fifty or sixty years of existence for her to get through, a vast expanse of Real Life in which anything could—and probably would—happen. She did not doubt her longevity. It seemed inevitable that, having endured so much, she would endure much more. If she had been a fictional character she was good for at least another four or five adventures, ageing with her readers and eventually bowing out around sixty, with many observations on the richness and variety of human life. Her return to Cambridge, the welcome narrowness and order of scholarship in this unreal city which seemed so much more real than Real Life, her resumption of the study of Russian icons, seemed not a conclusion but another episode in her legendary existence. Perhaps she was condemned to a life of genres: after the thriller, the serious novel of a brave and beautiful woman scholar, renouncing love. Perhaps a comedy after that, or a travel book. She was currently tempted by the idea of the Far East.

* * *

Pouring her glass of wine, she sat down in front of the athletics, putting aside the latest Anita Brookner. She admired those brave and lonely heroines, but tonight they seemed a little too familiar for comfort.

Scholarship and sensuality—her enjoyment of wine on her tongue, the cat's rich fur, the long limbs of the runners on the television screen—were her great consolations. Hero knew that her life was now as enviable as ever. Flora would come that weekend, flushed and crumpled after London; Cassie would arrive harassed the week after; her freedom allowed her to encourage the slight young physics supervisor from her new college who reminded her so much of an Irish Stephen Lewis. She was becoming flirtatious with an Orientalist from the Fitzwilliam. Life back in the shadows had many compensations.

The telephone started ringing, and Hero leapt up to switch off the Ansafone, which had a habit of butting in on conversations with its pre-recorded message, and irritating callers. Telephones ringing in cottage rooms still held fear for her: in a Pavlovian reflex, she always felt her heart thud as she reached for the handset: sometimes she never answered, but let the machine do it for her, and played the calls back later.

Nerved by another gulp of wine, Hero picked up the phone. Cat wove figures of eight about her ankles, calmly ignorant of Hero's sense of *déjà vu*.

'Hero? Did you get my message?'

Hero had some trouble establishing the caller's identity, but suddenly realised that it was the young physics supervisor she had spoken to the day before.

'It's Mike Mulholland,' he confirmed, sounding cheerful and rational and sanguine. It was perfectly obvious why he was calling her, and Hero was rather pleased by that.

'I wondered if you'd like to have lunch sometime.'

'Certainly.'

271

'Tomorrow?'

Hero looked around her calm and orderly room. Like a sanctuary, it would always be there to come back to. Though at present she wasn't sure that she wanted to leave it.

Hero stepped out on the high wire, simultaneously frightened and exhilarated by the danger. She wondered fleetingly if she had learnt anything from her experience and concluded that she had learnt the value of taking risks.

'Yes,' she said, smiling. 'Yes, I'd like that very much.'

Photoset, printed and bound in Great Britain by REDWOOD BURN LIMITED, Trowbridge, Wiltshire